The Auth

Owen Marshall's first collection *Supper Waltz Wilson* was quietly published in 1979. The late Frank Sargeson wrote that it was, 'As fine a book of stories as this country is likely to see this year, the next, or the one after...one that will stand close re-reading for many years to come.' Marshall is now considered one of the finest short-fiction writers in New Zealand.

The Master of Big Jingles 1982, *The Day Hemingway Died* 1984 and *The Lynx Hunter* 1987 preceded his *The Divided World*: Selected Stories published to wide acclaim in 1989. *Tomorrow We Save the Orphans* is Marshall's sixth collection.

He has received numerous awards and prizes, including the New Zealand PEN Lillian Ida Smith Award for fiction in 1986 and 1988, the 1987 *Evening Standard* Short Story Award and the 1987 American Express Short Story Award. He held the University of Canterbury Literary Fellowship in 1981, the 1988 New Zealand Literary Fund's Scholarship in Letters, and was awarded the Queen Elizabeth II Arts Council Award for Achievement in 1990 and the Robert Burns Fellowship at the University of Otago for 1992.

Owen Marshall lives with his family in Timaru.

For Janet
and Michael
with best wishes

Owen
Marshall

By the same author

Supper Waltz Wilson, Pegasus Press, Christchurch, 1979
The Master of Big Jingles, John McIndoe, Dunedin, 1982
The Day Hemingway Died, John McIndoe, 1984
The Lynx Hunter, John McIndoe, 1987
The Divided World, John McIndoe, 1989

Tomorrow We Save the Orphans

FICTION BY

OWEN MARSHALL

JOHN McINDOE

Acknowledgements

'The Rule of Jenny Pen' and 'Algebra' appeared first in *Metro*; 'Tomorrow We Save the Orphans' appeared in *Soho Square IV*, Bloomsbury Publishing Ltd., London, 1991; 'Heating the World' and 'Glasnost' were first published in *Landfall*, 'Aubade' in *Takahe*, and 'Saffron Walden' in the *Auckland Sunday Star*. ('Iris' was placed second in the BNZ Katherine Mansfield Short Story Award and the Mobil/ Sunday Times Short Story Award in 1991.)

The author acknowledges the use of the setting in V.S. Naipaul's *Finding the Centre: Two Narratives*, Andre Deutsch, 1984, for satirical purposes in the story 'A View of Our Country'.

The author is grateful to the Literature Programme of the QEII Arts Council for the financial assistance given through an achievement award in 1990.

Published with assistance from the Literature Programme of the QEII Arts Council of New Zealand.

ISBN 0 86868 139 3

First published and printed 1992 by John McIndoe Limited, 51 Crawford Street, Dunedin, New Zealand.
Reprinted 1993

Contents

For Jacqueline,
Andrea and Belinda

The Rule Of Jenny Pen

The heavy moonlight gave it all the appearance of quality linen, flattering the exposed walls of the Totara Eventide Home, and the lines of stainless steel trolleys and wheel chairs by the windows glinted like cutlery upon that linen. The moon was more forgiving than the sun, allowing a variety of interpretations for what it revealed. The shadowed places were soft feathered with blue and grey, like a pigeon's breast.

The only sound was Crealy pissing onto Matron's herb garden. The white cord of his striped pyjamas hung down one leg, and his bald head was made linen in the moonlight. 'Had enough?' Crealy asked the sage, basil and thyme. Residents were not supposed to come out and treat the Matron's herbs to such abuse. Crealy felt his life stir as ever at the defiance of rules. He could see the trim, summer lawn and the garden which paralleled the side path to the slope of the front grounds. The moonlight lay over it all as a linen snowfall.

Crealy had never before lived in a place so pleasant to the eye, or so well organised — and he hated it. Always a big man, he had never done anything with it; lacking the will, the resolution, the brains and the luck. At eighty-one and in Totara Home, he found that time had awarded him a superiority which he had been unable to earn any other way. He had given little; and lasted well.

Crealy's bladder was empty, so he put a large hand over his face to massage his cheeks, while he waited for an idea as to what to do next. Even in the moonlight the kidney spots on the backs of his hands showed clearly. He could think of nothing novel to do so decided to persecute Garfield. He went back through the staff door of the kitchen, and bolted it carefully behind him.

Before seeking out Garfield, Crealy wanted to be sure that Brisson was settled in the duty room. He went slowly through the kitchen and the dining room, through the corridors which were tunnels in the Totara of all their past lives.

Crealy stood in the shadow of the last doorway, and looked into the corridor which led past the duty room. He was like a bear which pauses instinctively at the edge of a forest clearing to assess possibilities of gain or loss. He walked slowly down the corridor of mottled, yellow lino, his breathing louder than the regular shuffle of his slippers. Before the duty room he slowed even further as a caution, but his breathing was as loud as ever. The door was ajar, and Crealy looked in to see Brisson at leisure.

The duty room had a sofa, a chair, a log book with a biro on a string, a coffee pot, a telephone, a typed copy of the fire drill on the wall. It had the worn, impersonal look common to all such rooms in institutions, whether hospitals or boarding schools, army depots or fire brigades. Brisson lay on the sofa, and held up a paperback as if shielding himself from the light. His head was round and firm like a well grown onion, and light brown with the sheen a good onion has too. He wore no socks, just yellow sneakers on his neat feet. Crealy was surprised yet again to see how young some people were. He'll lie there all night and do nothing, thought Crealy.

'Who's that huffing and puffing outside my door?' said Brisson without moving, and Crealy pushed the door and took a step into the doorway. 'Ah, so it's you, Mr Crealy,' said Brisson. He swung the book down and his legs onto the floor in one easy movement. 'Why are you wandering the baronial halls?'

In reply Crealy made a gesture with his large hands which seemed more resignation than explanation. Brisson was lazy, arrogant, shrewd — and young. He took in Crealy: the awkward size of him, the sourness of his worn, bald face, the striped pyjamas, and between them and slippers, Crealy's bare ankles with the veins swollen. Brisson gave a slight shiver of joy and horror at his amazing youth and Crealy's old age.

'Mrs Vennermann said you squeezed the blossom off her bedside flowers,' he said. Crealy itched his neck; his fingers sounded as if they worked on sand paper, and the grey stubble was clear in the light of the room. 'She said you pick on people. Is that right?'

'She took my Milo,' said Crealy. Brisson picked up the exercise book that served as the log for duty shifts.

'Shall I put that in here then? Shall I? Mr Crealy deprived of his Milo by Mrs Vennermann. For Christ's sake. And someone said that you have been making Mrs Halliday all flustered. Aye?'

'It's just all fuss,' said Crealy. He began to think how he could get back at Mrs Vennermann.

Brisson smiled at his own performance, looking at old Crealy, at the mottled lino like a puddle behind him, at the exercise book with the cover doodled upon and the biro on a string from it. He considered himself incongruous in such surroundings. He had such different things planned for himself. 'I won't have a bully on my shift, Mr Crealy. If I have to come down to the rooms then look out. And don't you or the others come up here bothering me.' Brisson hoped to be with Nurse McMillan. What time was it?

'I don't do anything,' said Crealy in his husky voice. 'It's Jenny Pen.'

'What's that?'

'Eh?' said Crealy.

'Go to bed,' said Brisson, and saw the old man turn back onto the puddle lino; heard the shuffle and breath of him as he went back to the rooms of the east wing. Brisson did an abrupt shoulder stand on the sofa to prove age not contagious, then relaxed again with his book and thoughts of Nurse McMillan.

WHEN Crealy reached the room he shared with Garfield, Mortenson and Popanovich he was ready for a little action. Jenny Pen time. Jenny Pen was a hand puppet that Garfield's grand-daughter had made at intermediate school. Although christened Jenny Pencarrow it looked more like Punch, or the witch from Snow White, for its papier mâché nose and chin strove to complete a circle. Jenny Pen had a skirt of red velvet, and balanced all day on the left hand knob of Garfield's bed. At night, ah torment, she became the fasces of Nero's power, the cloven hoof, the dark knight's snouted emblem, the sign of Modu and Mahu, the dancing partner of a trivial Lucifer, a tender facsimile of things gone wrong.

Crealy lifted Jenny Pen from the bed end, and thrust his hand beneath the velvet skirt. He held her aloft, and turned her painted head until all the room had been held in her regard. Garfield began to cry; Mortenson turned the better side of his face aside, and wished his stroke had been more complete. Popanovich was just a shoulder beneath his blankets. Crealy walked Jenny Pen on her hands up Garfield's chest, and she seemed of her own volition to rap Garfield's face. 'Who rules?' said Crealy.

'Jenny Pen,' said Garfield. Garfield had played seventeen games for Wellington as fullback, and later been general manager for Hentlings. It was all too far away to offer any protection.

'Lick her arse then,' said Crealy hoarsely, and Garfield did, and felt Crealy's hand on his tongue. 'You're on Jenny Pen's side, aren't you?' said Crealy.

'Yes.' Garfield's voice barely quivered, although the tears ran down his cheeks. He could scarcely conceive the life he was forced to lead: his soul peeped out from a body which had betrayed him in the end.

Crealy's eyes glittered, and he looked about to share his triumph with others. 'What about you, Judge; want to do a little kissing?' Mortenson gave his half smile.

'It's difficult for me,' he said slowly.

'Bloody difficult with only half of everything working.' Crealy walked over to the last bed, and shook Popanovich's shoulder. There was no reaction. 'What sort of a name is that for a New Zealander,' he said. 'Bloody Popanovich!' He banged his knee into Popanovich's back, but there was no defence of the name. It put Crealy in an ill humour again, and he went back to Garfield with Jenny Pen. He began to go through Garfield's locker. 'It's share and share alike here, Garbunkle.'

'Communism has the greatest attraction to those with the least,' said Mortenson in his slurred voice, knowing Crealy was not bright enough to follow.

'Shut up,' said Crealy. He placed a bag of barley sugars and a box of shortbread biscuits on the top of Garfield's locker. 'Is that all you useless bugger,' he said. He looked at Garfield for a time, letting Jenny Pen rest on the covers, almost basking in the knowledge shared between them of Garfield's weakness and his strength. And even more, the mutual knowledge of Garfield's former strength and superiority, Garfield's achievements and complacency, now worthless currency before Crealy who had achieved nothing except the accidental husbandry of physical strength into old age.

'What else have you got hidden after all them visitors?' Crealy slid his free hand slowly under Garfield's pillow, and withdrew it empty. 'Come on now you bugger,' he said.

'Just leave me alone.'

'Make Jenny Pen sing a song,' said Mortenson. Sometimes Crealy would have Jenny Pen sing 'Knick Knack Paddy Wack Give A Dog A Bone', or 'Knees Up Mother Brown'. It was an awful sound, but better than the beatings.

Crealy listened a while, to make sure that no one was coming who could take Garfield's part, then he pulled the near side of the mattress up and found a packet of figs. 'That's more like it,' he said. He sat on the bed as if he were a friend of Garfield. 'You selfish old bugger,' he said mildly. 'How many figs do you reckon there are here?'

Garfield didn't answer, and Crealy took hold of his near ear and shook his head by means of it until Garfield cried out. 'Don't you start calling out, or you'll get more,' said Crealy. He opened the packet and began to eat. 'For every one you're going to get a hurry up,' he said, and gave Garfield one right away.

So it began. Popanovich remained in hibernation beneath his blankets, Mortenson watched, but tried to keep the true side of his face as expressionless as the other, even though his good leg was rigid. Garfield covered his ears, and Crealy ate the figs, hitting Garfield's face with each new mouthful. 'Figs make you shit, Garfield old son,' he said, 'but I'll make you shit without them. That's rich isn't it. I said that's rich isn't it, Judge?'

'Exactly,' said Mortenson carefully. What time was it? He tried to remember some of the letters of Cicero he had been reading.

The one light from Garfield's locker cast a swooping shadow each time Crealy leant forward solicitously to hit Garfield, and when Crealy held Jenny Pen up in triumph she was manifest as a montrous Viking prow upon the wall. Mortenson had to accept the realisation that there were underworlds which he had been able until recently to ignore; now he was part of one, suffering and observing, powerless through reduced capacity and fear.

When he saw a little, shining blood beneath Garfield's nose he could contain his opposition no longer. Yet stress undid his recent progress and Stefan Albee Mortenson, barrister, solicitor, notary public could produce before the court of Jenny Pen, only, 'Creal youb narlous narl stapp awus nee.'

'Careful, Judge. I don't need your squark. I might come across and give you more than just this feathering Garfield's enjoying. I'll do the side of you not already dead, you pinstripe squirt.'

Mortenson had nothing more to say, and Garfield sat with his chin on his chest as if in a trance. 'Had enough?' Crealy asked him. 'You're gutless the lot of you.' Crealy was bored with his immediate subjects, and with Jenny Pen still on his hand as his familiar he went to wander the night corridors of the Home. No conversation began in the room he left. Popanovich feigned the sleep of death, Garfield remained slumped in his bed and Mortenson had no way of travelling the distance between them to offer comfort.

MRS MUNRO knew nothing of Totara's netherworld. She had her own room in the separate block before the cottages, and the sun was laid on the polish of several pieces of her own furniture which had accompanied her. Mrs Munro could never understand those who complained of time dragging. She herself delighted in time to spare for all those indulgences a busy life had denied her; all those intellectual and emotional considerations that the slog of a seven-day dairy had prevented her from enjoying. She wore the track suit which she had insisted on for a Christmas present. She liked the comfort, the lack of constriction, the zippers at ankle and chest which made it easy to get off. She liked the two bright blue stripes and the motif of crossed racquets, even though she had never played sport.

Despite something of a problem with head nodding, and a hip operation on the way, Mrs Munro was quietly proud that although she was an old woman, she was not a fat, old woman. She didn't complain about the food, and she drew more large-print library books in a week than anyone else in the Home. She rejoiced in an hour to wile away over a cup of tea, or in writing to Bessie Hambinder, or in putting drops in her ear, or measuring her room with the tape from the sewing basket. Miss Hails from the main block did visit too often it was true, and her repetitions tended to start Mrs Munro's head nodding, but there was always the bedding store-room as a sanctuary, and Mrs Munro had built a little dug-out in the blanket piles where she could rest in her track suit after lunch until Miss Hails had given up looking for her, and gone visiting elsewhere.

For the present though she counted the spots of a ladybird on her window sill, and watched sour, old Crealy smoking on a bench by the secure recreation area. Crealy was not compulsive viewing, and when Mrs Munro finished her computations concerning the ladybird she decided she would begin her next romance of the British Raj.

Crealy's cigarette was the last in the packet he had stolen from Popanovich, who was sleeping again. The days were not as enjoyable as the nights for Crealy, because he was too much under the eye of authority, and the spirit of his fellows was not as easily daunted when the sun shone. He wondered if Mrs Halliday was by the goldfish pond, but couldn't see her, and so he went back indoors to check Mortenson's locker before lunch. In the main corridor he came across Mrs Joyce, who had her blood changed quite regularly at the clinic. Her forearms and elbows seemed forever to have the yellows, purples and blues of ageing bruises. Mrs Joyce had made binoculars of her hands and stood with them pressed to the glass doors, staring out. 'What's out there?' she asked Crealy.

'Herbs and spices, sycamores and young people. And bloody work.'

'I can't see it,' said Mrs Joyce.

'You've gone daft in there.' Crealy rapped on her head with his knuckles, but she kept peering out into the sunshine through the tunnels of her fingers.

'Let me join Jesus,' she said. Crealy looked down at her pink scalp beneath the white hair. Because there was no resistance whatsoever that she could make, because she was not even aware of his malice, Crealy couldn't be bothered hurting her.

'Dozy old tart.'

'Let me come to thee sweet Jesus,' said Mrs Joyce. Crealy had a chuckle at that, and at how Mrs Joyce was peering through her hands and the glass, although everything outside was perfectly clear to him.

Matron Frew heard the chuckle from the office, and it reminded her that she wanted words with Crealy. She first of all took Mrs

Joyce's arm in hers, and walked with her down to the dayroom. She was back before Crealy could quite disappear from sight down the corridor however, and she told him with some bluntness of the indirect complaints she'd been receiving, particularly from staff who had noticed Crealy pestering Mrs Halliday and Mr Garfield.

'Mark my words,' said Matron Frew. 'I will be watching, and also I'm making mention of things in my report to the board this month. You show an unwillingness at times to be a reasonable member of our community.'

As she spoke Crealy hung his head, but not from meekness or contrition. He was counting the number of usable butts in the sandbox by the office door, and when he had done that he imagined himself in the mild, summer night standing over Matron's herb garden, and pissing on the chives, parsley, mint, fennel and thyme. A lifetime in the indifferent, hostile or contemptuous regard of others had rendered Crealy immune to all three. He recognised no value or interest other than his own.

ON Wednesday evenings Matron Frew turned off the television in the east wing lounge and organised communal singing. It was not compulsory as such, but absence meant no chocolate biscuits at the supper which followed. As a professionally trained person, matron knew that a variety of stimulus for the elderly was important.

The committed, the egotistical and the hard of hearing stood close around the piano, the infirm or less enthusiastic were rims at a great distance. Golden oldies they sang, to Matron's accompaniment. 'The Kerry Pipers', 'Auld Lang Syne', 'The Biggest Aspidistra In The World', 'On Top Of Old Smokey'.

Matron had begun her career as a physiotherapist and it showed in her playing; the keys kneaded like a string of vertebrae; each tune well gone over and the kinks removed. 'Waltzing Matilda', 'Home On The Range', 'The White Cliffs Of Dover', 'Some Enchanted Evening', 'Polly Wolly Doodle'. Matron Frew allowed her charges to respond in their own way and order, but she always had Nurse Glenn or Nurse McMillan guide Mr Oliphant to the uncarpeted area by the door because the pathos of any Irish tune made him incontinent.

A refrain, particularly with high notes, would sometimes trigger Miss Hails' weakness and she would begin the incessant repetition of a word. It happened sure enough during 'Riding Down From Bangor', and for several minutes Miss Hail sang only 'May'. Crealy was present not just for the chocolate biscuits, but because it gave him perverse satisfaction after the Matron's rebuke, to exercise intimidation almost under her gaze.

He stood on Mrs Dellow's toe during 'Annie Laurie', and stared into her face, daring her to respond. Her thin voice assumed even greater vibrato and her eyes misted. Crealy then leant in comradeship over blind Mr Lewin and sprayed saliva into his face as 'Christopher Robin Went Down With Alice'.

When the chocolate biscuits came at last, Crealy kept himself between them and George Oliphant until they were all gone, then he said, 'Now isn't that a bugger, George, they seem all gone.'

'Silver Threads Among The Gold', they sang, and 'Swing Low Sweet Chariot'. 'Home, home, home, home, home, home,' Miss Hails continued, until Matron Frew told her to suck her thumb until the cycle was broken. 'Knees Up Mother Brown' Crealy liked, but because it was his favourite the others found no pleasure in joining in.

Mortenson enjoyed the association the songs bore, even if not the singing itself. He preferred to be at some remove from the piano and his fellows, for then he could imagine other company and past days: his mouth would twitch and his good hand move to the melodies. 'Some Enchanted Evening' — he would sing it with Deborah as they drove back from ski-ing, ready for court work during the week. He hadn't realised then, that all roads led to this. 'Roo, roo, roo, roo, roo,' began Miss Hails.

BEFORE midnight, aware of an odd, sighing wind around the Home, Crealy made a patrol of his domain; only his harsh breathing and shuffle gave him away. In his own room everything was as it should be — Garfield was weeping, Popanovich sleeping, and Mortenson in his snores fell every few minutes into a choking death rattle which woke him briefly, then he slept and it all began again.

Further down the corridor Mrs Doone was talking to herself as she strung up non-existent Christmas decorations. Every night was Christmas Eve for Mrs Doone, and the wonder and *frisson* of it were freshly felt night after night. 'Compliments of the season, Mr Ah — ah,' she said as Crealy slippered by. Around the corner, Crealy paused outside the room Mrs Oliffe and Miss Hails shared. Miss Hails was doing her thing of course; for almost an hour she had been repeating the sound tee, while Mrs Oliffe was trying to find nineteen across which was Breton Gaelic for divine harbinger.

'Oh, stop going tee, tee, tee, tee,' Mrs Oliffe said, but the simple satisfaction of it set her off also, and she joined in. Outside, Crealy could hear them in unison, tee, tee, tee. He found his own head nodding and his mouth formed the sound. One night it might spread through all of Totara, and capture them in a transport of repetitious senility.

Crealy put his hand to his face to stop himself. He looked carefully down the corridor. 'Mad old tarts,' he said. He considered opening their door and frightening them into silence, but the chances of being caught up in their chant and left nodding with them indefinitely was too great. He went on, still with one hand to his face. Tee, tee, tee, tee, faded behind him.

Outside the Matron's office were chairs for visitors, and a varnished box with a sand tray in it for smokers amongst the visitors. Crealy was able to find several butts worth using again, before he noticed Mrs Joyce standing by the main doors once more. 'Jesus loves me this I know,' she said. She had two overcoats on, and stood with her hand on the catch of the locked door. 'I'm going home,' she said. 'I've been here nearly a fortnight and they are expecting me back now.'

'You've been here for years,' said Crealy.

'Oh no, just a fortnight, and I need to be at home for every special occasion. We've always been a very close family you see.' Crealy went through her double set of pockets as she talked, but all he could find was a small book of stamps. 'They may well send a car for me,' she said. They both looked through the glass doors for a moment, but there was only empty wind and moonlight: no car was parked on the linen of the drive.

'You can go home this way,' said Crealy, taking Mrs Joyce by the lapel and leading her towards the kitchens.

'Has the car come then?' she said, and 'God will provide, you know. Even Solomon in all his glory.' Crealy led her through the dining room laid for breakfast, and the kitchens, where worn, steel surfaces glinted like new bone. He unbolted the service door and set Mrs Joyce in the gap. 'There you are then,' he said. 'The main drive's just around the corner.'

'It's a clear path to home, thank Jesus.' The blue second coat would barely fit over the first, and pulled her arms back like the flippers of a penguin. Rather like a penguin she began walking, struck her head on a pruned plum branch, and reeled past the herb garden.

'What's your name again?' said Crealy, but Mrs Joyce didn't answer, and still unsteady from the blow made the best pace she could around the side path. She had the scent of freedom; she had a promise of home.

CREALY waited until Mrs Joyce was well gone and there was no sound of pursuit or return, then he went out himself and stood in the summer night, sniffing the aromatic air of Matron Frew's herb garden. He hung out his cock, and waited patiently for his prostate to relax its grip so that he could enjoy the physical relief and pleasurable malice of watering the herbs. He had both in good time, then he stood under the sycamore by the old garages and had one of the visitor's cigarette ends, after nipping off the filter.

The sycamore creaked and murmured in the night breeze which blew out from the land to the sea. Despite the ache in his joints, Crealy enjoyed being by himself there beneath the branches, and higher the summer sky, for he knew that he had always been unloved. Even though old age at Totara had given him a mirror image power and significance while always before he had been subjugated, he liked still to be alone, to have no sources of action or response other than himself. So he stood beneath the sycamore, and enjoyed his cigarette ends guardedly, shading the glow with a palm, and looking out to the better lit parts of the grounds. 'No bastard can see me,' he said. 'No bastard knows I'm here.'

Even a summer's night grows cold for old bones, and Crealy came in and bolted the door behind him. 'Had enough?' he had asked the mint and parsley as he went by them. He inspected Mrs Joyce's stamps in the dim light. He wanted to search her room, but had forgotten her name. Crealy had never been an intellectual, and at eighty-one he found it difficult to move and think at the same time. So he remained stooped in the semi-light between kitchen and dining room, and he tried to remember what he had been going to do before he met Mrs Joyce.

He went into the pantry beyond the stainless steel moonlight of the kitchen, and lifted out a large tin of golden syrup. He took a thick crust from the toast drawer and with his fingers as a ladle spread golden syrup on it. The syrup lay dark in the tin, but silver in glints as it twined from his fingers.

Crealy replaced the tin, and stood with the bread and syrup in his clean hand, sucking his other fingers. He looked into the shadowed dining room: the identical tables, evenly spaced, and an oblong of light across them from the corridor. The golden syrup was rich and energy giving. Crealy began to wonder if Mrs Halliday was having one of her spells in the Home. He made such demands on his old mind that his chewing slowly stopped, and his hand no longer held the bread level. He stood in the kitchen doorway as a Neanderthal at the entrance to his cave. The syrup made a silver necklace to the floor. Crealy couldn't remember: couldn't remember at all.

'Bugger me,' he said at last. He was unable to come up with anything, so he stopped thinking, allowed the motor-sensory centres priority again, and moved into the lino tubes which were the Totara corridors.

At the duty room, Crealy decided to check on Brisson in case he was doing the unexpected thing and actually making a round. There was no key for the duty room door, but when Crealy pushed lightly against it, he found that Brisson had set the end of the sofa hard to it. Then he heard voices. Nurse McMillan talked as she and Brisson made love, but her topic was dissatisfaction with conditions of service, not romance. Lovemaking altered the normal rhythm of her words so that odd, accentuated syllables were driven out of her. 'GOD we've all thought OF handing in our resigNATIONS,' she said.

'There's nothing in all the world to match it,' Brisson said.

The palm of one of Crealy's large hands still rested on the door, though he pressed no more. He listened to a tune which mocked him, and his arthritis drove him on, shuffling and disgruntled; missing out as usual. Mrs Doone had finished putting up her Christmas decorations for the night, and the corridor was as bare as when she first began. Even Miss Hails was silent, but as Crealy passed Mr Lewin's room he heard a talking clock. 'It is twelve o'clock, midnight,' said the talking clock. Like a fox at a burrow entrance, Crealy stood before the door, but the clock didn't speak again, and blind Mr Lewin who must have activated it made no sound either.

As he neared his own room Crealy could hear Mortenson's stricken breathing, and remembered with sudden vividness a time more than thirty years before when he had been a cleaner at the Nazareth Hall and Mortenson had been president of a group that banqueted there. Crealy had looked out from the serving hatch, waiting to begin clearing up, and S.A. Mortenson CBE, barrister, solicitor, notary public, city councillor and party chairman, had been standing at the top table; standing in his dinner jacket to give an erudite speech which was buoyed up constantly by delighted applause and laughter from the other tables. The recollection had such strength that Crealy felt again the flat ache of his own inconsequence, but it passed and he was aware of the cream Totara walls again, and the struggle Mortenson had to breathe.

Crealy laid Popanovich's open bottle of lemonade on the bed so that it would wet the sleeping man's feet, and plucked Jenny Pen from Garfield's bed end and held her briefly aloft. 'Wake up, Judge,' he said, and took Mortenson's nose between Jenny Pen's hands.

Mortenson's good side woke with horror. What time was it? 'Let's have poetry tonight,' said Crealy. He made himself comfortable on the bed with his room-mate. 'And I want to see you enjoying it, Judge; getting into the swing of it,' he said.

And where the silk-shoed lovers ran
with dust of diamonds in their hair,
he opens now his silent wing

began Mortenson indistinctly.

Crealy put one of Jenny Pen's fingers into the slack side of Mortenson's mouth and pulled it into the image of a smile. 'Let's not be half-hearted about this. Try something else,' said Crealy. Mortenson wished to disregard the setting his senses made for him, and the only escape was through the words. He did his best with a bit of 'The Herne's Egg'.

Strong sinew and soft flesh
Are foliage round the shaft
Before the arrowsmith
Has stripped it, and I pray
That I, all foliage gone,
May shoot into my joy.

'Eh?' said Crealy. He tired quickly of poetry, even when seasoned with humiliation. 'Had enough,' he said. His thoughts turned to Garfield. There were hours to go, years maybe, before it would be day again.

BLIND Mr Lewin was guided by Mrs Munro to the sunroom in the east wing the next afternoon. Mr Lewin loved the warmth, and found that he could sleep easily during the day in full sunlight. Mrs Munro kindly led him down, and Lewin could feel the warmth even as they approached the end of the corridor. Mrs Munro's head nodded companionably as she pulled a cane chair close to the large window; so close that Lewin was able to put out his hands and feel the glass while sitting comfortably. And she gave him his talking clock to cradle so that he would not be anxious about his meals. Mr Lewin thanked her, and listened to the departing footsteps.

He had never seen the sunroom, and instead of the meek, faded place that it was, looking out over the crocodile paving and lawns in front of the cottages, he imagined it cantilevered high into the sun's eye and with only the yellow, benevolent furnace of the sun to be seen from the window. Lewin had known far worse times.

While Mr Lewin slept, Crealy elsewhere watched Mrs Halliday. Mrs Halliday was only in her sixties, but subject to Huntington's chorea in recurring spells during which she often came into the Totara Home to relieve her family. Crealy always took a considerable interest in her visits, for her breasts were large, she still had firm flesh, and caught at the right moment she could be used without much recollection of it.

Towards the end of the long afternoon she was at her most confused, and Crealy watched from outside the television lounge until he saw her talking to herself and constantly folding and unfolding her cardigan. He went in and firmly led her along the trail of mottled lino to the sunroom, which visitors or clergymen sometimes used to have their talks. 'Has the family come? Has Elaine?' said Mrs Halliday. Crealy was quite pleased to see blind Lewin there, close to the window, for he could pass as a chaperone at a distance, but not act as one on the spot. Crealy sat Mrs Halliday with her back to the window.

'Your family are coming soon,' he said, and opened the front of her dress.

'Is that you, Mrs Munro?' asked Lewin.

'Shut up,' said Crealy.

'The family you say,' said Mrs Halliday. She allowed Crealy to unclip her bra at the back, and he scooped out her breasts so they made two full fish heads in the flounce of her dress.

Lewin was still groggy from his sleep, but he didn't wish to seem discourteous. 'Where would we be without families,' he said gallantly, and fingered his talking clock for reassurance. Crealy stroked Mrs Halliday's breasts, and clumsily rolled the nipples between thumb and forefinger so that she pursed her lips and put her hands on his wrists.

'You need to get changed for your family,' said Crealy absently.

'What time is it then?' asked Mrs Halliday. Lewin pressed his clock.

'The time is 4.42 pm,' it said.

Crealy took another minute of satisfaction in the sun, then refilled Mrs Halliday's bra, and with some difficulty fastened it across her back. Matron Frew might come looking for her soon. 'Stay here and talk to Lewin,' he said.

'Am I changed for my family?'

'Good enough,' said Crealy.

'Who is that?' said Lewin, turning an ear rather than an eye for better comprehension

'Jenny Pen rules,' said Crealy as he left.

THE impartial sun which Mr Lewin blindly enjoyed, shone on Mortenson who sat in his wheel chair on a landscaped hillock which looked over the SRA — the safe recreation area. Within it the bewildered or fretful, the complacent and serene could be left in security. Only the staff could manage the latch. Crealy called it the zoo, but it was pleasant enough, more like a kindergarten. There were seats with foam cushions for thin flesh, and raised garden plots which keen Totarans could work on without stooping or kneeling.

The SRA was overlooked by the wide windows of the dining room on one side, but to the warm north side there was a view across the grass and gardens towards the cottages and the spires of the great world. Mortenson could see the goldfish pond in the zoo, and George Oliphant dolefully shaking the back of his trousers because he was in trouble again.

The Matron and Dr Sullivan stopped beside Mortenson on their round, but finished their conversation before greeting him. 'I've no idea how Mrs Joyce managed to leave the block in the first place,' said Matron.

'It can't be helped.'

'It's a puzzle though.'

'I haven't told her family the actual circumstances of the death: to minimise the trauma you see. And how are you, Mr Mortenson?'

'Mr Mortenson is brighter every day,' replied Matron. Mortenson gave his half smile. He could see the exquisite glow on the sunlit tulips, feel the sun's good will on his faithful side, and hear Miss Hails practising her word for the day. The word was Nell, or perhaps Knell; how was anyone to know but her.

'Nell, nell, nell, nell,' said Miss Hails. Like a prayer wheel she gave a benediction over all the zoo, the lawn, the cottages, the totality of Totara and beyond. 'Nell, nell, nell, nell, knell.'

'Well, nice talking to you,' said Dr Sullivan, and they went on their way. Mortenson felt an itching tic begin at the corner of his eye. In all that ground of apparent pleasure he wondered what Crealy was up to. What time was it? It came to Mortenson that his karma had been assessed; that from the best of lives he was in a spiral descent of reincarnation from which he would emerge perhaps a six-spot ladybird, as counted by Mrs Munro, and would clamp the stem beneath the wine glow of the sunlit tulip blooms.

WHAT time was it? Dr Sullivan and Matron were trying to wake Popanovich. 'It's always the same. Ah, well, he seems healthy enough and sleep can't hurt him.' Dr Sullivan smiled at the other three in the end room, while Matron moved Popanovich in the bed. The doctor was not a dour person; he believed in good spirits and optimism. He looked about for something that would provide an occasion for light-heartedness and rapport.

Matron sensed that the mood had abruptly changed, though at first she didn't see that behind her Dr Sullivan had taken Jenny Pen from Garfield's bed and mounted her on his hand. Garfield began to shiver, and put his hands out, palms uppermost, as if to play patter-cake. Crealy hung his head to one side like an old dog, while the whites of his eyes showed as he kept things in his view. Mortenson felt a sweat break out on his good thigh beneath the rug, and his smile was slow to form and slow to fade. He smiled as a Christian might smile who catches the Devil out walking in the daytime.

'What a good life we lead at Totara,' said Dr Sullivan in falsetto for Jenny Pen, and he jiggled her to emphasise his humour. The only responses were those of Matron Frew's crepe soles on the lino, and at a distance Miss Hails saying her catechism for the day. It drifted to them down the corridor.

'Mi, mi, mi, mi, mi, mi.'

'Perhaps puppeteer isn't my calling,' said Dr Sullivan. He was disappointed by his reception and withdrew into professionalism. Matron knew how to keep that patter going.

Crealy's arthritis was giving him gyppo again. To appease it he walked the maze of corridors, and watched from window after window the sunshowers above the grounds. Dramatic clouds were towed across the sky, and when they met the sun they were lit with red and orange embers which glowed and shifted in the deep perspectives. From the dining room Crealy saw a travelling shower fracture the surface of the zoo pond, so that the goldfish lost their shape, and became just carrots in the shallow weeds.

On his second circuit Crealy noticed that Nurse McMillan had left the office, and that the morning's mail lay partly sorted on the counter. He eased in, and his stiff hands found envelopes addressed to Mortenson, to Oliphant and Garfield. He pocketed them, and was cheered by the petty malice even though he couldn't see Mrs Halliday in the TV room as he went past. For the life of him he could not remember when he last had a personal letter. Garfield on the other hand received far too much kind attention from outside, and Crealy decided to give him a hard time until the weather improved. He began a search for Garfield, but George Oliphant saw him checking the TV room, and afterwards went to the window which could be seen by Mortenson and gave a warning by semaphore, which Mortenson passed on to Garfield.

Garfield began his slow but urgent escape down the corridors of hours towards the bedding store-room. The door there had a plunger and cylinder to draw it closed without slamming. To Garfield the mechanism seemed to take an eternity to work, and the cylinder hissed as his view of the corridor and bathrooms narrowed. Garfield sat in semi-darkness, content with the little light entering from a glass strip above the door.

The broad shelves had stacks of sheets and pillowcases, and on the floor were piled blankets which rose like wool bales. Garfield sat on a half-bale to wait it out. He didn't trouble himself with the metaphysics of his situation: what he had come to. The former Wellington fullback and general manager for Hentlings sat grinding his teeth in the bedding store-room of Totara Eventide Home, and listening to the perpetual echoing orchestration which his tinnitus inflicted on him.

Crealy found him there.

IT was nearly four. The showers had become less frequent, and a rainbow stood clearly behind the cottages, fading up towards the sun. Yet Mortenson couldn't concentrate on his history of Rome; he felt a helpless consideration for Garfield, and a fear of Crealy. He knew that where there are no lions then hyenas rule.

His chair was very low-geared, and despite the busy noise of its motor, Mortenson moved only slowly along the corridors towards the bedding room. At alternate windows the day's strange weather was displayed as sunlit promise, then skirts of rain from fiery clouds, then blue sky once again. The door took all the thrust his chair could manage, and sank closed behind him so that the failing light and hiss half hid Crealy's torture of his friend.

'Hello, Judge,' said Crealy. Once he found that Mortenson had come alone, he was pleased. He had become almost bored with Garfield. Yet an advantage can be gained or lost quite unexpectedly and with such an absence of drama that it is easy to miss the significance. Crealy moved to get a better leverage, overbalanced on the soft surface and fell backwards just a couple of feet into the comfortable crevasse fashioned by Mrs Munro between the banded blankets. His old arms and legs moved silently in the shadows, as if he were a beetle on his back there. He was too stiff to turn easily.

Mortenson took a pillow with his better arm and pushed it across Crealy's face.

'Come on,' he said to Garfield. It was more a delaying tactic at first, with neither of them having much hope of success; even Crealy gave a sort of grin whenever he managed to free his face, as if he recognised his temporary difficulty, but would soon pay them back all right.

But the more Garfield and Mortenson pushed, and the more Crealy twisted, the deeper his shoulders sank between the blankets. He began to pant and jerk; the others saw a chance indeed and their lips drew back in the dark and they pressed for all their lives. Crealy's big arms and legs fell in harmless thuds against the embracing blankets. Mortenson felt strength and justice in his good arm even though it trembled with exertion, and Garfield was on his knees to use his body weight upon the pillow.

'Had enough. Had enough, Crealy old son,' he kept whispering. The competitive urge in Garfield revived one last time. Crealy's arms and legs moved less, but his body bucked.

'Now let us play Othello,' slurred Mortenson.

'Had enough,' sobbed Garfield.

For a good time after Crealy was still, they continued to hold the pillow over his face. Accustomed to such full tyranny as his, they could hardly believe that they had beaten him so completely. Even when they heard his sphincter muscles relax, and had the smell of him, they held the pillow down. 'Had enough?' said Garfield tenderly.

'Put the pillow back,' said Mortenson finally, and he wiped the tears from Garfield's face. They didn't look again at Dave Crealy, who was a big, stupid man lying well down amongst piles of blankets. Garfield opened the door a little, and when he saw that there was no one outside he held it back for Mortenson's chair, and the snake hissed behind them in the dark.

As they went home they met Mrs Munro guiding Mr Lewin to the sunroom. Mrs Munro delighted in being useful, and was thinking also of a nice cup of tea. 'There's a rainbow,' she said, nodding. Mortenson and Garfield could see its thick, childish bands behind the cottages; at the same time the sun was strong enough to cast shadows from the benches in the grounds. Who knows what Lewin saw, but he could hear with them the piping of Miss Hails at a distance.

'Na, na, na, na, na, na, na, na.' Mr Lewin pushed the button on his clock.

'The time is 4.19 pm,' the clock said.

Iris

Iris, my mother, had this idea that sooner rather than later something marvellous was bound to happen: a lucky break in life if you kept at it. She wasn't selfish about this, everyone had the same chance for something quite undeserved, like being approached out of the blue in the supermarket by a talent scout to become a model, or marrying an accountant as my aunt did who now spends money like water and has two homes. For my twenty-first Aunt Esther gave me a cream, silk dress, but I snagged it at the Polytech wine and cheese on a rivet in the plastic chair.

Even when Iris was too old to go on hoping to be approached in the supermarket for anything other than shoplifting, she believed magnificent opportunity was in the offing. She took Golden Kiwis and then Lotto tickets and worked out on the backs of envelopes how she would divide and spend the money. I was to come in for some pretty good stuff when she won, according to the lists. Each mail time was a high, never mind that she hardly wrote to anyone, had jobs without prospects and shifted a lot. Throughout the drizzle of magazine offers, bills, perfunctory greetings, community newsletters, demands on former tenants and coupon books, she kept a fierce hope in miraculous correspondence. An approach concerning political candidature perhaps, or an invitation from the Max Factor directorate to be a special consultant; gardenias from a secret admirer, or notification that she was meter maid of the year. Iris never did realise that her whole life was unsolicited. She intently examined each special offer and would speculate joyously if her actual name was used. But how would they know my name, she'd say, look, they use my proper name. So that I could be at my best she would roam the twilight, feeling in her neighbours' boxes for shampoo sachets sent as samples. Needs must, my girl, she would say firmly. Our time will come.

Iris answered an advertisement about Dr Asmunzov, professor of the mind, who came and said he could do a seance on my dad, even though he'd gone off, not died. I was seventeen and the professor of the mind had other interests as well, for he clasped my knee beneath the table. Being naturally blonde and with a good bust I've always had to deal with that sort of thing. Iris, my mother, said that it didn't necessarily mean anything and that men were just like that. Hormonal, she said, and nothing in it to blame anyone. When she was going to school in Taranaki a share milker used to undo his fly each day as the bus passed his milking shed. The association gave her a particular aversion to cholesterol she said.

Iris did win a Christmas hamper when I had chicken pox in form two, from the Super Doop, and once initiated a correspondence with a firm of Auckland solicitors acting for an unclaimed British estate. The hamper she unpacked on my bed and found lots of low cost, bulky items under the more glamorous surface layer: weetbix, dried lentils, toilet rolls, stuff like that, and the solicitors lost interest when we couldn't provide any evidence that the family on the Bleeker side originated in Dorset. I ate a small tin of sardines cold from the hamper and with my finger put their oil on all the chicken pox that I could reach. My second hand bed head had transfers of Pooh Bear and Cliff Richard that were nothing to me.

For a time, when we lived in Wanganui, Iris thought we had a fortune at our toes, because our Aramaho suburb neighbours said that the house we rented used to belong to a retired Greymouth dentist who must have been worth a packet, but left nothing when he died in my room. I did consider using the untainted third bedroom, but mine was so much sunnier and I could come and go from the big window without bothering Iris. She said he would have had it all in gold, being able to get it for fillings as a dentist though other people weren't allowed to buy it. She had a dream of gold filled Havelock Dark tobacco tins hidden under the brick paving between the back door and the laundry. We dug up the bricks, every one, but found no gold. The bricks remained stacked on the lawn and next winter we got muddy feet going to the laundry. They were a reminder of yet another false lead in the treasure hunt which was my mother's life. It's there all right though, Iris said, he just doesn't want a woman to find it.

My boyfriends seemed possibilities to Iris; opportunities for advantage. Being blonde and with a good figure as I said, I had plenty of guys coming on to me. You get used to it after a while. Not great, but not unbearable. It's just the effect you have on hormones I guess. Mum said that she'd been trim herself in her time, but her face had become a bit of a handbag. My father had been an All Black trialist who couldn't get used to his diminished place in life when he got past playing. He had these wonderful hands though, Iris said, and should really have taken up the saxaphone, or the piano. She took it up herself soon after he left, from an easy stage instruction booklet called 'Jazz Sax Made Easy'. She didn't find time for much practice, but made herself a black, sequin dress to wear when she played in cabarets. I wore it for the Leavers' Dance at Te Tarehi High School and Maurice Prentice told me that I gave him such a hard on that he could only dance stooped. Maurice wasn't one of those Iris had any hopes of, but Nigel Utteridge and Denzil Smith were. Denzil and I were both keen on roller-skating and won the under sixteen figure skating title in Marlborough, not long after Mum and I shifted down from Horowhenua. Iris saw a magnificent future for us on the international circuit, like Torvill and Dean, with her managing the television interviews and contracts. She cut down the sequin cabaret dress, sewed in bra cups, and I wore it for competitions. Nigel Utteridge was later. His parents were both doctors would you believe. Each worked in a different practice so they could have professional independence. Mrs Dr Utteridge was quite confiding and told me there were no children after Nigel because Mr Dr Utteridge was injured by the Big Dipper at the Tahuna fairground. Mr Dr Utteridge had the thickest most muscular neck you can imagine; wider than his head even. He must have taken up the sport of butting at a very young age. Iris imagined me getting married to the son of two doctors and neither of us having to work again; just sit behind the receptionist's desk, lift our heads occasionally and say, Dr Utteridge will see you now, I'm sorry Dr Utteridge has been delayed by an outbreak of anthrax, Dr Utteridge is at present examining your uterine x-rays. Maurice

Prentice was probably the best looking guy I went out with early on, but very hormonal, always talking about cars, and he walked with a stoop.

Sooner or later, Iris would say, our ship will come in. Over Kentucky Fried Chicken on her fiftieth birthday she told me about this Grandma Moses who at eighty started painting pictures of her farm and became famous. The Grandma Moses' in all walks of life were a marvel of reassurance to my mother. What can happen once can happen twice, she said, and she was not afraid to work. She formed a co-operative when we were in Palmerston North. Herself and two huge twins called McIntosh and they supplied hors-d'oeuvres at functions. Salmon or crab finger pastries, gherkin, prune and pineapple on toothpicks, cheese balls, home ground pâté and cinnamon sticks. They made a go of it too, though Iris said that people didn't appreciate the cost of the fillings, but then the twin five minutes older than the other had an experience when delivering to the Town Clerk's farewell. A lap dog ran up inside her dress as she was carrying trays into the civic chambers and she went right off the business. Iris said the filthy little beast had ruined what could have been a catering empire, because that twin had the flair and they couldn't carry on afterwards.

I don't want you to think Iris's vision was a mercenary one. Money wasn't an end in itself. What Iris wanted was to force life to yield her something of value, something from the top drawer. She had no belief in a heaven and wanted a greater share of life. We all go down to the grave in the end, she'd say. Behind the library building and no longer used was the old cemetery on the slope. When I had the job at Hendry's cosmetic counter we would meet some lunchtimes and walk through the alleys of crushed, white quartz between the tombs. She would sigh, but only to cool the meat pies she liked for winter lunch. Iris was in fact cheerful in the cemetery, for of all the people on that slope only she and I had any further hope of a shot at life. Died for King and Country, she might read for me, her meter maid shoes making a sensible crunch upon the quartz. Iris would eat strips from the top of her pie and the steam would wisp into the winter air. Meter maiding was only one of Mum's skills. She believed in a variety of jobs to lure good fortune. In Christchurch she was a fish splitter for almost a year. Well, Lyttelton she actually worked in, but we lived at New Brighton. A bach over which the fine, grey sand would whisper when the sea wind blew through the marram grass. A millionaire's view of the ocean, Iris said. I was still young enough to need entertainment and she played the water pipes for me. By turning on the taps to different positions we could hear fog horns, fire engines, the howling jabberwocky. My schoolbag on the lino beside me, the smell of fish all the way from Lyttelton, the millionaire's view over the fritz haircut of the marram dunes, as I crouched by the lion paws of the bath to hear tubas, or what Iris said was the farting of the elephants in the jungle. I wouldn't be surprised if there's a way to make a career from this she'd say, and the water is all free, she'd say. Called Home, or Till The Daybreak Comes, she read out in the cemetery of that later town. As I Am Now So You Must Be Prepare Yourself To Follow Me, as we opened up a bag of crisps, pausing by the dearly loved and much missed husband of Astral Pruitt while I explained the new gloss shades of half-pink, full-pink, mink-pink. Iris said that the pastie man had asked her to go to the trots with him, but she didn't like his lank hair. A man should have some bit of natural wave or curl in his hair, my mother reckoned. I had plenty of offers from men myself by that time, and while Iris never interfered, she did say that men made lousy friends and that women knew how to stick together. Her own mother was a grand friend she said, and in one tough year went into the city gardens and lopped off a branch to make a Christmas tree.

Mum was fascinated by those things which defy routine — a locust swarm, footsteps of Homo Erectus, Halley's comet, which was certainly a fizzer, the Brewster kid who used to run howling round the block in Te Kuiti when his parents were fighting. Iris would take a cold sausage or potato out to him and he would snatch it on the trot with his face gleaming with tears in the streetlights. Iris was a good neighbour, though a temporary one. She babysat scores of kids who we never heard of again. Later she would send me out to do it. We received neighbourly kindness in return of course. In the Brewster kid's Te Kuiti I remember sneaking over each night to plug an extension cord into old Mr Hammond's work bench. He was rich and never went out after dark. While we lived there most of our power intensive activities were late at night. We had an adaptor plug into the water heater, and a large frypan for our main feed at nine or ten at night. When we had to leave Te Kuiti my mother made Mr Hammond a green, double knit jersey with a vee-neck and raglan sleeves. Only it had a narrow yellow band at the waist, because she was one green ball short.

From what Iris said, my grandmother must have been the same sort of person, though I never met her because she had Iris late and died in a nursing home somewhere in the North Island while we were living in Tuatapere. Iris was a school cleaner. There was a mill just down the road and the sawdust piles were mountain ranges there; the oldest peaks with the richest colours. Iris said that once I asked for a packed lunch to take to climb them. She couldn't afford to go up for the funeral. Her sister sent some of their mother's things down to her, including a sealed envelope addressed to Iris in her mother's handwriting. For days Iris left it unopened on the mantlepiece, and speculated on the way the contents would change our lives: how it might be the title deed to her father's brick house in Seatoun which she could not remember having been sold, or evidence that she had an illegitimate brother who had become a Cabinet Minister in Brazil. The night we opened it we were having curried eggs for tea. The curry coloured the inside of Mum's mouth as she laughed to find clippings about my father's court appearances. This man deserted his wife and daughter, grandmother had written on the newspaper. Men are a different species, Iris told me over the curried eggs. Men are always alone, she said. My father had played squash twice a week for four years with a work-mate, yet never bothered to know where he lived, or how many children he had. Men don't ask anything of each other; it's both their weakness and their strength.

Iris was disappointed by the degeneration that happens to men as they age — hair grew all over my father's shoulders before he left, she said, as if he had died and the mould already begun. The oldest man I ever saw naked myself was the physiotherapist who took a fancy to me in Putaruru. Being in his line of business he kept himself from the most obvious signs of mould, but he had eerily white, caved-in buttocks and besides, as I lay on my back on the carpet, I grew tired of looking at the unvarnished underside of his desk with the lines of the carpenter's pencil still clear.

My mother did better work than that. When we were in Bulls she saved for my kitset duchess, and spent hours getting the tracks aligned so that you could open and close the drawers with the tips of your fingers. Just radiata, but how she sanded it, then umpteen coats of dark stain and a clear finish. I've still got it; each scratch and discolouration is a mark of our life. Yet see, the drawers open with finger tips, the tracks have traces of the candle grease Iris dripped on with puckered lips of concentration. The wood smell evokes the rose-hips that in one Marlborough summer were a livelihood for Iris and me. We spent weeks picking them from the briars growing wild on the Wairau terraces and river bed. It must have been my holidays and my mother had no better job. She picked into the pocket of a bag apron and try as I might I can't remember how we got out to the river bed each day. We sold our harvest to the rose-hip syrup factory. The syrup was a big thing for children's health at the time. Dry river terraces with their rabbit scrapes, foxgloves, bleached grass stems and rose briars. Iris with her bag apron, floppy hat, bloodied knuckles. We're not licked yet she said. We would have our sandwiches together on the stones, from a paper bag so often used that it had the soft creases of a dowager's face. She'd heard on the radio that the country was poised for great transformation and growth and she was determined that we would be swept along with it. The rose-hips were burnished in all that sun, almost ceramic with a red-yellow sheen. The last time I saw the sequin dress was when Iris offered it to me for Glenda's wedding dance. It had grown dull out of its time, as a lurid fish out of its element grows dull. Perhaps you're right, Iris said.

I'm surprised at all the places I've lived in. Ours was the off-season, budget sort of view of Wanganui, Blenheim, Lower Hutt and Bulls, Putaruru and Tuatapere. I never went surfing at Taylors Mistake, or had trout at Taupo Lodge, but I surely know the panoramic view of the Redruth tip, low before the sea, the gull flights wheeling like windmills above the plastic bags massed on the netting. A man putting tiles on the Oddfellows Hall in Invercargill was struck by lightning, yet not hurt much at all. Each working day as I went past I could see where the spouting was dented as he fell. The windows were small and high to stop the rest of us from seeing what the Oddfellows were up to.

Sometimes Iris and I walked past the hall together until we reached the lights, when she would turn right to old Mrs Brody who gave her one of the last jobs she ever had and I would walk on to Acme Smallgoods. Mrs Brody left Mum a Victorian washing bowl and jug used before plumbing was invented. Iris said the set would be worth a fortune today because it was stamped Duenly Pottery, Sussex, underneath, but the jug was broken when our neighbour's tom jumped up at the budgie's cage. I keep a plant in the bowl now. That bowl is big enough to bath a baby, with bruise blue embossed leaves on it and pink roses.

I've had at least two chances to marry rich apart from the son of the Doctors Utteridge — a sheep farmer from the Hakataramea and the owner of three rest homes in Mount Eden. By then though neither Iris nor I saw marriage as such an easy step to success. The merino farmer never spoke more than seven words at a time, yet Iris said you've got to think hard about marrying. You've a responsibility to ask yourself if you really want someone coughing in the same bed, walking in and out of your house at will, telling you things about his life. She thought that men were best as visitors.

Iris went at sixty-four: only sixty-four, and I was there. I'd come down to visit her in the first and last house she ever owned. A married couple's house in Murchison where prices were that cheap. Mum had put new iron on the laundry lean-to and when the rain began she took me out in delight to prove it didn't leak. Things were good for her, because she was on super by then and had plenty of work at the pub as well. She was a terrier for work. From the lean-to window we could see the rain cloud moving across the dark, native bush of the Murchison hills, and the rain dashed on the new, tin roof. Send her down, Hughie, cried Iris and she pointed out the good second hand washing machine and the red lino she'd put down. There wasn't a leak, or a spider's web, in the place. Send her down, Hughie. I think it rains a good deal in Murchison, for the grass on the flats below the bush was lush and there were rushes in the dips. She used to say send her down, Hughie, when she comforted me during a winter we spent in a Johnsonville caravan. We're snug as a bug in a rug here, she'd say. I turned to say something of this to my mother in her Murchison laundry, but she was falling backwards with a stopped heart. As if pole-axed she went down, and any murmur against it I certainly didn't hear above the rain that Hughie sent down. I reckon she died still with the satisfaction of her own home, the new red lino, tin laundry roof, and some great thing to come, even if she never made supermarket star, lost family heiress, or became a medium who told the police of a dozen murder sites, like Beryl Judkins' aunt.

Beryl Judkins' parents took her camping to the Coromandel and she raved on at school about moonlight swims, campfires and pohutukawa blooms along the shore. I must have whined at home about our failure to have holidays, as a ten year old will, so Iris made a tent in our backyard by putting a sheet over the clothes line and anchoring the sides. We had onion chips and lemonade. We lay rolled in blankets watching the sky through the tent end. My mother told me about the black, sequin dress she was planning to wear as a jazz sax player. I heard a hedgehog sorting for grubs in the currant bushes as Iris described the life of a cabaret star. Mr Thompson came out late onto his lawn for a leak and a spit. We were quiet until he was inside again. Sure, it wasn't Beryl Judkins' Coromandel. Mr Thompson once had his photo in the paper because an ancestor had been killed at the Wairau Massacre he said, and he wanted compensation from the government on behalf of the family. It can't have been far from the bright rose-hips of years later.

We shifted away of course before there was any response to his claim, but Iris checked at the library anyway to see if anyone with our name had been massacred there. She said Bleekers had been in New Zealand since before the Treaty. We shifted because she was offered a job as assistant matron at Stanhope Preparatory School in Johnsonville, but when we arrived the assistant matron refused to leave because her marriage plans had fallen through and so we lived in a caravan at the motor camp until Iris became car groomer at Crimmond Motors.

It was a shock at the time of course, Iris going like that, but I came to be glad she'd not suffered any sense of failure. She died in her first home and although Hughie was sending it down outside, not a drop could get through to her red lino and washing machine. The certificate gave Murchison as the place of death, I just thought it strange as about the only one of all those towns and suburbs that I'd not shared with her. All those uncaring places where she had fed and clothed me, and so much more. We're not finished yet, she'd say. Some of us have to achieve what we can despite our lives, rather than as a consequence of them. So there was no supermarket stardom, no Lotto first division, no Brazilian millionaire, no double doctor marriage, no jazz sax cabarets in the sequin dress, not even my father coming back reformed and freshly shaved to start again. Just Iris, my mother, and me.

The Rose Affliction

Myra was using the orbital polisher in the staff cafeteria at Proudhams when she first saw the rose. She had been working for five hours; her asthma was bad again and her shoulders ached from hauling the polisher from side to side on the brown and yellow mottled lino. The first rose was in the extreme upper left of her vision, and as her head moved with the polisher, so the rose moved, skimming over the cafeteria lino, or rising up the pale walls when she lifted her eyes. At first Myra thought it just a temporary continuation of the patterned whorls on the floor, or of the enamelled manufacturer's crest on the central boss of the polisher. But it was quite clearly a small, pink rose. The petals were flushed pink with the packed effort of escaping the green bud capsule.

Myra took one hand from the polisher to rub her eyes and then blinked several times, but although the rose blurred for a moment, it reformed perfectly again. She could see the slightly crimped ends of the small petals, like a delicate, miniature clam, and the deeper tonings of colour towards the centre of the rose. She turned off the machine and opened her mouth to call out to Ruby, who was doing the executive suites not far away. As the whine of the polisher vanished down the empty, night corridors, Myra thought how silly it would sound to complain of a rosebud in her eye, and how impossible to prove. She didn't know Ruby all that well, or trust her with personal things.

It was just that she was tired, Myra told herself; she would come right after a good sleep, and at fifty-nine she had experience of the tricks that body and mind could play on you, though menopause couldn't be blamed any longer. Her knees for example, after all that wear in commercial cleaning, rattled like dredge buckets if she had to get down onto the floor, and her left ankle on a hot day would swell over the rim of her shoe if she had to stand a lot. She had a frozen shoulder; found it an agony to have to work her right arm above the level of her head. Not that she mentioned those things to the supervisor.

But nevertheless, to see a rose was an oddity: like a transfer, or a logo, high left in her vision and superimposed on anything that she looked at there. Even in the bucket of water, milky with disinfectant, that Myra used for the urinals the pink rose could be seen, and as Myra had a lift home with Ruby, because Wayne was out in her car, the imposition of the rose continued. 'We'll get double time if we do the two extra hours on Sunday at the Super Doop Market,' said Ruby. As Myra looked at her to answer, the pink rosebud glowed in Ruby's straight, brown hair.

The rose was still in her eye when she woke: had gained company in fact, a darker pink, larger bloom, past its best so that the full petals exposed the straw coloured stamen of the centre — a round cluster like the cleaning brush Myra's dentist used on his drill. 'Weird,' said Wayne, as he asked her for a loan, and without waiting for an answer began scrabbling in her purse.

'What do you think I should do about it?' she asked her son.

'Does it hurt?' It didn't hurt at all; just the oddity of it concerned her, and what it might represent as a symptom or warning of something going wrong. 'Well I'd say just keep on normally then,' said Wayne. 'You don't want to miss work unless you have to. Not with double time at the Super Doop coming up.'

Myra was pleased with Wayne's matter of fact response, but she didn't say anything to Ruby, or any of the others at work, although there was a steady growth of roses over the following weeks. They massed to the left of her sight, roses of all colours and types, so that when she was cooking or cleaning, at home or at work, the blossoms were imposed on everything she saw. They festooned the cafeteria tables she wiped clean and softened the blatant commercialism of the Super Doop.

Myra developed a rather off-putting habit of cocking her head sideways in an effort to bring those things she wished to view into the clear area of vision that remained. 'What on earth's got into her,' said Ruby to the supervisor.

'You'd better see the quack,' said Wayne reluctantly at home.

'You realise that it isn't actually the image of a rose,' said Dr Neumann. 'Perhaps a vibratory retinal effect, but more likely organic particles in the vitreous or aqueous humour of the eyes. It is in fact quite common for some opaque cells to be there from birth or to detach in later life from inner surfaces.'

'Oh, they're roses all right,' said Myra.

'Indeed. Are they Charlotte Armstrong then, or perhaps Diamond Jubilee?' Dr Neumann was not accustomed to being contradicted.

'I don't know one from another,' she said, humbled.

'The images don't drift you say though. That's the difficult thing to reconcile with cells in the fluid. There's a drifting effect normally in such cases. I think that we had better make an appointment with Mr Hardie. There's nothing to worry about. He will introduce drops to dilate your pupils before the examination, but there's no discomfort.'

No discomfort, but a considerable wait, Myra found. A specialist's appointment can take months for all but the urgent cases. In the meantime the roses multiplied, white, yellow and red, until they were scrolled over much of Myra's sight and she saw the world through an increasingly profuse floral lattice of glowing petals and frog-green small leaves. The roses obscured the urinals, and the smeared tables and walls that Myra was meant to clean. Instead of stains and accumulated grease, scuffs and carpet fluff with blowflies, all of which had been her responsibility in life, she had a host of roses closing in.

'But no scents at all. That's the queer thing, and a pity really,' Myra told Mr Hardie, who looked up from his examination at that to smile to the nurse. Myra could see one side of that smile above a cluster of yellow floribunda.

'We'll keep a check on its progress,' he said. For all his kind intentions he could find neither cause nor cure. 'Don't hesitate to contact me if you experience the least pain,' he told her, and later on the phone to Dr Neumann, agreed it was an unusual and rather tragic case.

'She can't see to work any more,' Ruby said to the supervisor. 'I can't bear to imagine her cut off from us all. Oh, it's so sad isn't it. And there's no operation will help they say.'

'We'll have to get you right onto the sickness benefit,' was Wayne's opinion, 'and the car had better be put in my name, as you won't be able to drive anymore.'

The last roses to come were the richest — and the darkest. Though Myra sat in the sunroom with her face to the window, for her the roses were the enduring and exclusive view. The last roses fitted as if completing a cathedral window, and they bloomed so velvet, so red; downy black-red, red-black. The colour of the blood that goes back to the heart.

HEATING THE WORLD

Tucker Locke wasn't married until he was forty-two. A cheerful woman from the Taieri with good legs and three daughters finally decided to move north for the sun and take him in hand. Before that Tucker was one of a group of bachelor farmers so typical of the New Zealand heartland that they form a sub-species of the population.

After his mother died, Tucker had done for himself, as the saying goes, and with his cooking he just about did for anybody else who called as well. He had lived in traditional rural simplicity rather than poverty. He had an average downland mixed farm worth about half a million in bad years, and camped in his own home — a tartan rug on the porch bed, a laundry that still had a copper, and yesterday's paper as a tablecloth at breakfast as he read today's.

It wasn't that Tucker was a failure as a farmer, not at all, but his financial priorities and lifestyle were congenital. Super and drench, a new post-hole digger, or drill, the best stock and certified seed, were the natural expenses of life, but to buy a new lampshade, or replace the kitchen lino for reason of colour co-ordination would no more enter his head than to dine at the Victor Hugo restaurant in town when he had food in his own home. A four and a half thousand dollar skeet gun on the other hand, or an irrigation mule at twenty thousand, were perfectly justifiable purchases.

The sub-species of rural bachelordom is perpetually renewed of course by the very process of attrition which reduces its contemporary generation. By the time he was forty even Tucker had become aware that he was no longer typical amongst his acquaintances, and that there were deficiencies in a comparative sense. At the tables of his married friends he developed a taste for lasagne and apple strudel. His devotion to cold mutton, mashed potato and swede was somewhat undermined, and the sight of children forced him to consider the fact that his farm had no heir. So, advised by his friend Neville O'Doone who had taken the plunge a few years before, Tucker began the display which indicated that he was willing as well as eligible. He appeared in the retail area of his local town, wore a woollen tie with his sportscoat, and attended a few mixed gender events such as the trots and the show.

The community considered Tucker very fortunate in his marriage, and so did Tucker, nevertheless he had no knowledge of modern women and the marriage brought changes he had not predicted. Neville O'Doone was his counsel in such things, always in the informal and off-hand way that the sub-species deals with the deepest matters of the psyche.

Tucker and Neville were travelling together to an open day on shelter belt trials at Methven when Tucker first sought advice from his friend. They had been commenting on the management and condition of the properties they passed, doubtful of the future for Romney wool, when Tucker abruptly referred to Neville's wife. 'Margaret likes soap, I suppose,' he said.

'Soap?'

'Women like soaps: a variety of soaps and things,' said Tucker. 'I counted seven along the bath last night, and all partly used you know.' His laugh had good-humoured ease as its intention, but conveyed bewilderment instead. Neville told him that he meant shampoos. 'Shampoos, all different colours,' agreed Tucker. 'One oily, one normal, one dry, a body shampoo, a protein conditioner, an apricot facial scrub, and one enriched with the natural oil of some sort of pretzel which grows only in the Orinoco. And soft, pink soap which turns to a slush without use like snow, and vanishes as rapidly.'

Neville could recall Tucker's bathroom before his marriage: one block of yellow soap on which it was easier to work up a sweat than a lather, and with dirt settled into its seams as it weathered so that it was grained like a metamorphic rock. 'It's mostly liquid stuff they buy,' said Tucker sadly. 'It just runs away. You've no idea; it just runs away down the plughole. And women don't like to share a bath, do they. We've put in a shower as well. I could dip a mob of two-tooths in the time my girls take to shower.' In a half-hearted way Neville tried to persuade Tucker that shampoos and conditioners weren't really soaps. 'All do soaps' job,' affirmed Tucker. 'Can you believe seven different bottles, and others besides. Bath salts and that.'

'Oh, yes,' said Neville, but then he'd been married some years before Tucker. He felt a little superior; the sort of superiority you feel when up to your waist in quicksand, but observing someone else in up to his neck. 'But you wouldn't want to go back to being single again would you, Tucker?'

'Oh, no. Hell no,' said Tucker, but his face was pensive, as if regarding a mountain of expensive saponaceous products degrading in natural atmospheric humidity.

They were together at the gun-club when next Tucker raised his home life. Neville had commented on a flash, wine shirt his friend was wearing. 'Pull,' said Tucker, and fired. 'Yes, Dianne thinks I should have some new things. My clothes seem to be wearing out more rapidly these days.'

'How come?' Neville hadn't noticed Tucker working any harder than usual.

'I reckon my stuff is getting worn away in the washing machine,' said Tucker guardedly. 'Women love to get the clothes from my back.'

'Do they indeed, you old dog.'

'I mean for washing. I've always felt myself it takes a day or two to feel comfortable in what you're wearing, but Dianne has it into the machine before I'm hardly used to it. Continual washing is bad for the stitching I'd say, and seems to be shrinking the waistbands, but there's no telling her. I'm getting quite a wardrobe now you know.'

It was true. For twenty years Neville had identified Tucker off his own property by his blue check sports jacket, but he was becoming more difficult to spot since marriage, as his colouration varied. 'Women have a good deal of clothes, you know,' said Tucker with some vehemence.

'I know.'

'My daughters have a drawer of pants each. Whole drawers of pants.' Tucker lifted his hands to emphasize the incredibility of it, then let them fall helplessly to his side. Tucker had been accustomed to maintain three pairs of underpants — one to wear, one to wash and one to change into. He couldn't comprehend the necessity of any other regime. 'Scores of them,' he whispered absently. It was axiomatic for Tucker that clothes were used until they were worn out; the same sensible approach he took to cull ewes, or tarpaulins for the hay shed, yet he was confronted with a philosophy which discarded garments because puce was no longer in fashion, or because the pleats had a tendency to accentuate the hips. 'Margaret buys a fair amount of clothes?' asked Tucker.

'From time to time. Yes,' said Neville. Tucker's expression lightened. If headlong expense was universal in wives, he was human enough to feel pleased that he had company in being a witness and somewhat reluctant backer.

'You're getting to understand why women look better than men. One reason, anyway,' said Neville.

'I guess you're right,' said Tucker. 'I've got two suits myself now, though I can't see that people are going to die regularly enough for me to need to alternate them.'

Tucker still shot well however, despite his financial concern, Neville noted ruefully. He has an eye like a stinking eel, Tucker has. He shot everything out of the air with almost vindictive skill and won another top gun sash and a side of hogget. Neither he nor Neville thought to relate the cost of their day to the conversation.

Tucker and Neville met on sale days at the Dobb Hotel, the only one in town that hadn't put in a barbecue and outdoor seating. Tucker drank draught beer, but slipped in a Glenfiddich every now and again as a chaser. It was in the Dobb that Tucker confided further in Neville concerning his personal life. They had been talking about the Celtic-Old Boys game, and Neville said Ransumeen wasn't talented enough to bring on the oranges at half-time. 'I've rather gone off fruit,' said Tucker after a pause, during which they both watched through the window Gus McPhedron trying to climb into the back of his utility for a nap. Neville found it difficult to follow Tucker's claim, for old Mrs Locke had been a great one for utilising their own orchard, and their pantry had held rows of bottled plums, peaches, and quince jam. She had showed them even, in the produce section of the A & P show. There had been boxes of wrinkled, autumn apples in the laundry and Tucker normally had one or two in his pocket, or the glove compartment of the truck. He had a kelpie once which liked eating them, but Tucker had shot it for biting his best ram in a costly fashion. Neville said something of all that. 'No, no,' said Tucker. 'You don't understand. There's bought fruit, see.' His tone was one of shocked disclosure. Fruit was nature's bounty, something that arose naturally from one's land without great attention and with no mercenary aspects. Ah, but since his marriage Tucker had been introduced to mandarins and melons, paw paws and peppers, passion fruit, oranges and kiwi fruit.

'Do you know how much a feijoa costs?'

'Well, ah,' said Neville.

'Much more,' said Tucker. 'We have bananas often in a bowl together with oranges and pears.' Tucker was half defiant, half distraught, convinced that such hubris would bring his ruin. 'This morning I looked at the ticket on one of the bananas. They each have their own ticket you know. It had come from Ecuador. Ec-u-a-dor!' Tucker was silent after his syllabic exclamation, which had drawn looks from other tables. He was considering the number of chargeable exchanges and activities needed to get a banana from the plantations of Ecuador to his wooden fruit bowl in Te Tarehi. Gus McPhedron was asleep in the ute outside; the tail-gate down, the sun glinting on his tan stock boots. 'And the thing is, see, that often fruit goes off before it's eaten and has to be thrown out.' The concept of produce purchased from the ends of the earth and then thrown out was arsenic to Tucker's peace of mind. Almost bitterly he downed another Glenfiddich. 'No one bothers to eat a quince, or a plum, these days,' he told a sagely nodding Neville. 'The whole crop lies beneath the trees in the orchard for the wasps and the birds.'

'But what's that against all the advantages of marriage,' asked Neville.

'Oh, you're right there,' said Tucker. 'Of course I wouldn't change for the world.'

Yet at the Town versus Country game, in the first half, when the action was mainly down the other end, Tucker voiced further anxiety. He had picked up his family from town the night before and unfortunately been exposed to some of the prices. 'You know how much a lipstick costs; just one?' he asked. Neville was embarrassed in case some of their mates heard, but they were too busy abusing the town ref. 'Twenty-nine dollars thirty-nine,' said Tucker. 'It's true. It's true. And how often do you see a tube used right up. Answer me that.'

'You're blind and bloody half-witted with it,' shouted Neville.

'And Sarah wanted some shoes for aerobatics,' said Tucker as the Town took their penalty.

'You mean aerobics,' Neville said.

'Right.'

'You see aerobatics is —'

'Okay,' said Tucker.

'So she wanted sports shoes.'

'I went in with her myself,' said Tucker. 'Reddickers had a sale and I found a decent pair reduced to fifty-five dollars.'

'That's reasonable enough,' said Neville.

'Oh, but they wouldn't do. Not enough heel cushioning for the effects of aerobics the woman said. A lot of people did structural damage to their feet that way, she said, and Sarah said her friends had different ones. You wouldn't believe what I had to pay before I got out of that shop.'

'Tell me,' said Neville. 'Back up your man, Cecil, for christ's sake. That boy's all prick.' But Tucker couldn't bear to mention the actual amount in all its grotesque enormity.

'Six lambs at today's schedule prices,' he said, and even the sight of the Town's captain being taken off on a stretcher barely lightened his spirits. 'Six lambs; can you credit it. And all for jumping about in.'

On their way back from the match, Neville and Tucker heard on the car radio that there was progress at the great power summit. 'They're wanting more changes,' said Tucker pensively. Neville thought he was referring to the world leaders, but after some confusion realised that Tucker was meaning his wife and daughters. Perhaps it was just a matter of scale after all, though. 'Interior renovations,' said Tucker, as if giving Neville a medical diagnosis of some significance.

'So?' said Neville.

'First grade Axminster, designer wallpaper, new drapes.' Tucker was marking them off on his fingers as he spoke, and steering with upward pressure of his knees. It seemed that Tucker's wife was determined that the good room get the works. 'Ceiling repainted, pelmets removed, droop light fittings and new fire surround tiles of Tuscan red. We'll use the room a good deal more because of it, of course,' said Tucker to console himself, yet the car shimmied because Tucker's knees were trembling.

'It's improving your asset, Tucker,' said Neville. 'There's that as well.'

'That's true,' said Tucker. Neville's considerate response encouraged him to further revelation. 'We have all duvets now,' he continued; his tone wavering between pride and defensiveness. 'Yes, duvets on all the beds, and now we have a double dozen unused blankets folded in the cupboard.' Tucker had pressed past anxiety to a state almost of awe. The grandeur of the extravagance conditioned him to expect some providential punishment. All those blankets that had provided sensible warmth for generations of Lockes, now stored with good wear still in them, and duvets purchased in their bedstead. It couldn't be right in the view of a Calvinistic god. 'Of course I'm a believer in progress,' said Tucker stoutly.

'A lot of the improvements have been on you, haven't they?' said Neville. 'I mean Dianne's done you up proud since you've been married.'

'True, true,' said Tucker. Neville was thinking of Tucker's wet weather gear. In the old dairy next to the back door there had been an array of Locke coats going back into rural antiquity. Tucker's favourite had been a sou-wester which must have defied the last ice-age, and although the cuffs were frayed completely away, the coat itself remained so stiff that if Tucker took it off between cloud bursts, it would stand like a tent in the wet grass. And it blended in with the landscape so well that even the wiliest mallard couldn't pick Tucker out in the mai-mai.

'That new nylon parka for example,' said Neville.

'An anorak,' said Tucker. 'You ever heard of an anorak.'

'Oh yes,' said Neville complacently as a well-married man.

'A bright, red anorak.'

'Very fetching.'

In frosty July Tucker and Neville went to a euchre evening at Wally Tamahana's. Afterwards as they stood in the moonlight to enrich the nitrogenous content of the lawn, Tucker spoke with unease of the range of alternative milks with which he was forced to become familiar since he had been persuaded to abandon a house cow. Red tops, blue tops, green tops, banded tops; low fat, non-lipid, reduced cholesterol, anti-coagulate, mineral free. Tucker claimed he could see a logical trend in it all: the more things were removed from the milk the more the product cost. 'You know,' he said to Neville, 'soon we'll pay the highest price of the lot for milk with everything extracted — and it'll be water.'

'It's all progress I suppose,' said Neville, but he too could remember the cream jug of his boyhood in which the spoon would stand upright.

'Right. Right. Of course I wouldn't have it any other way,' said Tucker bitterly.

Neville was deliberately cheerful as he drove Tucker home, but Tucker, having lost fifty-seven dollars at the euchre to Wally Tamahana, was in a mood to resent any hint of extravagance in others. They rattled over the cowstop at the entrance to Tucker's farm and drove up the track. The median grass not yet brittle with frost whispered beneath the car, and the lights and the moon picked out the massed stinging nettles by the hen house and sheep yards. Tucker's house was a focus of activity and warmth; every room seemed to be lit and one of Tucker's new daughters was singing along with her cassette player. Neville thought it grandly welcoming, but Tucker gave a whimper. 'The door. Ah, god.' The back door was open in defiance to the vast, surrounding winter night, and the glow of double bar heaters could be seen. 'Look, look,' said Tucker brokenly. 'We're heating the world.'

309 HOLLANDIA

Ruth had an understanding with Gordon at Reception, and he rang and said there was this older guy in 309 who wanted company. Gordon knew her style, and Ruth knew the hotel. She placed a good deal of reliance on the type of hotel she dealt with, because it was a way of saving hassles. So she had a shower, and put on her new yellow. She was able to wear the slingbacks with higher heels. She wouldn't be on her feet much.

It's nice, the Hollandia. The reception area is in black and gold; there's black buttoned leather suites facing the second storey windows from which you can look down into the shopping mall. Guests at the Hollandia don't call out to each other just to draw attention to themselves, or laugh loudly. You can hear the businessmen folding their newspapers when they have finished reading, or when their clients and acquaintances have arrived. Gordon told her that a lot of those at the Hollandia were on delegations, or teams from government departments.

There was no embarrassment of hanging about in the corridor after knocking, or being turned away because of visitors in the room. Gordon would ring through first and Ruth would go on up if it was okay. It was okay right away for 309. So she stopped looking down at the people in Stabey's examining the silver bracelets, and sapphire and diamond cluster rings which are the thing right now, and she went up. There's a sense of discreet privilege at the Hollandia — private and select. After ten o'clock only guests with keys can use the lifts to the accommodation floors. Ruth was of a mind to appreciate the bold hachures on the lift carpet, and the photographs of Leiden and Haarlem.

She was interested to see what her client was like, even if it was business. Many of them put themselves out to be pleasant and entertaining. The man in 309 was impressive to look at in an ordinary sort of way, but Ruth thought he became less ordinary as she noticed things about him, for he dressed well and spoke well. He had an ease of presence which she found relaxing. His name was Hamish Green, and he thanked her for coming and poured drinks. They sat by the drapes partly drawn across the window, and Ruth looked down at his shoes. She knew that a man's shoes spoke of his place in the world. A man might splash out on a shirt or a jacket, but shoes gave the consistent picture. Hamish Green's shoes were European, probably German she thought. The uppers had double stitching and leather toe caps with punched whorls.

'I hope you don't have to dash off?' he said. Ruth warmed to that: the courtesy which made it sound as if their purpose was social, which perhaps it was, and her presence a favour, and that he would miss her company if she had reason to go.

Yet when they finished a second drink, sitting by the window with the Friday night passing below them, there were times when he didn't talk, as if he were thinking of some other place. Yet it was an easy silence, and he spoke well when he wanted to. He talked wryly of his fear of flying which never seemed to abate he said, and the petty humiliations it caused him, comparing the sensation to that he had in a dentist's chair. Even in his humour there was an unemotional tone which suggested a lack of affinity with the things he spoke of, or a belief in the final triviality of any subject that could be named.

'Are you warm enough?' he said. 'Would you like something to eat sent up?' The view was quite different to that which Ruth had in the reception area. The lights and the traffic made colours and angles of competition, and as the shoppers came closer they seemed to dip below until briefly they were reduced to a bird's-eye view of heads, hair, parcels, before gaining a length of body again. Ruth had become accustomed to observation, to waiting, to her own thoughts during the time which could otherwise bring boredom. Most professional people develop the skill and habit of maintaining a social presence quite successfully while all the time another enquiry of experience or reflection is underway.

It suited Ruth to change in the bathroom. On the folded towels was an envelope with two hundred and fifty dollars inside: left privately there, with no need for either of them to mention it. She put in her bag also the small hotel pack of hair conditioner, for she knew men didn't bother with it, and she turned her head in the mirror's reflection as a check without vanity. She had a three pack of condoms for the hand-sewn pocket of her night-dress. She admired the small, well set tiles of the shower, the heated rail, the sheen of new fittings. She remembered her first flat in the city, with a scornful califont over a bath stained dark yellow like an old tusk. She had learnt how to live better.

'Are you coming through, Ruth?' said Hamish Green, and as she did so he turned from the bedside table, and put down the hotel's black and gold biro. 'Very glamorous,' he said. 'I love to see lace on a woman's skin.' It was said with calm admiration, and as Green hung up his suit he talked about doilies as an extension of the topic of lace. He described them without knowing the name, and Ruth supplied it. He said he remembered in his grandmother's house all these things on dressers and polished wood tables. Ruth imagined him as a rather stolid, obedient boy, visiting his grandmother, and then leaving early so that he would be home in time to do his homework. He went into the bathroom in his turn to wash and change. He had large feet with expansive, milky nails on big toes. He came back in navy blue, with his large, soft feet like the paws of a bear across the carpet. 'It's not up to the lace is it,' he said.

'Dark blue is nice.' Actually, he was too pale for it. It drained him.

'I'll get it off soon enough,' he said.

'So you're beginning to feel hot-blooded?'

He continued talking about clothes as he made himself comfortable in bed, saying that because of his work he wore suits almost all the time, and had few sports clothes. His hands smoothed her breasts, and then Ruth massaged the back of his neck. 'That's it,' Hamish Green said. He took his navy blue top off. Their talk ambled from massage to tension to headaches to acupuncture. Ruth was interested in acupuncture after reading an article in which migraine sufferers had claimed relief with its use. Sometimes she had a bad head herself. While Green explained the theory behind acupuncture, Ruth thought of the times when her migraines had caused her embarrassment with men. Clients didn't expect a woman in her position to have a headache. There was even humour in it, although on each occasion neither she nor they could see it. Ruth imagined that Hamish Green would have enough detachment to appreciate such a situation, but she didn't mention it. She joined instead his game of finding improbable anatomical points for acupuncture.

A phone call interrupted them. It was about his work, for he listened for several minutes just saying yes, and hmm, with his eyes on the ceiling, and Ruth looked there also, noticed the nozzles of the automatic sprinkler system which marred the even surface. Each floor of the Hollandia had its own colour scheme, right down to the covers. The bed in 309 had a pattern in black, pink and lilac, and the pink was picked up in the drapes. Green said hmm once more, then he had his turn; talking of the next day and how he expected things to go, and it was the other person who did the listening. 'We don't want to get into the question of funding at all tomorrow,' he said. 'Surely at the moment we're concerned only with agreement in principle. Discussion on funding is another thing again, and for another meeting.' And so on. Twice he made mention of paschal lamb, and Ruth didn't understand what he meant. He ended the conversation by laughing in his deliberate way and saying, 'All right, but I wouldn't prepare the paschal lamb just yet.' Ruth lay beneath the black, pink and lilac and her lips shaped the syllables of paschal lamb so that she would remember to look it up in her son's dictionary.

Green had a good deal of grey chest hair, yet on his arms the hair was black and straight, lying the same way across his wrist and forearm. The cabinet above the small fridge was open, and the miniatures stood in ranks like the contents of a doll's cupboard — whisky, gin, brandy, liqueurs, red wine; all the things which didn't need to be chilled. 'I wouldn't prepare the paschal lamb just yet,' Hamish Green said.

As he had talked, sitting half-turned towards the table and the phone, for a while she had knelt behind him, continuing to relax his neck and shoulders. Next to the phone was the envelope on which she had seen him write when she came to the bed. It was addressed to him, and she felt satisfaction that he had told her his real name. In the corner he had written her name — Ruth. She imagined he had done it to save the embarrassment of forgetting her name; having to ask again perhaps in the midst of their loving. There were things she liked about the man; not his middle aged neck and bear paws, but there were things, she thought.

'Sorry about that, Ruth,' he said when the call was over. Maybe he looked at her name on the corner of the envelope before saying that, maybe not. She herself never forgot a client's name until business was over, and never once had a man complimented her on that consideration. On the other hand she had been honey to a hundred men, darling or nothing to more. She had been Wilma, baby, hot pants, sister, Chattanooga Choo Choo even. For a weekend in Sydney it was an auctioneer's sense of humour to call her his opening bid.

Hamish Green talked of how tired he'd grown of staying in hotels, despite knowing that as he had no dependent family anymore it made sense that he was often his company's choice. But hotel room after hotel room, he said. 'Well, there's no dishes to do,' Ruth said. She could find little reason to pity the life he led. She had to bite her tongue sometimes when men complained about such things.

'That's true,' he said. 'I suppose it sounds absurdly indulgent to complain about living in hotels. You're quite right.'

'But I can see what you mean. A hotel's not a home.'

He moved a hand to her thigh. 'Where's home?' he said.

'Right here,' Ruth said. 'You don't mind wearing a sheath? It's better these days.' He stroked her shoulder, and enjoyed slipping the strap of her night-dress up and down, and when he started he was content with the usual missionary position. It was fairly practiced and fairly long, but the earth didn't move for either of them. He then lay on his back with his eyes closed, and began to talk to her again. No confidences or revelations, just his half-serious complaints of the effects of travelling long distances, and how to work effectively despite them. He talked also about those interests and ambitions that he had been obliged to slight for the sake of his work and family. Commonplace topics in most respects. As Ruth listened she sensed that behind the even tone of his indifference, and despite his influence, education, his German shoes, he felt headed in a direction not of his own choosing. She responded to that feeling in two ways natural to her; a selfish satisfaction that he had his problems as she did, and a greater sympathy towards him because of it.

He asked her opinion about diets, said hmm and yes when she was talking, and soon fell asleep. He had moved while she was talking, and slept with his hand on the rise of her hip as if it was a posture he had been long used to. He snored, but not in a way exaggerated enough to disturb her as she lay thinking. She wondered if she could keep her son interested in school, so that he could go on and get a degree in law or accountancy. Then surely he would be able to have a job like Hamish Green's: a job that allowed confidence, self-respect and freedom of choice in little, day to day things even though powerless against the general pattern of life. That way her son wouldn't have to be like her, and she didn't see that in the narrowest sense, for she knew from experience that there were plenty of people of both sexes in the same situation, even if their barter was not so direct or categorical. Later, quieter, when Green's light snoring was as regular as the noise of the sea at a distance, Ruth calculated her income and expenses for the week, and was comforted by the outcome. Yet at the back of her practical mind she posed a question as to how many years she could continue to make the sort of money she did, and how far away was the time when Gordon at Reception would begin to call her less and less.

Almost asleep herself, perhaps even woken by it, Ruth heard Green talking in his sleep. He slurred a few words, then clearer and louder through urgency he said, 'Is that you, Dianne? It's you at last. Don't stand on ceremony.' The words were startling not for themselves, or because uttered in sleep, but rather that the voice was so apart from any tone he had used before. The voice was vibrant and full of sudden appeal, as if another man lay there. Green said nothing more, and continued sleeping, but without any snoring for a long time. Ruth was left to wonder. She thought that Dianne must have been his wife's name, and she moved her lips to remember, don't stand on ceremony, the way she had with paschal lamb. She wondered about his voice and what special world of imagination, memory or emotion was its source. Ruth was interested in patterns of speech; the individual differences helped her in her work to pass the time. When the subject of men's conversation was most predictable there was still the variety of expression. Words, like shoes, she considered useful clues, but the words had interest in their own right too. Thinking of Hamish Green's sleep-talking she smiled, and began to sleep herself.

Ruth woke first in the morning. She found that she didn't sleep in when she was working. Green had moved away in the night towards his own side. He still lay on his back, his jaw dropped somewhat, and his breathing a small gasp on the indrawn air and a sigh on the outgoing. Ruth renewed acquaintance with his face, and noticed most the growth of bristles, so that what had seemed one piece the night before had become two faces; pale above, flint grey below the cheeks. A pirate combination. And on the angle of chest exposed, amongst the ash of curled hair was one incongruous nipple like the wasted kernel of a nut. Yet he had a good head: the face although not handsome suggested reason, and wasn't completely animal the way some men's faces were in sleep.

Ruth went from the bed quietly to have her shower, and when she returned, Green was shaving. 'I've asked for some fruit to be sent up,' he said.

'It's time I was on my way.'

'Me too,' he said. 'A quick shower and then to work whatever the day.' She knew to be putting on a little make-up, out of sight in the bathroom, when room service came, and then she sat close to the window while Green made coffee. They talked of what a city had to offer in a weekend. They weren't completely at ease. She found it more difficult with an intelligent man, once the object of the exercise had been accomplished, and rarely stayed the night in any case. She had her son to consider. She half-regretted having stayed, but then it wasn't fun getting up and leaving the hotel at two or three in the morning; demeaning even. Ruth wished she had some better experience to draw on in her conversation with him. If the feeling had an outcome it was only that her comments became knowing, sharp, even at the expense of people they could see in the Saturday street, or issues of mild interest raised between them. 'You're no fool, Ruth,' he said. She had an answer to that too, but didn't make it, just took her bag and prepared to leave.

'Goodbye, Ruth. I'll remember your lace night-dress. Lovely.' He held out twenty dollars: for a taxi he said.

'Oh, I can walk. I can find my own way all right.'

'No friend of mine walks home alone from the hotel,' he said. That was the right thing to say, Ruth thought, and she didn't find any sarcasm in it. Yet behind all he said she felt some malaise, some lack of expectation. She thought of his sleep-talk in the night; the voice of a different man she had heard just that once.

On impulse she said, 'I won't stand on ceremony then,' and Hamish Green smiled at the phrase, but there was no sign it meant anything to him. She had a last glimpse of him and 309, with the black and pinks well caught in the low morning sun, the envelope with her name on the bedside table, Green's quiet suit and the silver watchband on his wrist.

It was nice wasn't it, the Hollandia. The carpet was obsequious beneath her slingbacks, making no distinctions. Even in the mornings at the Hollandia there was a sense of ease — as if all had been paid for, and quality given for that payment. It was nice, she thought, the Hollandia; with photographs of Groningen and Emmen, Amsterdam, Hilversum and The Hague.

Literary Fair

Yes, folks, it's Lit-rature land at its very best; a stroll down the culled de sac of cultural bequests. Our British light section is the envy of all arcane arcades. (Believe me, madam, he'll be perfectly secure with us. Pick him up in ten minutes at the Moriarty gates.) Just keep to the track, follow me, and don't touch the exhibits for they're completely irreplaceable you see. Smooth your dress down, Anna my dear, and look after the little ones; rendezvous at the Cheshire cat, or the Dr Doolittle zoo. Take her hand dearly beloved, there's a treat in store for you: off to that wonderful world inside the Pied Piper's mountain. Oh, a land of no mummies and daddies, just kind aunties and nannies, barber striped candy and chocolate fountains, and pierrots and carousels, and wise old owls that philosophise and tortoises that instruct. There's fairy dust to sprinkle and a never never land. There's tin soldiers and tinder-boxes, and mice with mustard spats. Little black sambo and gollywogs, and handicapped people as villains. Blind Pew, fingerless Black Dog and Captain Hook are nonconformity. A land of innocent frilly dresses and suck a thumb cherubs, and goose-girls, and Cook all warm in flannelette who lets us steal Madeira cake while the adults are dressing for dinner. Come potter in the land of Green Ginger, where plovers and curlews are calling. Hear the rattle of the tilt cart and the fairy caravan. Everybody pitches in you know, even Milly Molly Mandy. The mock turtle's a standing joke for his mathematical creator: the single print of the day of the week is acknowledged as living theatre. The fox uses a Latin tag in talk with a well-dressed drake, and every stump has a small red door which leads to another land. Meet me there, Anna my dear, meet me there. Bunter of the lower fifth foils the mad scientist once more, by sagacity and loyalty and crumbs laid on the floor. Oh, it's the boys' own annual fête with China or Indian tea, and the Lord of Blandings nonplussed fours are seen in baronial halls. Oh, Fritz the Hun is on the run from constable Plod my friend, and a white Russian princess is gloriously saved by the charge of the 9th Hussars. And Prepington-Smythe of Scotland Yard heads down to Paddington Quay. The Queen's word is clearly heard in a hundred tribal districts, and law has come back with the drums' beat to subjugate the jungle. The Commissioner brushes a ginger moustache and narrows his eyes in the sun. Day after day with fairness and calm he rules the vast Mungapopo, and at night in his tent with a gin and a lime he says not a word of why he is there for the honour of Lady Cecilia. See Ellen will take in the tea things, for the gypsies are camping again by the oaks of harpenny field. Oh, it's Wooster's sauce we must laugh at, he's the devil's own chap for a prank. Yes, and cut along young Delacombe or you'll be late for chapel. They're changing the guard at Buckingham Palace; it's shoulder to shoulder with Englishmen and follow the fun to Khartoum. It's potted ham and honey for tea, and the curate's a fatuous ninny: it's striding along in the wolds and the fens and not caring for stains on the pinny. Oh to think of it, oh to dream of it, fills my heart with tears. Come and eat our fill again at the wonderful Wodehouse café. It's Saunderson's last race, and the price is paid in full. Squeers is blamed — and Joe Gargery? We're ashamed to be ashamed of him. Mungo Park and Livingstone are modern Marco Polos: assegai are raised on high at the mouth of King Solomon's mine. The capstan winds a tale or two for cabin boys and bosuns. There's an indrawn hiss as the black spot's sighted; ah, Jim lad so there is. There's grottos of immortals and each lingers in the mind: Edward Whymper, Captain Trotter and R.E. Prothero. Oh, huzzah for E.J. Trelawny and the adventures of a younger son, huzzah for Peacock's English prose from Mandeville to Ruskin. Oh, huzzah, huzzah, for the rallying cry of the indomitable 9th Hussars. Camping holidays what a wheez, with Wodger and William, and no hint of panky in the dark; not even thoughts of hints of panky in the dark. Oh, it's mistletoe and holly, and a communist robin all the year. And a chimney sweep to be discovered with talent, scrubbed up and sent to Grammar. The wreckers are out on the Cornish coast and the revenue men are massing. The mad woman in white flits over the moor: the laird reviews his crofters. So cut along young Dewkesbury or you'll be late for chapel. Three cheers for threequartermain: hurrah for Ralph and Peterkin and dinghies on the Yar. But psst, psst, beware of the man with the scar! Cads and bounders, rotters and blighters, sneaks and heaps of uriah. We'll cut them dead without a nod of the head, and pass with a careless laugh. And Kitchener's grim and determined for the sake of the old country. Oh, steady the blues, steady the blues, don't fire till the light of the Khyber glints on the blades from Kandahar. Don't trust the French master new to the school, we've always judged him a rum 'un. It's nine wickets down, two runs to win, and the captain's taking the strike. He's a good type of chap and plays a straight bat, and tries to take after his pater. Though whether the family is really quite county we're bound to find out later. Oh, the Afghan passes from hand to mouth, and Purun Bhagat is seen again in grinning Kali's shrine. Absolutely everyone is part of our kith and kin, we'll have no rank outsiders to tamper with the cellars, for there's some jolly splendid Medoc, laid down by the fourth baronet. The game's afoot I surmise, Watson, bring the slipper and a service revolver. Now you girls follow me and try to keep from blubbing. Do what you're told, be good scouts, and we'll fox them yet against the odds. And cut along young Pountney, or you'll be late again for chapel. It's rotten luck for Archie, but Biggles is coming you'll see. There's the code of silence, the stiff upper lip, law of the jungle, the done thing, a fair crack of the whip, and the honour of the British Raj. The svelte veldt is a customary place for the regiment to die. All in the donger together, with a jibe at the fates as they wait. And in the south quad late tonight there's Queensberry rules between the Head of House and the foreign chappie with a shocking cut to his jacket. Oh the sounds of the Kerry pipers, oh the shouts of the 9th Hussars. Stand by the captain against mutinous crews; rescue the runt of the litter. Play in the attic and orchard, stomp in the mud with your wellies. But is that a hunchback at the darkened window! He at the Hall is frightfully grand, but never puts on any side; he's even developed a stutter it seems, to put other chaps at their ease. When the Toad comes home: when the Toad comes home. How splendid a recitation. And Ratty and Mole are always loyal to the muscular

Christianity of Badger. It's Baden-Powell for ever, and never a thought of panky. It's Kaffirs and Boers falling neck and koppie before the 9th Hussars. And brother Mycroft from the smoking room of his cherry leather club, summons a hansom woman to carry an esoteric clue to Prepington-Smythe of the Yard. Pluck, puck, luck and the good old school will surely see us through; and we'll never be found a shirker. There's watchers along the paper chase, with moleskin trousers and hair on their cheeks, and ominous dark, felt hats. And you know old chap, deuced if it doesn't, it all comes down to you. Play up and all that, do your bit, we know we can rely on you. Up and at them the Blues. Take my hand upon the truth of it, and follow to the ends of the earth; for when the salt of the Government's taken there's no turning back at the pass. Nancy's for it, I'm afraid, she sees what no woman should. The subalterns grow pensive in their cups, and the children from the orphanage sing thankful carols in the snow. It's a damn near thing, but we'll see it through at odds of thirty to one. Goodbye Mr Potter, goodbye farmer Meek, goodbye Aunt Polly and the road to Manderley. Goodbye to Cook and Nanny and the pert little parlous maid. Goodbye to midnight feasts, and goodbye school bully with a squint — the beast. The hare and the houndstooth are nearly done, the race of life is nearly won. And a Gothic moon leers in at the madmen in all the secret rooms. So here's to Landseer paintings, and here's to the 9th Hussars. Here's to life at the Grange, and to Prepington-Smythe of the Yard. Here's to the purple sashes and blushing rosettes all on the harness room wall. Here's to Toby and Runnymede Glen, and the turrets of Baskerville Hall. Here's to the Forsyte an Englishman shows in planning for his future. Here's to endless summer Hols. Here's to pikelets and scones and strawberry jam; bluebells and hyacinths, cobblestones and slates, cousins in the country, new people at the manor. Here's to furling the topsoil gallants; and claymores raised by the tartan clans in honour of '45. Here's to the little people and animals that talk; here's to the toadstool kingdom and cowslip wine. Here's to the hills of Simla, and the Pathan of the days. Here's to the sense of duty and regimental ways. Here's to roses over the cottage door and plaintive minstrel lays. Ah, here's to all those things so bravely done within the covers. Here's to every decent chap, as British as an apple. So cut along young Fethergill or you'll be late for chapel.

Yes, folks, it's Lit-rature land, and all your old friends were there: some of the paint is chipped it's true and the costumes a little soiled, but we move so much from place to place to satisfy the punters. Ah, no photos, sorry, we're very strict on that. Keep it all in the mind — it's our livelihood you see: but come again, come again, if you've the genuine price of admission.

Guest Of Honour

'On the other hand,' said Willcocks. 'On the other hand, a centenary is an occasion for some recognition of history, and Adrian Webb is the oldest living former club champion who isn't completely gaga. What a pity though that Gavin Buttery's not alive.'

At that moment Webb was turning round and round on the spot, trying to get his right arm into his pyjama top. It was an arthritic waltz. Each time he completed the circle he kept himself up-to-date on the migratory patterns of the snow geese on the screen. He felt no telepathic pride as on the other side of the city his invitation was decided. He stood still finally, his awkward arms clad in blue flannel, the collar turned under at his thin neck, and he watched the snow geese sweep together with unblinking eyes far above the tundra. Just for an instant Webb caught the exultation of it; caught his breath against the Arctic wind.

Willcocks was the senior partner in his firm; accustomed to respect. Also as president he gave a good deal of time and expertise to the club. So Webb was invited as a guest of honour to give a speech at the centenary banquet in the summer. He was put on the menu before the main speaker — a Davis Cup player with no affiliation with the Holly Park Club, but known on the after dinner circuit for a wonderful repertoire of locker room tales.

Sixty-nine is not all that old. Webb was still capable of some concern for others, still capable of organising his own modest finances and getting back from the shops without forgetting his address. He could give a speech, Willcocks said. After all they didn't want a complete dodderer, but Willcocks' father had seen Webb bearing up pretty well in the supermarket, and Webb had been men's singles champion in 1947 and 1948, not long after the war.

Webb's invitation was accompanied in the post by the notification of a rent increase and a letter from his ex-wife extolling her quality of life since leaving him in 1974. She wanted the monogrammed teaspoons from Rotorua and Queenstown, she said, as she had become a collector. In the circumstances Webb felt a surge of affection for his old club. Being flattered, he persuaded himself that he had learnt at Holly Park aspects of character and fellowship which remained significant. He thought back to his playing days and was disconcerted by how little he could recall: only the great Buttery for skill and presence, only Nellie Hambinder for incorrigible beauty.

What to wear at the banquet was just as important as what to say. At the back of his wardrobe Webb found his club blazer, grown shabby in obscurity, but he thought that a good dry-clean would spruce it up enough for one night. Some insect had dined on the backing of the pocket crest; there were small holes which showed pale material through the gold thread of the crossed racquets. Webb bought a yellow felt pen at the supermarket and inked over the holes so that at a distance nothing seemed amiss. There is no appeal for pity in all this; such measures are merely the prudent decisions of a man retired and self-reliant. Adrian Webb was not in physical want. Four or five good shirts, a drawer of socks, a clump of broad ties like a kelp bed. He drank a glass of beer quite regularly and a bottle of red wine perhaps half a dozen times a year — more often than the great mass of mankind had such enjoyment. He didn't fret that his estate could be cleaned up in two or three tea chests when he died. He no longer had a car, for a working life in the motor trade had taught him the real cost of running a vehicle. It took a great many taxi rides to equal that total, and Webb took few. He intended, however, to arrive by taxi at the Holly Park clubhouse on the night of the banquet.

Over several weeks Webb assembled the combination of clothes best suited to his newly dry-cleaned blazer. He laid everything out on his spare bed as a check, including his good shoes. The natural creases and welts held slightly more of the hundred polishes over the years, and gleamed more deeply brown than the smooth toes and sides. The clothes, the chosen shirt and striped tie, the cuff links even, lay on the bed as if he himself had been there, then taken just his flesh away. Like the eyes of the snow geese, his outline in apparel posed a riddle that was discomforting.

It is the nature of the human mind that there must be a motivating priority and if there is no immediate threat of death, or glorious fame, then such things as the unusual sight of a black rabbit, or a neighbour spitting on the path, will be elevated to that significance. The banquet became the centre of Webb's life. When he was satisfied that his clothes would pass muster, he began to consider his speech. He hadn't given a formal speech since his retirement from Astor Motors, but as a salesman he had no fear of words. Despite not maintaining an association with the club since his playing days, he would find things of interest for modern members. He told this to Mrs Beardsley from the next unit as they put out their rubbish bags. Mrs Beardsley nodded in excitement and asked what sort of a spread there would be. Webb was good-natured enough to mention it also to the girl selling Guide biscuits. He asked her opinion on the influence of professionalism in modern sport.

What Webb didn't admit to anyone, least of all himself, was that the rise of Holly Park had lead to an inflation of reputation for earlier players such as himself. In his day Holly Park had been just another club struggling to win a pennant here and there and lucky to keep a team in the A grade. Only the great Gavin Buttery had any class. The club's expansion came in the later 1950s and 1960s as a result of energetic fundraising and administration by Willcocks senior. Six all-weather courts were added and lights for evening play. By the eighties the club's trophy cabinet groaned and the top two or three players were rarely out of the provincial squad. Yet people you see have little understanding of historical forces and Adrian Webb's 1947 and 1948 titles ranked him with later champions who could have wiped the courts with him. In his heart Webb knew that Buttery was the only Titan of the early days, but we are not bound to acknowledge our hearts, still less to impart the truth.

Gavin Buttery had won the men's singles on seven occasions, and it was only because he was on an agricultural exchange to Nebraska that Webb had won the title in 1947. In the absence of the great Buttery, minnows were left at Holly Park to divide the spoils. The gods smiled again on Webb in 1948. The great

Buttery, when two sets up in the final against him, ran back for a lob and tripped over Nellie Hambinder's spaniel. Buttery wrenched a ligament in his playing arm, and Webb by playing above himself won 12–10 in the fifth. There were no tie-breakers in those days Webb liked to remind young players, with just a suggestion of disdain. The coming banquet revived in Webb memories of that triumph: he could see Buttery wince on that final cross-court backhand, the ball strike the netcord, bulge for a moment at the brim and then fall back to the great Buttery's side. Webb had again the salt taste of victory, the scent of mown grass, the glint of summer leaves above the clubhouse, the shamefaced, sideways glance of the Hambinder spaniel.

One week before the banquet there was a page in the sports section on the Holly Park centenary. Webb's name was listed among the speakers, but he didn't rate a photograph. There was a bird's-eye view of the facilities, a picture of the Willcocks, father and son, and one of the great Buttery when Canterbury champion. Webb was dismayed at his youthfulness. Webb carried the page in his wallet and spontaneously produced it at the supermarket checkout, the barber's, and a quiet, Maori nurse on the bus was made aware of the Holly Park celebrations and Webb's part in them. Webb practised his speech as he prepared his one hot meal a day, or washed the dishes afterwards, unaware that he was a laughing stock when he did so for the Crimmond children across the way.

On the Saturday Webb was dressed by half-past five, having filled out at last the clothes assembled: a risen Lazarus. For an hour he fretted, pushing his face often up to the mirror, checking his blazer for fluff, wondering why there was such a gap between his shirt collar and his neck. He recited parts of his speech, watched at a section's remove by derisive Crimmonds. When the taxi came at last — quite on time — Webb bent the driver's ear with the significance of the night.

With such anticipation Adrian Webb was bound to find his arrival an anti-climax. The clubhouse was strange to him and even the gate lock a puzzle, so that another guest had to show him how entrance was gained by using a plastic membership card in the locking device. But there was still sunlight and the trees of the park massed behind the new pavilion. Some players still hit about after the centenary tournament, others sat on the grass bank, or the wooden forms behind the courts.

Formality was confined to the clubhouse, for there Willcocks presided as chief official on the steps, and the trestle tables for the banquet covered the verandah behind him. Some committee members had wished to have the function at one of the large hotels, or in a public hall, but Willcocks had held out for the club's own premises as a backdrop, even if it meant eating on the verandah. *'Dejeuner sur l'herbe,'* he claimed blithely. *'Potage al fresco.'* Webb recognised Willcocks from the sports page, but would have known him in any case by his position at the top of the wide steps; the posture, the dinner jacket with scarlet cummerbund all bespoke a barrister and president. Webb in his way was equally easily identified: his out-moded blazer, the shirt collar too large at the throat, the well-preserved leather shoes polished to an apoplectic glow in the evening sun, his hair grizzled at the back. He had an air, part indecision, part elderly presumption.

'Our past champion,' said Willcocks as he took Webb's hand. 'We look forward to your speech. My father sends his regards, but is unfortunately too ill to be here. I understand that you knew Gavin Buttery?'

'Oh yes.' As the great Buttery was dead and none of his real friends present, Webb assumed a greater familiarity than had in fact existed.

As he talked Willcocks glanced over Webb's shoulder to see if the Davis Cup player, guest of honour, was arriving. 'Let me get you a drink,' said Willcocks before Webb had completed his description of Buttery's service action. The president led Webb inside to the bar and gave him a glass of the rather *spritzig* white bought in bulk. 'This is Mervyn Harrod of our committee,' Willcocks said, and having previously deputised Harrod as Webb's minder the president moved back to the verandah as official greeter. Webb glanced after him and had a sense of loss as he watched the young people still nimble on the courts and the vast self-sufficiency of the leafy trees in the park beyond.

Harrod was a thin, buckled man. His hair ran left to right across his balding head and the scalp glinted like a tusk beneath. Although not listening to Webb's conversation he had a habitual chuckle at the conclusion of anything said. Webb wasn't too old, or too silly, to recognise the insincerity. What did surprise him was the casualness with which the centennial banquet was treated. Many of the guests wore no tie; some even came to the clubhouse in tracksuit trousers and leisure shirts. 'Young people can be too relaxed about social occasions, don't you think?' he said to Harrod, who gave his easy chuckle as a reply.

The Davis Cup player came at last. A slim face so reduced by fitness that it seemed a hatchet; good nature and ease of manner from his success in life. Willcocks primed him with several glasses of wine, then tried to herd people back from the bar onto the verandah. Even his voice of advocacy took time to have an effect, so he winked to a rural member of the committee who put his fingers in his mouth and produced a whistle of such shrill intensity that it brought the crowd to heel. 'Ladies and gentlemen, please take your places for this our centenary dinner,' said Willcocks. He was a queen bee amongst more humble members, resplendent in dinner jacket, cummerbund and bow tie in matching scarlet. Even with the Willcocks assurance such magnificence seemed a little much in the slanted sun and amongst the trestle tables in close rows on the verandah boards.

Willcocks began with a ten minute speech the main thrust of which was that they wouldn't be having speeches at that point of the evening, and advising members that only the top table would be served; all others to satisfy themselves buffet style, as he termed it. Webb knew that the meal was his payment as a speaker so he determined not to sell himself short. He held his plate up obligingly whenever he was aware of someone passing behind his chair. Sometimes it was a committee member on errand, or a guest seeking the lavatory, but usually it was a waitress who added to his plate. Also he was careful not to leave that mouthful or two of wine in his glass which might serve as an excuse when refilling was done.

It was a solid enough meal, particularly at the top table. Webb avoided the drumsticks, because they took longer to eat and the debris tended to build noticeably on the plate. The cold ham and silverside however, left no evidence of their passing. Yet Webb's hands were not as steady at sixty-nine as in the days he could play a drop volley from mid-court, and as the main course progressed a ring of peas was a necklace for his plate. When the plates were cleared for dessert, Webb showed presence of mind by sweeping the peas clear with a single movement. They fell to the floor, or lodged on Harrod's lap. Pavlova had never been a favourite with Webb, a lack of substance in proportion to bulk disappointed him and he timed his helpings so that it was the heavy, sherry trifle that he ate. The veins of custard, the sherry sodden sponge, the compacted cream, all slid down his throat so easily. Webb continued with his trifle, strange misnomer, even when the other diners had moved on. Harrod couldn't help noticing Webb's determined appetite and his ready laugh took on a note of derisory admiration.

'I make no apology for touching on my father's contribution,' said Willcocks in his speech proper. He had already summarized the 1920s and the twenty years after in the history of Holly Park. 'Would that he were present with us to witness the strength and vitality of the Club he so ably supported as player, administrator and patron for so many years.' Webb could vaguely remember Willcocks senior as a thick-set, sad man who repaired the court netting, or marked the grass courts with wet lime from the small wheeled trundler while people around him enjoyed themselves.

'Wasn't he a very sad man?' Webb enquired of Harrod, lifting his head to scout for more trifle.

'Pardon?' said Harrod after his laugh.

'Always sad,' said Webb loudly, exasperated with Harrod's vacuous company, so that Willcocks raised an eyebrow and continued more forcefully.

'My father had a vision for Holly Park, and the willingness to back that vision with hard work and financial assistance.' Harrod and the other management committee members Hear, Heared, and tapped the trestle table tops. 'I hope that I may say I have maintained both that vision and that practical support.'

'Hear, Hear,' chorused the tapping committee, and a fox terrier on the number two court howled rapturously and annointed the net post.

Something magnificent was happening in the sky as Willcocks spoke. The summer evening still had light although it was almost nine, but a transformation was taking place. Purple and mauve clouds heaped like candy floss in the bowl of the heavens, and the park tree shivered in a new breeze. The sky held menace of both sound and fury, but for the moment postured in eerie silence. The heat drained from the verandah and those diners at the outer tables felt quick, chill paws along their backs. 'It may be true,' said Willcocks, 'that my experience in the legal profession has shown the necessity to me of forward planning and adequate financial structures.' There were rumblings of thunder and a cold gust of the approaching southerly swirled into the clubhouse. The president went on to document the era of the sixties and seventies when Holly Park established itself as a premier club, yet his speech did not receive the attention of before, partly because after twenty-five minutes the impressive, orotund delivery was losing its novelty, but more because of the dismay felt by those people on the open side of the verandah. The top table was distinguished by social not physical elevation, nevertheless it was closest to the inner rooms, while for those by the broad steps the night encroached and the first rain spun in the air. A few of the told-you-so members began to grumble at the venue after all, and point out that even Willcocks was not capable of manipulating the elements to serve his purpose, but everyone had eaten and drunk too well to be vindictive in criticism.

'Mr President, distinguished guests, members of the committee, past and present members of the club, fellow tennis enthusiasts all,' began Webb. How often had he rehearsed, yet he still enjoyed the flow in its proper context at last. 'How fitting Mr President that we should be in the environs of our own club grounds this evening to celebrate the centenary.' There was vigorous assent from the top table and others well protected; some contrary comment from the outer reaches. The grounds were being lost to encroaching darkness. The wind flared out the nets and rain drops glinted like harried whitebait shoals in the verandah's light.

'My thanks for your kind introduction,' continued Webb. In fact he felt a grievance at the inadequacy of his introduction which stressed his age rather than his achievements. 'As I stand here tonight I am reminded of the great Gavin Buttery.' There was a reverential murmur from the club elders. Willcocks by saying Hear, Hear was able to both ease and disguise the passage of a little flatulence. Webb had made Buttery the vehicle for the themes of his speech. He listed the great Buttery's club and provincial honours, stressing the graciousness in victory and defeat; his custom of choosing a different partner for each year's club doubles so that the honour of winning was shared around. As Webb made his speech, fresh, separate images of Gavin Buttery paraded in his own mind. Buttery sipping Ships' Lime Juice at the courtside between games; the idiosyncracy of a muslin cloth loosely tied around his neck to absorb the sweat. A host of Holly Park juniors had followed the habit, as if a muslin cloth about their eager necks could bestow the great Buttery's back-hand floater, or his drive volley from three-quarter court.

'Learning how to win and how to lose in the game of life,' continued Webb, having quoted Kipling's poetry and a Churchill speech. The wind and the rain, the caterers behind him and the guests before, provided a background chorus. 'As I look about me here I recognise the same adherence to fundamental sportsmanship . . .' The members on the outside of the verandah rose from their seats, not in endorsement of Webb's sentiments, nor in mutiny against them, but to escape the rain which began sweeping fearsomely along the side of the clubhouse. They took their glasses and crowded amongst the more sheltered tables further in. Some of the women sat on proferred knees amid giggling and by-play.

'The game's called off because of the weather,' shouted someone.

'I've played and won in worse than this,' said Webb and was clapped for it. Yet he felt obliged to finish hastily and his pleas for the great Buttery's virtues of sportsmanship to be exemplified in every day life were largely lost in the noisy migration from the open side of the clubhouse. In all the steady rehearsals of Webb's address there had been no thought of such conclusion, but the search for physical comfort is a priority for the human animal.

Willcocks decided that the Davis Cup player, as a funded speaker, should give his speech inside. The guests crowded in after him. Even so, some had to be content with getting close to the doorway, while others gave up and sat drinking around the most sheltered tables of the verandah, or playing the goat so that one of the trestles was upset and brought down a table with uproarious crash. The wind and the rain gathered to a storm: water gushed from the overhang, the trees behind the clubhouse and the courts could no longer be seen, but they howled and shivered. The table newsprint flapped and the frame gates at a distance rang out of tune.

The Davis Cup player had nothing uplifting to say, and consequently was very well received. What did he care of Holly Park. He knew what was expected of him to earn his fee, and he told locker room anecdotes of Jimmy, Stefan, Steffi and Gabrielle. The faces of his audience mirrored his expression of insider privilege. Second-hand was so much closer than they were accustomed to. Their mouths remained half-open so that they could trip their laughter the more readily.

The unplanned move into the clubrooms broke up the hierarchy of the top table. Webb found himself hemmed into the kitchen doorway. He could hear just the echo of Harrod's placating laugh as the minder worked his way through the crowd towards Willcocks and officialdom. Webb's view was blocked by the bulk of a freckled, ginger youth of amazing muscularity, and whose ears were moulting several layers of skin. 'Good speech, pops. Way to go,' he said to Webb, but then gave offence by observing that the moths had been at Webb's blazer monogram. 'Seen a fair bit of service, the old jacket, pops,' he said. Webb drifted back into the kitchen without reply. The throng, the ginger Titan and the Davis Cup player's quips were distanced somewhat.

Yet Webb was aware that the feature speech of the evening was being enjoyed more than his own. 'Oh, it's all very amusing I dare say,' he told the catering woman who was scraping dessert plates above a plastic bucket, 'but it hasn't much to do with our centenary has it.'

'I've never been much at sport myself,' she said. 'It's an outgoing rather than an incoming, you see.'

'Pardon?' Webb hadn't expected a reply.

'An outgoing. An expense rather than an earner,' said Pauline. Her name was clear on the red, plastic badge. As she worked the flesh shook on her large arms, but she was very quick, very sure and adept. The dessert remnants were flung like jellyfish into the bucket; the cream, green and powder blue plates were stacked for washing.

'There's millions made in sport: millions. There's sponsorship and endorsements as well as prize money you know. There's lecture tours and coaching. Speeches for two or three thousand dollars a time in the States. There's income in sport all right.'

'Not for you and me though,' said Pauline. 'I bet you never made any money from it.'

'No,' said Webb honestly. There was a burst of laughter from the crowded lounge as the Davis Cup player told another one.

'Push them along. There's a love,' said Pauline. The kitchen windows were misted with condensation; a cloud grey which kept back the dark storm outside. Webb didn't know what she was talking about.

'Them plates,' she said. 'Push them along the bench to make some room.'

'Right.' Webb thought he could hear Harrod's laugh, cranked up almost to a squeal, and because he was cut off from its source he found the braying of his fellows empty, even disheartening. The mounting slops in the bucket began to make Webb queasy: the pavlova, fruit salad and trifle scraps all flung together in a mucus of slow subsidence.

'Imagine,' said Pauline, 'if the human body retained everything that it consumed. Think of the size of the average person at sixty after say five pounds of food for every one of those days.'

'My god.'

'Imagine it,' said Pauline. 'Think of all the difficulties. The effect on public transport for instance.' All the time she worked on quickly, her large, deft hands washing plate after plate.

'I'll just nip through.' Webb nodded his head at the passage.

'Get rid of some of it,' said Pauline kindly.

At the end of the corridor was the committee room, built in the time of the club's new affluence and success under the family Willcocks. The trophy cabinet covered a wall, and cups like catacomb skulls were laid in ranks. The honours boards of presidents and champions were surrounded with photographs. There was a gloss to things that was strange to Webb. He recalled the humble clubrooms of the forties and fifties: unlined changing sheds, two shower roses, like watering can spouts, and the challenge ladders with names on cardboard cut from a shoe box.

In the new committee room the honours boards had gables of polished wood and were faced with green vinyl which bore names in gilt lettering. Webb's name appeared twice of course, for 1947 and 1948. All that remained of the actual events, apart from his own memories. He could see again the great Buttery dancing backwards, eye on the ball, racquet arm rising, and then Nellie Hambinder's spaniel scampering out to be an obstacle where no obstacle should be. Yet Buttery had his name up often enough, and his presence central in one photograph after another. There was even a separate head and shoulders of Buttery; the muslin tucked around his neck and his hair amazingly neat and flat. The great Buttery's aquiline face had the confidence of a Caesar. Webb could find himself only once; third from left in the back row on an opening day.

It was all very well for Gavin Buttery, for he had gone in his prime, killed instantly by a helicopter monsoon bucket during the Te Tarehi scrub fires of '61. Webb could hear Pauline talking in the kitchen while she worked, could hear the braying of the mass in the lounge, and the fury of the storm about the Holly Park clubhouse, but in his mind's eye were white lines on the sweet grass, a white hem across Nellie Hambinder's brown thigh, and the lithe figure of Gavin Buttery as he reached the net to drive another volley for a winner. How that man could middle the ball; and he would never grow old. Webb turned out the committee room lights. Only a random selection of names then glinted in the lesser light from the kitchen corridor. G.B.Q. Buttery and C.R. Noble, G.B.Q. Buttery and B. Smith, G.B.Q. Buttery and N.A. Hambinder. Webb recognised part of the record of the club mixed doubles. He felt his arthritis begin to niggle as he went back down the corridor.

Pauline was making progress: clear areas of bench top were appearing. She worked with abundant energy and efficiency, her priorities being to finish her work, earn her money and be gone. Pauline had no intrinsic interest in Holly Park, President Willcocks, the great Buttery, or even Webb. Functions were not weddings, reunions or centenaries for her, but thirty-eight dollar apiece three cold meat hot vegetable buffets, twelve dollar table served continuous savoury suppers, or a nineteen dollar silverside cold cut and salad on paper plates with club sandwiches and a coffee gateau dessert.

'Feeling better?' she said.

'Oh, I wasn't sick or anything.' He stood by the bench; watched the clean cutlery in jugs of hot water.

'Just shaking hands with the unemployed,' said Pauline's colleague, Viv.

'Any more glasses in the lounge they can do themselves. We can't wait all night,' said Pauline. From habit triggered by Webb's presence at the bench, she gave him a tea towel and he began the forks without complaint. 'There's one anaesthetist puts his hand on your boobs when you're under,' she said.

'Never,' said Viv.

'It's a known fact, but nothing's done you see, because it's their calling.'

'They cry out you mean.'

'I mean the doctors. Their occupation. No one stands up to them.'

'At a time like that you'd think they'd keep their minds off it, wouldn't you.'

'Marjorie Saunders said her nipples were quite sore after she woke up, and she was having the veins in her legs done.'

Willcocks had finished his final speech some time before. Some banqueters were leaving. They built up like lemmings on the verandah, milling apprehensively and peering into the storm. From time to time a group spilled out and went splashing and squealing past the misted windows of the kitchen. Willcocks, Harrod, the Davis Cup player and others from the top table went back to the president's house to continue a more select celebration. No one sought Webb out with an invitation. A hard core of club members remained in the lounge. With a certain ostentation they stock-piled beer and prepared themselves for an all-nighter.

'You wouldn't know a thing. They could be up to anything,' said Viv.

'That's why the nurses are so important. I'd never go into theatre without several of my own sex.'

'Well anyway we're just about done here,' said Viv. She watched Webb drying the last of the knives, tolerant of his clumsiness.

'Nearly cleaned up,' said Pauline. She lifted a soft rope basket onto the bench, and displayed four bottles of the slightly *spritzig* white which Willcocks had bought cheaply. They had been opened, but not used. The corks were driven back into their mouths. 'One's a present for you,' she told Webb. 'Where's your car?'

Pauline and Viv said they wouldn't think of letting Webb go home by taxi. So Webb carried one of Pauline's baskets and walked between her and Viv across the verandah and into the storm. The women held the collars of their coats tight at their necks, and Webb was protected by their bulk. The hard cases were still drinking noisily in the lounge. The night was slick with wetness and the wind worried in the trees, the poles and the netting. 'We shouldn't by right have to wash our own smocks, I reckon,' said Pauline.

'You're right.'

Webb hurried to keep up, and coughed to keep in the conversation. He found it difficult to realise that the Holly Park centenary banquet was over. A priority for so long, it had finally passed beyond the need for preparation, or the provision of anticipation. He felt as an explorer who has had a mountain peak in his sights, then climbs it at last and must face a bare horizon afterwards. Sixty-nine run of the mill years, and the club monogram of his blazer yellowed with felt pen to hide the moth holes. He should have known better than to think the centenary offered anything out of the ordinary; that the great Buttery could be conjured up on his behalf to spin the straw of trivial experience to gold. Webb decided to concentrate on his free bottle of wine and the possibility of new friends. 'In return for the ride, you must both have a night-cap at my place,' he shouted into the wind. He sheltered between Pauline and Viv as they passed through the storm towards the carpark.

Aubade

The Justice Department Hostel was as all hostels, as all institutions which are held in common and by an unwilling or transient population. It declared itself by signs of piecemeal maintenance and general, inexorable decay. It was grey like the enamel of an old tooth; the strip of cloud in the still, early morning was the same grey. How exact and unremarkable it all was she thought: how difficult to shake off. Nothing moved, lest it become a target for the watching chill of dawn. Nothing moved, for a movement would begin the day. Jessop had it coming though, no doubt about that, she thought. She remembered how far his face tipped back when it was over.

To the right of the high window ledge was the flat roof of the service area, with the aluminium sheeting in raised strips. Patterns of dust and fine debris had formed, and there was a pink sweatshirt which had been lying there for a long time, for it was much faded and set in rigid folds like the skin of an animal long dead by the roadside. Jessop was still somewhere though, wasn't he, despite what she had been told? He'd often said that it would take more than a mean slut like her to put him down. A stiff drag and the weed was at its job. The smoke hung as a mist in the still air.

Concrete sides, and older wooden sides of buildings were at all angles, and above the strip roofing of the service block a long board had been fastened between the side of her building and the next, and on it were fastened a pipe and wires, like a life line. Birds had found it a pleasant perch, and on the roof below, mimicking its course, was a line of chalky droppings. On the high buildings the paint had cracked from the barge boards, particularly at the corners where the moisture was able to get in, and a mildew like mustard flourished. On the old wood of the nearest corner a new spotlight for the quad had been fitted. Its outer case was of bright, green aluminium, as if a single leaf bud had burst from the whole warped length of that wooden stem. Once perhaps she had loved Jessop, or wanted him anyway: the inverted pyramid of his torso, wide in the shoulders, a sharp point at the loins. Yes indeed. In the firelight the flat of his chest had often been a table for two glasses and their fish and chips.

An amazing number and variety of snorkels rose through the roofs: thick chimneys, round ventilator ducts with conical tin hats, lavatory vents with archaic, wire bulbs at the top like the little traps in which yellow soap used to be shaken in the sink. And hot water over-flows; delicate reeds amongst the other fixtures. The roofs showed so much more sign of life than she had ever realised, whereas it was the sides of the buildings which were barren. Just cliffs of uniform descent, with only windows as a break, all closed and all in rank and file. While on the roofs tufts of grass could be seen above the gutterings, and T.V. aerials were the hieroglyphics of the new world. A forest up there, she thought. Jessop's last emotion she was sure was surprise, rather than fear or anger. Surprise that after all she could start his blood flowing, and he couldn't staunch it. Surprise, amazement even, that he was not going to teach her a lesson as he always had before.

She had supposed that at the end it would be just a general image; vaguely realised buildings and sky, yet definition remained exact. Rather the inner world was flux, and the irrelevance around her had the detail of a fingerprint, the authenticity of the sky's cold sheen. She was cold on the ledge; goose pimples and hairs stood up on her pale arm. Her fingers whitened in their grip on the frame, and beside her thumb with its peeping moon of cuticle, a rust stain through both putty and paint gave away the hidden head of a nail. The blue leather of her sneakers picked up an odd dust weathered from the ledge, and when she began to fall she took her breath with a gasp because the air was suddenly colder, as if it had all at once begun to blow, instead of hers being the rush against it.

Gideon At The Walls Of Party Talk

I was attempting to be completely honest with the woman.
Never be honest about sex.
Good lord, no.
It's far too important.
Good lord, yes.
And never with a woman.
What, honesty, or sex?
Ah, now there's a question.
What's your view on that, Jenny?
On what?
Anyway, let me freshen up your drink.

Gideon was one of the greatest of the Judges. Warlords in a sense; warrior leaders who could inspire confidence and unity in the tribes of Israel and provide protection from all those that threatened them. Gideon belonged to the tribe of Manasseh. He was the son of Joash of Ophrah. Times were nasty and brutish, as Hobbes would have it. This is way back you realise, Old Testament stuff with a vengence; twelfth, eleventh century B.C. The Midianites were the trouble and their allies the Amalekites; desert people as numerous as a grasshopper plague. For seven years the Israelites had to live in mountain dens and caves and look down on the valleys crawling with Midianites, and weep.

You've never had an Achilles go on you then, aye?
Sorry?
You've never had an Achilles go on you.
Can't say I have.
Pow. Just like that.
Just like that.

Pow! Just like a rubber band snapping and you're on the deck wondering who kicked you from behind. Exactly that.

I've had my knee lock with a damaged cartilage. It was a very abrupt thing.

No, no. Pow. Just like that. A rubber band couldn't be cleaner. I had a thigh to toe cast for over six weeks.

With my knee though it popped back after manipulation by the doc.

I was playing touch rugby and just went to sidestep off my left foot. Pow.

Really.

Hell of a thing, an Achilles.

If you read Judges you find it's a very clear statement of cause and effect, over and over. When things were very bad the children of Israel repented their godless ways and cried to Yahweh who raised up a deliverer from amongst them, a true believer, and through him smote the enemies of his people. But success and prosperity always led the Jews to forsake their God and worship Baal again — a most hedonistic, persistent deity. He has even greater success now than in Gideon's time. Yahweh himself is powerless in the 20th century. It's fascinating: the scholars have discovered that the Deuteronomistic historian, probably Jeremiah that bitter supporter of Shiloh, made insertions in the text of Judges to emphasise all success and failure in terms of the covenant with Yahweh. Infidelity brings misery and subjugation, which leads to repentance, which results in deliverance. After all, what is the first commandment? It is the most rigorous, didactic history. Oh, you must, must read it.

You're so proud, my mother said to me when I was still in short pants: so proud you'll choke on it. I was as usual refusing to admit that I was a liar when the evidence was clear.

Before the Midianites Israel had been oppressed by Jabin, king of the Canaanite city state of Hazor. Yahweh punished his people thus because they had turned away from him, but then through the prophetess Deborah he raised up Barak, son of Abinoam, who with 10,000 men defeated Jabin's general Sisera at the Kishon river, and went on to overthrow the king. Then the land had rest for forty years. The Israelites reverted to Baal of course, so their God withdrew his power and allowed them to fall into the hands of the grasshopper Midianites and Amalekites and we're back to Gideon again.

When I think back, I'm appalled at how little interest as a boy I took in my family. I find I know little of importance about my parents. The direction of my curiosity was always outwards.

Power dressing you mean? In Christchurch. Never forget you're in the South Island now. Every instruction must be given with a smile.

But obeyed all the same.

Certainly.

But you'd rather suits than dresses?

I give myself a rule. Now that I'm over forty I never wear anything shorter than the knee.

Ah, but you're tall you see. You're lucky.

Byron said he hated a dumpy woman.

The poet? Dumpy. Did he actually use the word dumpy?

He did.

Sounds very modern, very colloquial, dumpy.

And I never tell jokes. That's the other thing.

Well, it's worked for you all right, and neither Benjamin nor Anna seemed to suffer. A doctor and a lawyer. Have you been to Britain again recently?

June, actually.

I'll be there next month.

So will I.

Maybe we can meet up to see a show together. Plenty of dumpy men make it big though, don't you find.

Well, self-made, entrepreneurial men can, but there's American research which shows that in corporate structures a tall man has better chances of promotion. A study of the British diplomatic service showed the same sort of thing. It's interesting to consider such general forces at work. I have a theory myself that the first two advancements are the most important, most influential on a career. Early promotion sets the angle of ascent; establishes a fast track expectation that is self-fulfilling. You must get ahead of the pack early.

I'm sure you're right. That's why private enterprise has swept away the old seniority practices.

The other thing I've learnt is not to drink anything except natural fruit juices when travelling on business, or dealing with people that matter.

How's your drink now?

Thanks. Rum and coke.

I had left home, I'd been away several years, before I discovered that my mother had once been a sportswoman. At my aunt's I was shown a photograph of my mother in the Marlborough hockey team at a tournament which must have been in Wellington because the photographer was Sinclair Vene of Willis Street. She was lanky, her eyes took up a lot of her face, she held a teddy bear with a scarf as the team mascot. When I asked her about it she said she'd almost forgotten, it was so long ago. You don't think that your parents might have had a life before your awareness of them; a possibility of less sullied personalities. Dad and I would watch sport on television. My mother was never interested. She would be with my sisters in another part of the house. She had left it behind and had her life taken up with more immediate things, unlike most men who carry any sporting past like a credit card for the rest of their lives: a proof of masculine identity. And my aunt said that she was notorious in their family for her fierce temper, yet I never knew my mother to be anything but conciliatory. Her typical sign of disappointment, or displeasure, was to back off. I wasn't offered the photo and I never saw or heard any other evidence that my mother was once lanky, wide-eyed, spent a lot of time playing hockey. Dad of course was an authority on all sporting codes. In his case the expertise came with middle age.

A C-1. Is he a C-1? I never knew he was still that good.

He has been a B-1.

Has he? As high as B-1: the wily old bugger, and he still doesn't get beaten often does he. I watched him playing Norman last week and he kept slowing the game down, slowing it down, lobbing along the walls, or dropping into the corners and often coming up with a shot into the nick. Cunning old bugger.

You try to move him off the 'T'. He dominates the centre so well.

Right. Crafty old bugger.

What are you having? Let me top it up.

And you watch how he plays the stroke out of sight. Always seems to have his body between you and the ball so you're late to see his shot.

You're right. What a cunning old sod.

And have you been getting a few games in yourself?

Na. Flat out. I really should make more time for it.

I'm the same. We should jack up a few games together.

Anyway, Gideon overturned the alter of Baal at Ophrah to show he was the chosen one of God. He mustered a fighting force from his own tribe and from the northern tribes of Asher, Zebulun and Naphtali and they assembled near the well of Harod. The spring's still there today; isn't that a marvellous thing. Give me the old in everything the poet says, except in women, Jenny, of course, except in women. I've been there; drunk from it. Rock outcrops form a surround and there's trees on the rising ground behind. It was tactically suitable, because if need be the Israelites could escape into the hills and not be pursued by the Midianite camels.

Gideon had an army of 32,000 and they could see the enemy camped on the low ground to the north. Gideon had his doubts of course. No one likes to appear a fool, a false prophet, and so he'd asked the Lord for various signs — a fleece wet with dew though the ground around it was dry, then again the fleece dry and all around heavy with dew.

Faceless bureaucrats every one. I have to steel myself to be civil whenever I enter the municipal offices.

I work in the Council offices.

Ah, I meant the Planning Consent Department of course. The rest of the Council is chokka with sound people.

Actually that's where I am. Planning Consent.

Really. Fascinating job I shouldn't wonder. Just let me freshen up your drink though.

Do you know Stephen?

I think we have met before. I know. You're a yachtie. You were in Christchurch at the national sunburst class regatta on the estuary last year. That's it, of course. You came with us drinking at the King Dick. Old Miles Welby and that lot played up.

No. I work for one of your suppliers. Snee Light Engineering. Sometimes I've been round with all the bull-bars for your utes.

Right. Of course. Here's to you. A big success they've been as well. We're very pleased with them and so are the cockies. So you don't sail at all then?

No.

You're the spitting image of the fellow I had in mind.

I'm into stock cars more than anything else. I've got two chevs that I heave around the track at Redruth each month. Do you get to stock car meets?

Can't say I do. After all the noise during the week I like peace and quiet. You can find that in yachting.

I can imagine that.

Essen.

Pardon?

The yachtie that you reminded me of — somebody Essen. He lived in Port Chalmers and once sailed with Adrian Hayter.

Sin took the form of my mother's handbag. Not just because I pilfered from it, but because it was so personal, so female, and I transgressed those boundaries as well. Each of us knows the scent of our first sins. Mine was compounded of leather and lavender, powder and peppermints. The bag was shiny black with radiating pleats like the heavy folds of theatre curtains. A nest of the trivial essentials of an everyday world. A pocket calendar, Post Office account book, bus tickets, Rawleigh's cream, notebook with a gracile pencil in the spine, emery board, discount cards, lipstick, paper napkin, comb, bowls' chalk, lavender scented handkerchief, letterhead dockets of green and pink, keys, powder compact, tiny scissors with shafts that folded in on themselves, shopping lists. At the bottom loose peppermints had the scattered gleam of a diviner's bones and two lead pencil points were like the droppings of some handbag mouse.

Amongst all these aids to womanly security would lie the note purse and the change purse, with brass catches as firm as the jaws of an asp. Notes were taboo; known individually, but not coins. Yes, the coins! A handful of silver could be reduced with less risk. A shilling, a florin perhaps, or that great, glittering flounder prize, a half-crown which promised whole days of pleasure and silky guilt. A half-crown, was a purse in itself; could give entry to the pictures and still return two silver coins. I have a conscious gratitude that the names have been lost with time. I can deal with these dollars and cents and attach no guilt to them. I longed for the forgiveness that my mother denied me through ignorance of my wickedness. On the other hand of course, I would have picked the gold fillings from father's teeth with joyous righteousness.

Local people are quick to think that one among them is getting too big for his boots. The people of Ophrah didn't take kindly to Gideon demolishing the idols, but his father stood up for him; challenged Baal to do the punishing himself.

So what's your line Brian?

Richard.

I'm sorry. I thought Jenny said Brian.

Richard Bryan. Bryan's my surname.

Of course. I'm sorry. And what line are you in then, Richard?

I'm a tenancy adjudicator for the Housing Corporation.

Right.

I spend a good deal of my time with business external to the Corporation in a way. Mainly conciliation between landlords and tenants on matters to do with the compulsory bonds that we hold and so on. You know that it's a legislative requirement now?

Right.

In the present economic climate there has to be an institution to hold the ring as it were for the fair operation of contract between the parties.

Right. I'll just freshen up my drink, Brian, and be back. It's quite true what you say. Absolutely true.

Everyone has now gone over to Baal, on a scale and with a fervour not imagined by any of the Judges. But there will in the course of things come both a time and a cry for a deliverer. There's a prophecy from a modern Gideon.

It suits her colouring I suppose, the yellow. She's always so tanned in the summer. I must say it does suit her okay. Usually she's mutton dressed up as lamb according to Paul.

But he doesn't say it to her face, I'll bet.

Who'd dare.

She's got the nerve for anything, that one.

Did Jenny tell you about the off the shoulder black dress she wore to the kindergarten do?

I remember. Lovely emerald buttons down the front.

She had it on appro from Modes Moderne and took it back on the following Monday.

Really.

Jenny knows the manageress there and she said they could tell it had been worn, but Anna denied it point blank. She said she'd only tried it on and it was too small in the hips.

She can be very hard, can't she.

Anything to get her own way.

It's not an attractive quality is it.

I don't know why Jenny bothers with her.

I suppose it would be awkward otherwise, with the husbands being in partnership. Hardly a natural tan, I'd say.

The best known bit is when God told Gideon that his army was too large; that a victory by 32,000 even against the Midianites would be taken as their own doing. So Gideon followed his instruction and allowed any without a stomach for the coming fight to go home — and 22,000 went. But Yahweh was still not satisfied and told Gideon to take the 10,000 down to the Spring of Harod and watch them drink. Almost all got down on their knees to do so, only 300 eager and impatient men lapped from their hands and these were chosen to deliver the Israelites from their oppressors. A holy war you see and only the select few were fit for it. Such occasions in the Bible mark the first steps towards the professional army that began under Saul and was completed by David. And Yahweh's tactics showed a long experience of war, for the nomads dislike of night fighting was notorious and their tents vulnerable to fire.

I bought a cord myself last week. I thought I'd get in before the first cold snap sent the prices up.

And what was it?

Split pine mostly. Some bluegum.

It sparks in the open fire, the bluegum, doesn't it? Sparks a fair bit.

Willow you mean. Willow sparks at times.

Bluegum as well, I've been told.

No. I've burnt a lot of different woods over the years. They're all different. A lot depends on how wet or dry they are when cut. Macrocarpa; now there's a great heartwood for open fires. Glows as fierce as a knob of anthracite and the grain in it can be absolutely superb. My neighbour took out this old hedge and before he could deal with the knots and swollen roots a carver from the Polytech was round and made an offer. He barked it and wrapped it in oiled cloth to mature: said he'd leave it that way for three years. There's a market for almost anything. The Polytech guy had just been passing. He said he was always on the lookout for first-rate wood.

He's welcome to come round and have a hack at my hedge free of charge. A mammoth task each bloody year. Like the wall of China — bloody thing.

If I could detach some listeners from the accountant's free seminar on tax avoidance, I would explain to them my idea of the essential psychological distinction between childhood and the rest of our life. The reason for that vaunted clarity of early experience. For a child you see the present is all, hence its power, immediacy and vividness. Past and future are shadowy and insubstantial wings to the stage of here and now. The future is nothing in the scales until suddenly, inexplicable it is the fearsome present. A certain beating to come is easily traded for any sliver of on-going life: a yellow jelly bean, or twenty minutes more fishing for spotties in the sighing tide of the sea. And I suspect it is the truth anyway, despite the intellectual substantiation of past and future we maintain as grown-ups. For you realise in the end that the cost of life is always everything you have.

Yes, and Gideon was only one of the chosen deliverers. Some came after, like Jephthah, a prostitute's son who became a mighty leader of Israel, and Samson, but that is a Hollywood story and done to death. Some were earlier, like Othniel, nephew of Caleb, who led his people to victory against Chushan-rishathaim, King of Mesopotamia, to secure peace for forty years. But in such good times old Baal was dusted off, reinstated, and because the Jews did such evil then Yahweh as a punishment allowed their conquest by Eglon, King of Moab. In time God raised up Ehud, a left-handed Benjamite who was an assassin though not called this, and Ehud paid court to Eglon then stabbed the well-fed king while he was in his summer house. The scriptures say that the fat closed so upon the blade that Ehud couldn't draw the dagger out.

The next Judge was Shamgar who never quite caught the headline in the same way as the others and rated only one verse, although he killed 600 Philistines with an ox goad. Perhaps the writer knew something dishonourable of his clan, or perhaps his feat was eclipsed by Samson's slaying of 1,000 with the jaw-bone of an ass.

Mother loved a picnic, god help us. The concept of it, I think now, rather than the actuality. A sort of merchandising image of family harmony in the great outdoors. Parked on one of those bridge turn-offs that lead down to the shingle of South Island rivers, dad would sit in the custom line V8 with his shoes off and listen to the radio. In high summer the water level fell gradually, leaving a band of scum on the stones as if in some vast, neglected dunny bowl. My sisters would wade cautiously, and as a duty, past the willows, their cotton dresses tucked into their pants — the legs of course not the top. I wore khaki shorts and sandshoes. The fabric had a smell of the sun's bleach and more faintly of the mint beds I trod down in the lanes of old side streams. Each picnic began with the selection of a stick fit to aid exploration and ended with its whirling farewell into the lupins and broom.

Mother would sit on a tartan rug after she had carefully cleaned the ground there of sheep droppings, stones and any thistles. Her magazine was often laid aside as she warred with spiders, sandflies, beetles and catkins dropping from the branches above. She would tell us how much more fortunate we were than big city kids, while Dad dangled one leg outside the car and looked at his watch. Once at the Rangitata a fox-terrier burst from the dry grass and lupins, bit Dad's foot as if for a dare, then raced away again before anything could be done. Even my father laughed, I give him credit for that, though the bite drew blood on his toes. What I always wanted on those picnics was a black, inner tube like Willie Deng's to float on. I also wanted on those picnics to know what it was we all waited for and why it never happened.

They say he's got this woman in Wellington.

Never.

Is that a fact.

Hey, Jenny. Come and listen to this.

Set up a flat there and all. Tax deductable of course. He takes a three day business trip every fortnight and comes back complaining he's tired.

The old dog.

Tired! We should be so lucky.

Well, he's got the money, the confidence and the time.

All right for some.

You're a long time dead is what I say.

And she's a looker I suppose?

I'll just top up our whiskies.

Sammy says it's the idea of such perks that keeps all the rest of them working hard.

What are they laughing about over there, Jenny?

About Roland having a mistress in Wellington.

They never grow up, do they. Look how happy they are at the thought of it. Look at their happy faces.

It's the only explanation they can come up with for him being willing to work so hard.

Anyway, Gideon divided his 300 into three groups and he gave each man a trumpet and a flame hidden in an up-turned pitcher. They crept down to the camp of the Midianites and Amalekites at the beginning of the middle watch and at Gideon's signal they blew their trumpets, broke the pitchers to reveal the torches and cried out the sword of the Lord and of Gideon. They set fire to tents, and the Midian host panicked in the dark, fought each other, and fled in disarray. Then the Israelites could see that they were onto a good thing and they poured out of the hills over the next few days and pursued the Midianites and Amalekites for vengeance and loot. They seized the fords and when the Midianites and Amalekites tried to cross over, the Jews slaughtered many of them, taking their golden ear-rings and the precious ornaments from their camels' necks.

A few days after people stopped coming to the house, Louise and Megan sorted out her things. There was the jewellery. My sisters encouraged me to take something as a keepsake from the box which was sandalwood, or perhaps cedarwood, and had decorative brass corners and a jade inlay on the lid. Even a ring they said. Take any of them. I felt quite humbled by their genuineness, because although it was never spoken of, I imagined that at times both of them resented my being the favourite when I did nothing to deserve it. Maybe they had always understood that it was the customary expression of the importance of males in the family rather than any special bond of affection. I tipped the lid back and saw the rings in the velvet channel made for them, the necklaces, bracelets, brooches, studs, in the rest of the box. Instead of a hard, mercenary glitter there was a softness in appearance and the delicate chains stirred beneath my fingers almost like an oil. It all lay packed like small, vivid coral fish: gleams of lapis lazuli, paua iridescence, the glow of pearls. Just a handful of treasure at the end of a woman's life. There was nothing for me there, and I went out and thanked my sisters and said no thanks. What I wanted was something like my aunt's old hockey photograph, but Megan and Louise said no, there was nothing like that. No tangible record of our mother before she became the possession of her family.

So your illustrious namesake was the big cheese amongst the Jews. I never knew so much of the story before. And later he and his men blew their trumpets again and the walls of Jericho came tumbling down, didn't they. Must have hit a high C.

No, that was Joshuah.

Aye?

Joshua fought the battle of Jericho. You know the song.

It's all too complicated for me.

Tell me mother, what was behind each act of everyday kindness; larger the share of cake, smaller the share of domestic chores. Not primogeniture the birthdate proves, but being the boy of the family it seems to me. Some stamp of my father. A lucky pip-squeak — you called me — who would grow to be a man. I mustn't suspect in you the selfish reticence I know in myself. Most likely you didn't share with me the things of value in your life because you sensed I had no curiosity concerning them; no interest in anything about you which was not part of my own comfort and advantage.

I was telling Howard and the others about Roland.

Yes, I heard.

He's got a tasty mistress all set up in Wellington.

So you said.

You knew about it then?

I wouldn't say I know. Sammy's dined out on it everywhere of course, but since when has he been a source of either fact or goodwill.

No. I suppose not. There may be nothing to it. I just mentioned it: you know what parties are.

It passes the time, I suppose.

Well, that's it, isn't it. Old Sammy himself is something of a stickman.

Gideon asked the Israelites to give him the ear-rings worn by the Midianites and he ended with 1,700 shekels of gold. He made an ephod with it and set it up in a shrine at Ophrah, where it was consulted as an oracle. Yes, he was one of the greatest of the Judges. They wanted him to become King of course, but he refused, saying only Yahweh should rule over all Israel. Like Sulla before the Caesars, he saw the danger to his own soul I suppose.

Frome's new rosé is an interesting one.

I'm not big on rosé, although I will drink Mateus.

No, but this one's based on cabernet franc and isn't overly sweet.

Well, I'll tell you. After all the tastings and patter I've come down to one rule of thumb of my own — I don't trust any wine that I can see through.

She had a rash below her left ear and on that cheek when she was dying. She turned her head away and it was as if she blushed to be dying in my presence. Not old by any means. She liked to talk about the garden and I told her lengthy lies about how much work I'd done for her there since her admittance: how I pruned the roses and managed to rid the dry, front strip of both oxalis and twitch. It must be reassuring to die with a conscience so at rest that the only things which need to be rooted out are weeds from the rock garden.

I'm not much of a gardener, not just because of laziness, but on philosophic grounds. Surely it's hopeless to oppose the blind, ceaseless onslaught of nature. The magnolia that sulks is out at last I lied. How wonderful, my blushing, dying mother said. What is the intent of such horror within a scene so mundane. I sat quietly there, aware of the heavy, corporeal self as a burden. Oh, you'll be pleased to see how the garden looks when you come home, I said. Perhaps like negatives in algebra such double lies combine to form a sort of truth.

Not you again. The guy who's been talking about Daniel and the lions all night.

Gideon.

Who?

Gideon. It's my name. I've been talking about Gideon.

Jenny, who is this guy?

Anyway, let's freshen up our drinks. What do you say?

Almost every group I'm in tonight this prick comes up and starts reciting from the Bible or something.

It's nothing. Just party talk; to pass the time.

Hey, no big deal.

What is he? A holy roller, or something.

Gideon, known as Jerubbaal, had a mass of children and died at a good age. There's a lot more to tell if you care to listen: about the men of Succoth who refused Gideon help when he needed it, and Jether his first born who wouldn't execute Zebah and Zalmunna, the captured Midianite Kings, so Gideon did it himself.

Do we have to put up with this?

He's had some bad news recently.

Well let him keep it to himself; the weirdo.

The Israelites all went back to worshipping Baal after Gideon's death, of course. Would you like me to start on all that?

ALGEBRA

Yes, it was typical of Norman to be more than half an hour early at Te Tarehi, for he was a careful man who allowed for what he liked to call — contingencies. Contingencies such as heavy traffic on the motorway, or a second coming. On this occasion he allowed chiefly for not having been to the Samsons' before, and so wanting time to find the address.

'Oh, a pleasant enough place. These service towns are ideal in many ways,' he said. Just as he would if his wife had been with him as usual. 'Now, number one hundred and thirty-seven.' He drove slowly down the street he had found from the map drawn for him by the Samsons. 'Thirty-eight, forty-two,' he said, to establish which way the numbers ran.

He parked by a one section reserve, between numbers 50 and 52 which had green slat and wrought iron benches donated by the local pride of Lions, and one see-saw with a semi-circle of tyre embedded at each end to absorb the impact that no children seemed interested enough to make. Despite a sign forbidding bikes, a narrow rut cut across the grass on the diagonal and out onto the equally quiet street on the other side. The grass at the base of the sign had been sprayed; on the bareness there something caught the bright sun. A thin knife, and on the sign Norman could see where it had been thrown and struck several times. It was not a fearsome weapon; rather like a letter opener. Norman smiled at the inconsequence of its discovery and fiddled with the blade as he walked on along the meek, predictable street to find which house was the Samsons'. He then intended to return to the park and relax on one of the green benches until it was half past. A prepared life is the more comfortable.

Dianne and Rex Samson had come to his polytechnic course on pre-European New Zealand, and he looked forward to examining a collection of moa-hunter artefacts that the family had turned up during two generations of working their farm at the river's mouth. 'Argellite mostly, I expect,' he told himself, and did not dispute it. The sun blossomed in a fierce, blue-silk sky and Norman folded his sleeves to the elbow. A red Honda parked in the quiet street was already shimmering. Norman wondered if the Samsons were beer drinkers at all.

Number 137 was roughcast, tile, unremarkable, with a pebble garden along the block fence. Norman was about to turn back when the Samsons came striding down their path, laughing as they talked. Norman carried on walking, an impulse to avoid the small embarrassment of being discovered at their gate half an hour before he was expected. As he went on he smiled to himself at the odd circumstances that trivial conceit may cause. Behind he could hear the Samsons still talking. Norman crossed the road at an angle so that his face remained hidden, and he turned up the first street on his right before he realised that it was no exit and that the Samsons followed on. 'God damn,' said Norman and laughed. It grew worse. To turn and be recognised by the Samsons became less tenable with each step: more difficult to explain without some loss of face.

Sallust Street was short and ended in a lolly-pop turning circle with a golden elm in the central plot, but the countryside was a fifth column in Te Tarehi's suburbs and to one side a vacant section offered a grassy escape. Norman walked through the nodding twitch and brown-top, past the mouldering clippings tossed from the backing houses, and at the section's end found a line of jerry-built hutches. Large, white rabbits were chewing and dunging contentedly there. With relief Norman heard his acquaintances pass on to the golden elm at the conclusion of Sallust Street. 'You didn't! Don't tell me that. Oh, you didn't,' he heard Dianne saying happily at a distance and Rex's indistinct reply and chuckle.

'It's all right,' Norman told the nearest rabbit, whose bulging pink eye had a seemingly impossible meniscus. 'You don't have to hide me in Wonderland after all.' As he waited just a minute so that the Samsons would not see him as he returned to his car,

Norman began to sense a less pleasant reality beneath the surface charm of the rabbit enterprise. They were very white and soft, sure enough, but their dung pellets were heaped and malodorous, the wooden frames were gnawed and tortured, and although some hutches were two and three high along the fence, others were free-standing; had been dragged about the section in search of new grass, leaving soiled rectangles in their wake.

Norman turned to make his way back through the section, then abruptly felt his turning caught up by greater force and so continued further than he wanted. There were hands on his shoulder.'Not this time. Not this time,' was shouted, and a long, old face grinning with inexplicable fury was hung before him.

'Pardon?' said Norman weakly.

'Pardon! Killing my rabbits, coming into private property, and all he can say is pardon!' He was an inordinately tall, thin man who needed only farm overalls with braces and a pitchfork to be mid-American gothic, but instead he had a cream cardigan in the heat and blue felt slippers. 'Eh!' he said in an edgy way, precarious of control.

'Eh! Eh!' repeated a woman hidden behind him.

'I was just looking at the rabbits,' said Norman.

'Oh yes,' said mid-American gothic, 'and how did he know they were here when they can't hardly be seen from the road? Eh! Eh!'

'Eh! Eh!'

'What about that then,' the edgy voice continued.

Norman thought he was going to faint, not so much because of the malice in the situation, though that was real enough, but because of the suddenness of it, the brittle heat, and the inexplicable interpretation that developed from innocent intentions. He moved back slightly towards the tiered hutches to regain personal distance, and from the corner of his left eye saw a pink and white rabbit chewing insolently on fast forward as if nothing had changed.

'Bob. Bob,' said the invisible woman. 'We've caught the rabbit killer. He's at it again,' and a grave, olive skinned man eating a carrot and with eyes immensely wide apart came cautiously to join them. Norman spread his hands, palms uppermost, before his accusers.

'Look, I'm sorry. I haven't killed anything. My name's Norman Hewitt. I just walked in for a moment on my way past. That's all.'

'Who knows you? Eh! Eh!'

'Eh! Eh!'

'He can't see the hutches from the road hardly, yet he said he just came in to see the rabbits.' Mid-American gothic insisted on this as the essential Perry Mason point.

'Mr Keysey's had a lot of rabbits killed and stolen. Valuable animals,' said Bob judiciously. His olive skin had a liquid sheen in the glaring sun and his wide eyes slid past Norman in search of an accomplice.

'It wasn't me,' said Norman. He stood again, as he had a short-pants boy, accused, and said it wasn't him.

'Who knows you? We've never heard of you,' said the invisible Mrs Keysey.

'You're not from round here.' Bob took the carrot from his face. 'What did you come for?'

The gothic American leant forward and with sudden, heron movement plucked the knife from Norman's pocket. 'Why a knife then, eh?' he said. 'Look, a killer's knife.'

Bob gripped his carrot with greater resolution.

'He uses a knife on them,' quavered the invisible woman. 'I can't bear it.' Her husband's candle-wax face twisted as he imagined Norman using the knife on the dove-like breasts of his rabbits. The blade became a compass needle that lined itself on Norman's navel.

The heat and the threat were almost too much to bear. Again Norman swayed on his feet. He felt like the gingerbread man closest to the element. All his skills, his intelligence, his logic, and yet he couldn't conceive the right words to say. Surely it wasn't happening.

'Let's start again, please,' he said, then heard the voices of the Samsons at the cul-de-sac as they walked back to their house to wait for him. Norman pointed eagerly. 'I know them. I was on my way to visit them.'

'You know Dianne and Rex Samson?' said Bob.

'Eh!' chorused the mid-American gothic and his invisible wife.

'Please call them here,' said Norman. He didn't trust his own voice.

The Samsons stepped through the heat and polished grasses, saw Norman still with his back to the hutches, and blocking his way Mr Keysey with his wife so close behind him that they resembled the two-humped Bactrian camel. 'Why, Norman,' cried Dianne. She and Rex came towards the group bringing civilisation once again. The sun itself retreated to indifferent animosity. Dianne's eyes had concern and perplexity. 'What are you doing here?'

Who could answer? Norman gathered his wits to make a clear statement, and wondered why the simplest human things are the most difficult to explain.

IMMORTALITY

By that time it was not completely unexpected. The continued accomplishments of science, including outreach to Venus and the tapping of the Earth's nuclear core, had created expectations in people's minds. Also the life expectancy was already up to eighty-five for women, though somewhat less for men and neuters. Nevertheless the break through to immortality was considered a wonderful thing, and Academicians Neblinskov and Brown were awarded the Einstein Medal and grade five recreation rights. Their names would live forever, the Global President said, but the irony was that despite the discovery their own death could not be averted. The Neblinskov-Brown process wouldn't work for those much older than about eighteen you see, for after that the hormonal ageing process had begun and could not be reversed.

Oh, it was a time for fine optimism and delight. Treatment was begun in all areas irrespective of class, wealth or race, for the Neblinskov-Brown process was not particularly expensive, less than AIDS immunisation for example, and it either took the first time or not at all, which could be determined by a blood test six months later. Celebrations of the new epoch for humanity were held all over the world, and the media trumpeted material pointing out the grand effects of the discovery in every walk of life. Think of it! What a rugby team of exceptional once in a million talents could be built up over two or three hundred years say. In literature and art genius could mature and ramify without being cut short, and in politics the wisdom and experience of the greatest statesmen need never be lost. The great, lurking cause of melancholy and depression throughout our history — a consciousness of inevitable death — was itself finally defeated.

A triumphant mood remained the tone for a year or more, and then there was a tapering of interest and insistence: a slackening, like the pause at the turning of the tide, then gradually, as the ebb tide reveals new outlines, other tones and attitudes could be seen.

Initially the change was thought something of a natural reaction; an anti-climax to be expected as it was realised that immortality did not solve all problems. But it became clear to the thoughtful amongst us that more curious and sinister forces were at work than that. The realisation came that the last great schism had been created in humankind, far deeper than that of gender or of race: a schism between the last generation bound to die, and those who were immortals. For the trained observers in society, myself included, the terrible psychological consequences of the Neblinskov-Brown discovery began to be discernible. Amongst older people welled up a complex despair and resentment that by a quirk of fate they must die within an age which had discovered the secret of perpetual life. Like Moses they could view the promised land, but were forbidden entry. The new generation on the other hand were filled with a sense of complacency and arrogance that sprang from the knowledge that, barring accident, war, or the few remaining serious diseases, they would live forever.

The mortal generation did not admit the extent of their envy of course; some did not realise it. Instead their criticism took other forms. Churches began to preach on the theme that humankind had taken unto itself God's power over life and death; philosophers began to question the decision to apply the Neblinskov-Brown process before all the ethical issues had been considered; the social scientists warned of unmanageable population problems; sociologists feared a creeping lethargy of purpose once people had never ending tomorrows in which to do their work; psychologists predicted a growth of self-loathing as people could never escape their accumulating guilts and inadequacies.

The immortals and older people found themselves uneasy in each others' company. There was a separating and reforming of social groups, as oil and water seek themselves. The immortals formed large communities of their own where they could enjoy themselves without constantly giving offence to those who must die. Amongst the immortals was a marked sense of destiny and preferment. The more insensitive began a cult of jokes at the expense of mortals, even claiming that older people had a characteristic and unpleasant smell about them.

The rest drew together too, still powerful, holding wealth, political dominance and cultural supremacy because of their age. The SFHG was established, the Society of the Final Human Generation, and although criticised publicly as an extremist organisation because of its claims of moral superiority, nevertheless it was powerful within the mortal community.

Many reasonable older people still thought that with further research the threshold of immortality would soon be advanced, and enormous amounts of money were put at the disposal of the scientists for that purpose. After three years however the experts began to doubt if any advance on Neblinskov and Brown's work was possible, and the distinction hardened.

In my opinion the murder of Academician Brown was the first sign of things to come... An extremist group claiming links to the SFHG blew up the Rutherford Clinic where the initial breakthrough had been made, and Theo Brown, Einstein Medallist, was killed. Also a bitter argument developed as to whether the immortal generation should be allowed entry to positions of influence and responsibility as they came of age. The SFHG claimed that the attitudes of these young people were so different from any that had gone before that they could not be trusted to maintain the human civilisation carefully nurtured over thousands of years.

To protest against such views the immortals held a great demonstration at Alice Springs, southern capital since the Greenhouse Effect, and some 170,000 marchers supported demands for an immediate share in political decisions and greater access to the means of production. The new generation had its own radicalism. One of the leaders of this, Alphonse Diderolle, claimed that his group had nuclear capability, and openly questioned whether the old generation should be allowed any say in the direction of a brave, new world. Diderolle wished all mortals to be dismissed, retired, and confined to hospice communities.

Outbreaks of violence and irrational cruelty have become commonplace, and there is a persistent rumour that the military command has been secretly radiating the immortal communities so that they will die after all in their own turn. If such activity is ever detected the reaction must be catastrophic.

We have reached a sad situation of barbarism, so soon after the joy and anticipation which followed the Neblinskov-Brown discovery. Extremists on both sides have capitalised on fear, envy, and lack of trust. Who knows what we unleash within our minds, once we change the order of things.

I have decided to encode this brief summary of events, together with the documents supporting it, and enter it as a record in the high satellite Omega. If the whole business passes over without tragedy, I shall later update this information. If the file is not added to, then you will know what has happened in regard to the magnificent achievement of immortality.

Booke's Country Life

The sun swung udder full over the downs, and huddled any shadow as Arthur Booke crossed McKeeklin's cattle stop, and drove towards the yards. Stones chattered beneath the tyres, and the dust which arose was outdistanced, but followed in its own sweet time so that when Booke got out and approached McKeeklin to talk, the dust gathered there gentle in the air and on the tongue as the very spores of the land itself. There was a scent too of boiling offal, and the dogs beneath the trailer squeezed their eyes with the ecstasy of it.

Booke had been a coming man in the city, and he was determined to succeed. He took his vinyl folder of insurance tables and his urban knowledge to court McKeeklin. 'Arthur Booke, Amalgamated Western,' he said, ensuring a rich timbre to his voice. McKeeklin lifted another bag of fertilizer in a bear-hug from the ramp and stacked it on the trailer. 'We believe that safe-guarding assets in the present economic climate is doubly important,' said Booke. 'Take that shed now. I'd say 35,000 replacement and is it insured? One small flame sir, one small flame.' Booke stepped close to McKeeklin to take advantage of the moment. The farmer had a dark green singlet, lighter than his skin, and his work boots, grey with age, were unlaced so that he could slip them on and off like slippers, from house to yard.

'Watch how you go,' he said mildly. He continued loading the trailer; not hostile but seeming to lack any connection with the imperatives of Booke's world. When the agent left his card on the trailer deck, McKeeklin absently placed a bag of fertilizer on it, and while Booke read from his tables some of his most arresting incantations, McKeeklin looked beyond his scrum machine to the far gullies of native bush, then watched a pair of paradise ducks come down in the lucerne. McKeeklin climbed onto the high pulpit seat of his veteran Farmall and drove slowly away. His dogs annointed Booke's hub-caps with twitching accuracy, then followed with scarcely a backward sneer.

Failure was an unpleasant novelty for young Arthur Booke. In the city he had a reputation as a pressure salesman, and he had imagined that the rejuvenation of Amalgamated's business in the rural district would be a cinch, a doddle, a piece of cake. Yet in one full week he had been unable to perturb the face of pastoral recession by the threat of drought, fire, flood, pestilence, and least of all, death. Booke travelled through the bountiful heat, and his face retained the agent's set configuration of confidence, yet in his commercial heart was an apprehension that the simplicity of the countryside was a cloak for ciphers more difficult to construe.

Booke was a young man, with no hair on his shoulders at all, and not completely corrupted by Leviathan city. When he saw a man and bicycle lying side by side in the barley grass at the stone bridge, he stopped to help. It was Trevor Dooit, who had been returning from metaphysical discussion and beer at the schoolhouse when the ridge left by the grader undid him. As Booke assisted Dooit into the car, old Solitary Aimes the rabbiter walked by with his haversack and gun. 'How is it?' said Dooit.

'The grass grub flies this night or another,' said Solitary without breaking stride. A single cloud passed before the sun.

In his youth Trevor Dooit had attended Lincoln College for a year to improve his play around the base of the scrum, but he had returned to his people and lived thereafter as a sage on one of the smallest Dooit properties with his sister, Lettice Dooit, who had to be locked in her room each March and September. Since the abolition of subsidies Dooit had little money, yet as a sage he had the ageless caravanserai of country life — tin-kettling and tupping time, whitebaiting and moonlit hunts for the mint princess, the club wind-up, first footing, and watching the Dutch elm disease add to the autumn tonings.

The red roof of Dooit's home was an old ember beneath the antipodean sun, and the warped boards of the implement shed bore bleached skulls and splendid antlers as a form of reverence perhaps for Dooit forebears. On a verandah half spread with drying walnuts Trevor Dooit rested on an Edwardian *chaise longue* recovered with sacking, and spread veterinary salve on his bruised knee. Lettice Dooit put her finger in her mouth with intent, and glanced at young Arthur Booke. She made mutton sandwiches, prepared scones as huge as horse mushrooms and running with fruit jelly as though slit from the throat of a cull ewe. And rice pudding and gooseberry fool she brought to the table.

A horrendous behemoth blundered from behind the shed, making Booke start up with a cry, but it proved to be just Dooit's bull performing its duty in conjunction with a silken heifer.

'I's ready,' called Lettice.

Old Solitary Aimes passed the secret pines with his soft, relentless step. 'Them cabbage trees flowered very heavy this year,' he confided hoarsely.

Trevor Dooit appeared not at all surprised when Booke told of his singular lack of success for Amalgamated Western. Booke's kindness had disposed Dooit towards advice, though for a time he just listened, and noted where in the outbuildings his white-leghorns were going to lay. 'Who looks the sun in the face,' he said finally. Booke could only smile, so Dooit gave his advice in another form. 'Would you introduce yourself to a woman by placing your hand on her breast?'

Booke was not altogether a fool: he could still learn. He recalled those most civilised societies of Africa, China and Tibet in which true courtesy renders it uncouth to begin with one's intentions. 'You're saying don't state your business; don't push,' he said eagerly. Dooit lit one of Booke's dark cigarillos, and from the creek they could hear a faint whistle of goatish tune as Solitary Aimes checked his traps.

Armoured in the new knowledge, Arthur Booke was keen to try again. Dooit told him to avoid Naylor Naylor though; the old man had suffered some sort of collapse when penalised for producing fat lambs after a lifetime devoted to that very purpose. Dooit said old Naylor Naylor spent his time singing with the frogs in the top stock dam, and carving effigies of Sid Holland. 'Take the High Down Road,' said Dooit, and then, 'see if you can accept something. Remember that once a man gives you something he's obliged to you.'

Arthur Booke waved to him in gratitude, and to Lettice, who happened to be changing her blouse at the window. The stunted orchard trees were like parched spiders upturned along the track, and the shadows of the trophy heads made an antique script upon the shed.

The High Downs Road showed the Kooti stream, and the Dooit properties, the clumps of willows and the lines of pines. A bulge-eyed hare did have a run from the noise of Booke's car, right into the muzzle of Solitary's gun.

Arthur Booke parked at the entrance to Leevitt's farm, and left the folders and table books of vinyl behind. He walked slowly towards the yards, stopping from time to time so that Leevitt would become accustomed to the thought of a visitor. Leevitt was cleaning out beneath the grating of his shearing shed. He bent in a steady rhythm and the broad shovel did its work. Leevitt had blonde hair with an excellent crimp, and shoulders to support the world.

Booke sat on a drench tin, and turned a little from the power of the afternoon sun, and so that Leevitt could know his face before he spoke. A flock of yellowhammers passed like a hail shower. A lark drew up and down in the unbearable blue as a plumb-bob. Booke rested his arm on the top of the trough Leevitt's grandfather had made for the work horses — almost as large as the primary baths. His fingers broke the surface, and larvae jacked their way deeper into the green water.

'Peet wiik,' sang a fantail.

'Townies like the birds,' said Leevitt. He had stopped shovelling, 'but insects should be a man's study it seems to me.' He took a step towards the trough and kicked a rotten rail aside. A millipede, slaters, a green mush-worm swelling, and blue and purple hover flies crawling off as if from sin. 'These fellows are part of the soil you see,' said Leevitt companionably. 'As are we.' Old Solitary Aimes appeared from the nether shed, rabbit legs visible from his haversack. 'There you are, seeing to my land,' said Leevitt.

'Rape's not a willing crop on this ground any more,' said Solitary with a sad shake of his head. He went on remorselessly; the bird song dying before him.

Booke and Leevitt were left one each side of the trough. There was a sound of a harvester in the valley, amiable as is all sound of labour at a distance. 'I've been on the lookout for a forked willow stick for divining,' said Booke.

'It may be that I can help you there.'

'My name's Arthur Booke,' said Booke. And when shortly, on their way to choose a divining rod, Leevitt asked Arthur what line he was in, Booke mentioned insurance in all diffidence, and turned away to regard the dark pools of stinging nettle at the side of the sheds.

'I've been thinking about insurance myself lately,' said Leevitt. 'On and off like.'

Arthur Booke lifted his eyes in homage to sage Dooit. He knew he'd cracked it; nutted out these country matters. Yet from the corner of his eye he saw Solitary Aimes climbing the knoll towards the high swamp where he claimed the pukeko danced in strange formations on election nights.

Choice

As the Board of Proprietors had a policy of internal promotion, there were several at the Laystall Gazette who fancied their chances, but unknown to all but two of them the selection had already been narrowed to those very two — Rebecca Hanley-Hammond and Nigel Boone. Each had strengths in journalism. Rebecca had a talent for discovering what was influential in people's lives, and Nigel an instinct as to what they wished to read.

'You know how much I value you both,' said the retiring editor, sitting amidst the rubble on his large desk. The skin of his forehead and scalp was calloused and the hair worn to a few, grey bristles. He had wearied himself, an old truffle-hog, digging up delicacies for his masters. 'I won't state a preference between you,' he said. 'Which ever one gives me the better story within a week will swing it their way. I can't say fairer than that. Let's keep it a professional thing. A big pulling lead story is what people like,' he said reverently, 'is what will swing it.' The heavy creases of his brow lifted and the bristles above his ears became erect, as if he could scent one last, dark truffle in the rich soil of people's lives.

Rebecca Hanley-Hammond was prepared to accept the challenge. She was younger than Boone, with a better degree and she had for some months been working on an important story concerning the build up of trace elements in the city's reservoirs. She had gained the trust of the local authority scientist whose painstaking research was almost at the point of proving that long term pollution lay behind the deterioration of mental health in the area. Rebecca shook hands with the editor and with Nigel Boone. She wished the latter luck, and went briskly to shape her story.

Nigel Boone had no leads and little enthusiasm. He strolled back to the rat-hole of his office and put his feet up. He relied on the Sargasso Sea principle for his stories; the concept that if you locate the eddy point in human affairs, then in time all that you need will drift into sight. There wasn't time to set aside for the immediate quest of a headline in any case, for Nigel had arranged to take a weekend trip with a woman from the Practical Arts Emporium who thought that Boone might have useful publicity contacts.

Burrsnaithe On Sea was an eddy certainly; quiet, provincial, circular. While having a pint of bitter in the house bar before his friend's arrival, Nigel from professional habit established that there were only two things of note planned in Burrsnaithe that Saturday: the marriage of Miss Burrsnaithe On Sea and a donkey race on the sands. Neither promised easy access to the editorship of the Laystall Gazette.

While Nigel Boone ate plaice with the woman from the Arts Emporium and drank Australian Chablis, Rebecca Hanley-Hammond travelled to London to corroborate her friend's research with a Professor Mycroft. Her story grew sounder and more significant with each busy hour. Rebecca was not unaccustomed to success, but increasingly she felt that she had found the big one.

Nigel experienced a certain ennui on the Saturday. He was no longer a young man, and the woman from the Emporium was active and talkative; very insistent as to what posture she should adopt in regard to publicising the Arts Emporium. After a light lunch *en suite*, Nigel stepped onto the wrought iron balcony of his room which overlooked a cobbled lane leading to the esplanade. A score almost of donkeys were coming past for their races on the sands. Their hooves rang on the cobbles and their braying made for a moment in the English seaside a cameo of the Serra da Estrela, or Andalusia. Abruptly however the gleaming limousine carrying Miss Burrsnaithe On Sea was attempting to come from the other direction, and towards the church at the top of the town. The donkeys milled and bared their teeth; the driver left the car and stood shouting with the donkeys' owner. Finally the bride herself lost patience and resplendent in full nuptial dress of white satin and Belgian lace, advanced with the authority of beauty and pageant success towards the mêlée. One large jackass with the Jerusalem cross clear on its back became so excited that it began a torrential urination which splashed upon the wedding gown itself. The donkeys and owners were put irrevocably in the wrong. Shame-faced, the race men herded their animals quickly back the way they had come, and the wedding entourage also withdrew, loud with threats and lamentations. Nigel Boone was left alone upon his balcony, silent and thoughtful, a forgotten cigarette smouldering at his lip.

Rebecca Hanley-Hammond had finished her article, had checked its syntax and its sources, had already decided on her follow up. All her energy and ability, her tact and investigative skill was embodied in an article of genuine public concern and value. She was tired, but convinced that she had done more than enough to secure the proprietors' support: and swung it, as the old truffle journalist would say.

Yet at that very moment, Nigel Boone, sitting on the side of the hotel bed in Burrsnaithe On Sea wrote on the back of an envelope the headline for the piece which would ensure the editorship of the Laystall Gazette for himself. It read — Donkey Defiles Virgin Bride.

Don't Wake Beside Me

Don't wake beside me, for there's no continuation here, no ending even, that can complete our night. The rocket falls unseen from its fiery ascent and rainbow burst. The hair is still pushed back from your face, roughly combed by my fingers in the dark. Your lips have wet the pillow while you sleep, and as you had no time to take your face off, the chinked light from the curtain's edge smudges your eyeliner. So, you Cleopatra you.

Honk, honk. Yes old Baz, I admit the ridicule is clear. Every jest and verse he knew to pass the time. A German officer crossed the Rhine, parley vous, parley vous. He told the world that the angle of the dangle depended on the heat of the meat. A hard case, bit of a dag, real joker, always good for a laugh. A manifest old goat and smelling like it; we can pin our sins on him and despise him for it. Honk, honk, old Baz, gaga now in an eventide home I suppose, and boasting to the wall of how many he put in the pudding club. How coarse a fabric he could weave from the stuff of life. Inky pinky parley vous, as the actress said to the bishop.

When you sat across from me and talked to Wilkinson of your campaign for individual employee contracts, it was your hands I paid attention; supple, strong tendons like the ribs of a fan. Your nails were water clear and short in a practical way. And the light woman's voice of you. Your smile tugged at the corners of your mouth: your blouse was ruffled on your hip.

Don't wake beside me. Don't tell me with a smile, or deadpan face, there's no obligation because of it. Don't talk of it when all that is left of a good red and the cheeseboard is my stale breath above the covers. When you wake, the real time will end, or start. The evolution of our nature has accustomed us to value continuity in our experience, which is not always the benefit we assume. Any discussion of what we have done imposes boundaries and definitions; is a process of reduction.

Honk, honk, old Baz would say. His office desk was closest to the window, so that he could see the women passing in the mall. Built for comfort not for speed. What a pair! Thighs like a wild mare. Wouldn't mind getting my balls caught in that rat-trap. A month's wages, oh my god, just to slip a link in there, Baz would say. Get up them stairs. I'm only thirteen. I'm not superstitious; get up them stairs. Honk, honk. Does old Baz speak for us all, though we deny it and despise him? Baz confided in me that everytime he scored (and that not often, surely, old Baz) he wondered if it would be the last woman for the last time. He found it incapacitating, Baz said; the event and opportunity suddenly invested with such significance. The end of that life faced him. I suppose that I am about now the age that Baz was then. An ugly thought. Honk, honk, he'd say; I need my rations. The whippet needs a run. The wick needs dipping. Honk, honk. Mrs Palmer's the young man's friend, but not first choice of company, Baz always told us. Shut up, we said. The louder he gave his jackass laugh, the more lonely were his eyes. And somewhere, of course, there will be the last woman, for the last time.

Don't wake beside me and begin the disintegration. Full light will discover the wear on your blue shoes, and on my balding head before I have the chance to comb my hair in a disguise: that you have a toenail blackened perhaps by a falling breadboard a week ago. Don't tell me with enthusiasm of the T.V. show I find most moronic, or let me bore you with oblique aspersions on my peers. The air conditioning has dried my lips and throat, and anyway I'm never much at breakfast conversation. I find it awkward to balloon the trivial and would rather make a face and go.

Never quite strangers, you and I; we saw each other in the course of similar work for similar employers, but the juxtaposition of our routines was set and so formed our feelings in the same way. Now, however, a symposium no less, with mutual accommodation and chairs revisited from plenary sessions in the Conference Room. You were the only one to laugh at the keynote speaker's malapropism, then looked down and bit your lip.

They laid on a happy hour each night, with all the jollity that instant friends create and Willcocks from Whangarei charmed us long enough with his Muldoon impersonations. Those sisters from Christchurch were more vocal than you. Their laughter added balance to the middling wines; laughter which prevented the business bores from perpetuating their tyranny of the day. Yours was the breast though; the perfect form the bra cup could not duplicate, so that a little space was there which diminished with a breath, and formed again. I watched with the sad envy of middle aged desire, and squandered a friendship in my conversation to raise a laugh — from you. The few dark hairs on your small wrist were like commas on ivory paper.

Yet that night I dreamt not of your supple wrist, but of being vacuum cleaned in the main street along with other passers-by. In the common illogic of that world my concern was not that it should be customary, but that the prying nozzle would expose my old fellow — soft, wrinkled, the shrivelled filling of a cold sausage roll. Such a fear that I almost woke to the whine of the air-conditioning, but then lapsed back to meet my first boss, who died bungy jumping at fifty-four. He sucked his teeth in the old way to ponder a problem and asked as always for Indian tonic in his drink. All the same in a hundred years he told me. Siss-ss-ssh; the breath drew through his teeth. Did he have time for one last, indrawn breath, I wonder, on the bungy cord? Will it all be the same in a hundred years, and what consolation is that?

I shall burst, old Baz would cry, if I can't get a shot away. His eyes would be bloodshot with the pressure. Honk, honk. Old Baz whose soldier stood to attention, so hopeful of an engagement; so seldom called to arms. Tell us the one about the elephant and the librarian; that's a good one, Baz. Honk, honk. Who else in the firm knew the twenty-seven verses of Eskimo Nell, and the chugalug refrain, or the nipple song, yet to remember any more than a single professional task, Baz had to use the office memo paper, which he then usually misplaced. A deep understanding of women, had old Baz. They all like it, but some like it more than others, was the basic tenet of his creed. Honk, honk, sings Abdul abulbul Emir. Get up them stairs. My mother won't like it. Your mother's not getting it; get up them stairs. He had the loudest office laugh, but I never saw him smile to himself in all those years. Baz, the old mutton gun soldier. The old pretender.

Let me be most truthful while you sleep, and take your silence as assent. Other explanations are more comfortable, more laudable, more convenient, but the truth is I don't need your friendship, though I'd welcome it, can get by without your expertise in workplace equity management. Yourself is all you have that I find indispensable, or ideal. How bad does that sound to you? Yet it is the truth — I think. If you complain that I want only that, then isn't the disparagement your own. Only that! Only the smooth belly and the matchless thigh, the shoulder blade beneath my palm. Only that. Only the gift of beauty and of joy. If men express themselves so poorly that women have cause to feel demeaned, then accept apologies for the deficiencies, not the need or the gift themselves.

A knowing hand to make a cowling for my cock: those mild loving pornographies which make life more than the living of it. Can you laugh in your throat again, can you whisper, can you flutter. Your eye make-up is smudged, Cleopatra. I watch a pulse in the curve of your neck. Shall I kiss there? So don't wake beside me. Don't ask what follows the pulse in the neck, the fine laughter lines at the corner of your mouth; a night well spent, spent.

Didn't you know, would cry old Baz with delight. Oh, yes. A real porker, hot to trot, an absolute nympho, never gets enough. I thought everyone knew that. Honk, honk. We could be in there old son; though somehow events usually conspired against old Baz. He told me gloomily that he'd seen firm statistics that at any given moment only point five percent of the earth's population was copulating, and that even amongst men only the figure was less than two percent. Oh, look at the bristols on her, Baz would say. I wouldn't mind a piece of that. Towards the end I had to talk to him officially about his language to the women on the staff. An awkward task given to me on promotion, when it was Baz who'd kindly helped me when first I joined. With righteous tact and understatement I gave him a reprimand; censure for his dirty mind.

Honk, honk. Old Baz saw all of his life as just a context for the act of union, yet had no language to give it dignity. Am I the same as Baz, despite all my denials? Sleeping you require no answer.

In our night to bear down and hear the tempo of breathing and of words altered by our mutual grasp. That must mean a unity of sorts, don't you agree? In the act of love is life most strongly affirmed, and death most scorned. This French little death is an inoculation against the form most grim and absolute — for a time at least. A brief assertion which defies intellect, but by which instinct is assuaged. Oh, yes indeed. There are realms where words and logic have no power: red and golden tulips flare and jostle there, with no stems to grasp. So don't wake beside me; don't even whisper in your sleep.

Honk, honk. Be quiet old Baz and wipe your chin. Toothless in your eventide with the candles closing in.

Don't wake beside me, when in art one of us would take leave, take and leave, leave a single red rose against the white sheet. So let me write that clean, quick ending of our night, as if it could be. Your arm across the bed to seek the bloom, the tremor of the petals on your skin, Cleopatra, and myself withdrawing. In every man is that hunger for a woman he has not wounded.

Don't wake beside me.

Saffron Walden

See me as a nimble, slim and amorous fool, with a small town voice breaking through more formal education. On a pub crawl after the last of our exams — Benny, Raf and me. My final paper was Greek Political Thought; Protagoras, Antiphon and so on. I am a shoo-in for a B-plus at least, the beer assures me. From the punters' bar we can oversee the riverside with its quarrelling mallards and banks shored up with bricks and planks. To draw attention to ourselves we switch to stout and raspberry. Landlord, quoth I, tankards of stout and raspberry if you please. Dissipation is a concept rather than a practice with us. Dark Benny is man enough to have a full beard, yet the rest of his face is smooth and brown; a copper kettle.

Each empty table is testimony to the majority who work Thursday afternoons; captives in a wage driven world. A few shoppers and late lunch office people are outside on the benches, or on the grass far enough from the river's edge to be free of duck shit. Raf walks out to woo two girls in blue blouse tops and though they won't come and drink with us, they wave towards the punters' bar. Raf swaggers back because he hasn't been entirely rebuffed. The ridged plug of his Adam's apple ascends his thin neck.

The exams have lifted from us all at last. We expand in the sun, conscious of the yeast of our youth. Surely I can reach out and pluck the river oaks, or float like a blimp over the modest skyscrapers of our city. In fact I find myself puffing to climb the lavatory steps before we set out for the next hotel; swaggering like Capulets.

Beer, mein host, your finest. The new barman has the massive face of a prop, and the room has lattice windows which pattern the powder blue sky. Yet from that blue shimmer only white light is barred across the faces and table tops inside. Sweet Jesus, I have years and years to enjoy my life: almost everyone I see will die before me.

In some way, a mystery to me, we have increased our number on the walk along the river bank. This Keith, who claims friendship with Benny, grins at me on the strength of it, calls me cocker and chief, drinks the beer I buy, belches in my face with easy familiarity. The dark partitions are cool to lean against and the clocking of snooker balls from the next room lulls me. I have a fancy that each unseen colour has a slightly different sound. To the blue for example must belong the very clear, ringing voice.

This Keith is an intrusion on the last day that flatmates spend together. Benny is to go back to the Hawkes Bay to harvest peas, Raf to the Timaru woolstore and I will work on trucks in North Canterbury. Oh, the pay is good enough, the work almost all outside, but toughening up in the first week or two is a bloody thought. It could be several days first up of carting lucerne hay, each bale a test for unaccustomed muscles, so that you turn quietly aside if you can to throw up. I had intended this year to keep up my fitness rather better, but I wasn't called upon much to play for the Varsity fourths and my jogging fell away a good deal in the winter when the frost barked in the mornings, or the smog lapped the tree trunks of the park.

But now, now, as I pause in the doorway with two jugs I can see the brazen marigolds sneering at the sun from their tubs in the courtyard. The glitter drives me back to the high cubicules and the lattice bondage of the sun. I feel my throat swollen and moist. There is an Australian with large freckles on the backs of his hands explaining the intricacies of League to the barman. Dr Logan is an Australian. In July he told me that I had too narrow a research and reading background to be sure of a future in the subject. Do you want it straight from the shoulder, he asked me. These Aussies consider it a virtue to be outspoken. He told me that even if I had the ability then almost certainly I lacked the application. I resented it of course, though it was true I'd missed several of his lectures and asked for extensions on my essays. These Australians should be denied any positions here.

Raf has begun a friendly argument with a passing snooker player over who is the tallest person in the bar. They make a wager of five dollars and I do the measuring in the poolroom doorway with a cue. I do my best for Raf who is six two, but the snooker player is blessed with a natural stoop and unwinds in the doorway to damn near six four. My other task is to pay the five dollars. For most of the winter I tried to become the lover of Anna Sledgely, who wasn't at varsity at all, but worked in the fruitmarket. I had an idea that her seduction wouldn't be as long as that of varsity girls, who have to be intellectually conquered in a considerable campaign before they succumb in any other way. One foolish comment about Virginia Woolf, or a slip in scanning the trochaic metre can lose you a landfall. I reasoned that Anna would have a more immediate, physical response. She had a way of watching me beneath her lashes as I chose cabbages, or brussel sprouts, and she wore her smock tightly belted so that when she breathed in it was me who turned giddy.

However, we must move on. Benny's beard is now pointed in the direction of the King Dick, whose afternoon barman is friendly to students, unlike the anthropoidal brute who comes on at six. In early November a really hot sun is still a novelty and we pause at the Armagh corner to bathe in it; to enjoy our conscious idleness within the business rush. This Keith now finds he's left his jersey at the last place and runs back waving his arms to get it, while Benny, Raf and I carry on to the King Dick. If he doesn't catch us up I won't worry. He wipes the beer from his mouth in an irritating way and keeps calling me chief and cocker.

My grandmother is dying in Wellsford: dying of Wellsford perhaps. She should have stayed on the Northland farm with the warm rain and the sea visible from the ridges. Totara stumps from the original felling are still on those ridges, weathered white as driftwood and clutching in the green grass. Grandad had a soft moustache that same driftwood colour and it drooped in a way that gave his mouth and chin a gormless, caved-in look. He would point out to me the sunken places on the farm which seventy years before had been pits in which the totara were sawn to slabs before being sledged down to make planks for the house, or to be sold. I fossicked for kauri gum and found giant snails in the last of the native bush, with their great scimitar shells the colour of cow shit. My grandmother never talks of such things while dying in Wellsford of course; her condition gives her the right to choice of topics, which are the heinous effrontary of all political policies and the goings on of her neighbours. Two visits ago she gave me my birthright: the 500 family shares in the Te Tarehi Dairy Co-operative which failed in 1933.

Raf says that the draught beer at the King Dick is the ideal temperature for summer; too cold and the flavour of a bitter is numbed. There is a view into the entrance of the mall. We see the shoppers walk towards us, then turn left or right into the street. Most don't see us watching from the shadowed window of the bar and hold their smiles or conversations as they near. One or two women so admirable that in coming from the mall they must not turn aside at all, but maintain their graceful stride and smile, move through the hotel window to join me. Raf is making his despondent boast of three overdraft accounts with separate banks. His old man must just stump up, or it's all over for the next year. Overhead the brass tipped ends of the fans are idly turning. The barman who tolerates students is listening to the races while he cleans his shoes on a newspaper. On a drinking day I reach a stage at which the beer and I are no longer disparate. The tissues dissolve, the bones emulsify and all is tidal equilibrium. The expression to have a skinful is wonderfully apt. From the barman's crown one tuft of hair stands up like the crest of a quail and it shakes as he buffs his shoe caps. I lean back as I talk to Benny of our year and find my syllables oddly synchronized with the circling fan.

Benny has complexities of character; twin allegiances to rugby and art. He plays for Varsity A. Raf and I have become accustomed to watching him bulldozing in the winter scrums, then afterwards on our sagging sofa in the flat, usually with a bruise, or a split lip, he will talk quietly of Goya and Crome. My own sport has been a disappointment. I'm not successful in the cross-country any more. Too many guys built like ostriches go away from me on the hills with hawsers working in their featherless thighs. When I should be training I read Updike, or Cheever, lying on my bed, or have coffee with Anna Sledgely, not lying on my bed more's the pity.

We are having a discussion about our next port of call, and Keith assumes equality in our voting so that it's a tie even though he isn't one of us and went to some co-ed school without a decent first fifteen. It is agreed to accept the barman as arbitrator. He uses beer as a mild corrosive to remove shoe polish from his fingers as he passes judgement. I'd say the Star and Garter, he says. They know how to cellar beer, the yuppies don't gather there, and in the old bar there's a collection of coins nailed to the wall.

As we turn the first corner, full into the late afternoon sun, Raf stumbles on a sewer cover and does a header into the exhaust pipe of a Commodore at the lights. There is very little blood however and Raf soon remembers how to lift his feet. He tells us that when he was eleven he broke three bones in his shoulder falling from a yacht drawn up on the Picton slipway. He holds a handkerchief to his cheek and there is from somewhere in the shops we pass the smell of onions frying. Heaps of onions surely, being rendered down in some vast pan. There is an inevitable sadness about the fragrance of frying onions. Something of lost conviviality and simplicity, I tell the others.

Probably the best thing I did this year is my essay on igneous dykes on Banks Peninsula. As well as hitting the books I spent several days on site making sketches and taking photos — I've always had a good eye for proportion and perspective. An A-plus and Dr Waugh said that there were some pages which were not an imposition to read. I like a subject with a practical aspect. Arp, arp — excuse me. It's rather gassy, this bitter. Some people are great wafflers; running on amazingly with interpretations of this and that based on the premise of gold as a colour particularly significant to the schizophrenic mind, or one sixth Magyar blood on the mother's side. Dr Logan, the Aussie, delights in this sort of thing, while on my work writes — a barely competent, orthodox account from secondary sources. In this Armagh Street second hand shop there is a bear. Its snout is dusty, the eyelids shrunk back from its glass eyes. Benny has christened it Halpern after our landlord, because of its similar smile, and we go in to furtively punch its stomach a few times as a ritual. Don't you find yourself drawn to such things? The scales sloughed off assorted lives. Embossed volumes about David Livingstone, ink stands in cut glass, brass containers for wax matches on fob chains, a silver mug from the officers' mess of the fourth Gurkha Regiment, an astrakhan coat, a gentleman's riding boots with the wooden plugs to maintain the shape. A place marvellously uneasy with memories and aspirations not put kindly to rest. As we go on Benny searches for a phone box so that he can ring the real Halpern and abuse him. Raf grips his shirt to restrain him. Halpern is not a man we wish to be aroused against us: better to assault the cathartic bear.

I'm sweating in the street sun and welcome the shade of the Star and Garter when it comes. Our bar is half a flight up, with regularly spaced circus prints and more students than the other pubs of the day. We join a group from the Hall which includes the Boswell twins. In my first year I took Rebecca out, but I can never distinguish her on sight from Natalie. So I'm always extra friendly to which ever one I meet. All over then, I ask one of them. She mentions sociology and philosophy so I know it's Natalie. I'm no fool. A good listener though, is what I am; even as I nod to Natalie's recital I note the closest print has a very thin clown with a ruff, pedalling a one-wheeled cycle, and the next a troupe of acrobats with Italian moustaches who salute from the high wire. After that the glass surfaces are at an angle which catches the sun and each is a golden plaque as I drink and listen. I have a say myself in time, horrifying Natalie by telling her how we locked the neighbourhood corgi in our house by accident at the start of the May vacation and came back to find it dead by the kitchen door, a nasty mess at each end. And then there was a bad week in July when my teeth packed up and drove me to extraction — two of them and six fillings. I went into overdraft and the dentist told me not to ignore the need for regular checks. Otherwise though, a good year, I tell Natalie. A hundred laughs, a few knock backs and smothered apprehensions, and a stuffed bear to punch from time to time. I see a great future for myself. This Natalie has a nice pair on her.

Maybe I should revise my opinion of this Keith guy. He has bought a jug for me and listens thoughtfully, eyes on my face, to the account I give of my unequal struggle with Dr Logan. Attaboy, chief, he says, but without the cynicism I detected in it earlier. Raf on the other hand has pushed between me and the Boswell twins, and Benny doesn't pretend to listen to anyone, but gazes at the circus prints with such deliberation that as his head stretches up his mouth is drawn open. He could be praying. Both the clown and the acrobats are very stylised; a pointillistic technique almost. My eyes are running, my guts squeamish and I'm burping a lot. Someone is loudly insisting that we move on — and it's me. The door is inconveniently small, so buffets my shoulder as we leave. Let's take a route away from the homeward traffic and the crowded bus-stops. My powers of deduction are still sharp. By the river are some railings where we rest a while and I lift my tee-shirt to feel the sun on my stomach. I notice now that Raf hasn't come with us; just dark-bearded Benny and Keith. I have been wrong about Keith: I recollect a long history of comradeship between us.

We decide on one more stop. The Redux we call it, for we often visit it both coming to and going from the flat. We will make it for that quiet time when the respectable population have their tea. There are a few rilled clouds over the Port Hills and the smell of vehicles close at hand. The unruffled surface of the stream slides by without a sound; a voice behind the parapet calls that it's Sally, it's Sally, but we see no one. There should be a greater sense of relief and satisfaction at the closing of an academic year, but it's an anti-climax of a sort. Friends reassert their other lives: have separate homes to go to, vacation jobs, responsibilities, relatives and dreams not in common. Though Keith does invite me to go cane-cutting in Queensland. Great sums to be made on the land, he says. My grandfather's place proved intractable in the end; so much steep country was opened up early which should have been left alone. The bush is coming back now they say, and the farm houses are mostly sold to alternative lifestylers who have been spun out of Auckland by centrifugal force. In the first years of the farm he used to turn the cows into the bush for the winter; it was warmer there he said, and they found feed aplenty, coming out in the spring quite sleek and often with a calf at heel. By the time I remember most of the slopes were cleared, and suffering because of it. The moreporks would gather when I visited though and report the watch times to me in a haunting way. I was too afraid to go outside to the longdrop by the hedge, and would pee from the bedroom window into the night.

Quite often this year I've had a foreboding that I'll die young, particularly when I'm not doing so well with Anna Sledgely. The damaging effects of sexual repression are not sufficiently recognised. It comes over me too when I'm playing poker, swotting, or in that first, vulnerable moment of waking before daylight certainties take hold. I could weep for myself at such times. Benny tells me it's just a subterfuge to avoid concentration, but Keith says that such things shouldn't be disregarded. It's very important to listen to what your mind is telling you Keith says.

At the Redux I find that I have been robbed. There is no way that I could legitimately be left with so little money. Why, I can account to within two or three jugs for every purchase of the day. You've got to watch the people in a lot of those places says Trevor behind the bar. He knows me well, but can't break the house rule of strictly cash even for me, he says. I had hoped to have enough left at the afternoon's end for fish and chips. Fish and chips are a very sobering meal. The absorbent qualities and the salt I suppose. The Redux has round, wooden tables with ashtrays as large as coffee pots sunk into the centres. Raf, Benny and I invented a game tapping twenty cent pieces from the edge of the table into the ashtray. Some of the other regulars have even taken it up. I have become so skilled that I can hole out three times out of four. During the year I suppose I've spent a hundred hours tapping a coin into ashtrays. But then any sport can be made to seem ridiculous if described in terms of time and consequence. In September I had a sequence of eleven straight wins over Benny and Raf. I was the world champion. Trevor asks how my exams are going and even as I lean to tell him that I've finished, as I smile and raise a glass of Keith's beer, I have that abrupt, hollow certainty that I will die young. I feel my face blanch, and turn back to our table with a start of self-pity. For reassurance I borrow a coin from Benny and pot it expertly on the table top. My old friend, Keith, refills my glass. Feeling all right, chief? Maybe I will be spared for just a few years — time to achieve something and return by invitation to address my old school.

You need at times to just sit and let the mind settle. Some people use the bog for such relaxation; some take up yoga, or trout fishing. Chekhov spent hours fishing in a pond on his Melikhovo estate, but a visitor discovered there were no fish in it at all. During the warm months I found relief by lying on the garage roof. I could take my pipe and climb the plum tree onto the garage. It is completely private there and I could consider the reasons for not being more appreciated by the world.

From the Redux we walk through the church grounds and down the bowling club alley to the park. The alley has pipe barriers at each end to deter the cyclists and we have a gymnastic competition there to see who can complete the most rotations without stopping, or touching the ground. I run a very close third to Benny and Keith, but afterwards have to lean over the fence and overflow into a camellia bush. Things have lost distinct identities. Blurred in the sun the large trees closest to the river topple slowly towards the placid current. Yet there is no splash. An avuncular statue of a city hero centres the lawn and even as I pass the goblins drop from his arse and scuttle into hiding amongst the rye grass and japonica. Everybody is speaking German, even Benny and Keith have atrocious accents. Raf has surely betrayed us by remaining with the Boswell twins instead of coming home. Yet from some fortunate place is the fragrance of bacon. I could weep at not being invited there. In fact I do, and am only cheered by my close friend, Keith, who promises to buy me fish and chips. The ducks come over in flights of five and seven; fast wings from the sun. Anna Sledgely has golden hairs on her arms and after swimming at New Brighton the sand clings to her like sherbet powder.

Benny tells me to stop shouting at the ducks. They've done nothing blameworthy I must admit. Keith says when a bird shits in flight it must stop flying, just for that moment of release. Keith says it's something to do with the musculature that birds have. I believe him and stop to watch, but staring straight up turns me dizzy and so I kneel for a bit. There are old coins of chewing gum on the pavement and stones worn smooth at the surface, pressing like cockabully mouths at the meniscus.

The villa welcomes us; weather boards a warped smile and thistle heads swollen in the heat. I'm amazed how quickly my learning slips away. Only last week I could recite whole chunks of Donne and Marvell — verbatim mind you, verbatim. I knew all the details of Xenophon's espousal of discipline and the anecdotes of Diogenes of Sinope. How that old cynic would love today's fierce sun. Benny claims I have the key to the back door. I reckon he has. Neither of us can find it, but after a leak beneath the garage plum tree we sit on the verandah to wait for Raf. By the logic of elimination he must have the key, and if not then we will be sober later and will find our own. There is a chair and a sofa to sit on. The horse-hair stuffing shows where the velveteen is worn through. The sun knocks Benny into a rumbling sleep, while Keith and I solemnly accept each other's confidences. Show me the man who is never sad and I suspect a fool. Although my most recent knowledge is slipping from me I can remember the exact and marvellous crimson of the cloth lining in the box which held my grandfather's microscope, and the steady voice of the morepork when others had been silenced by the night.

Yet Keith and I take the trousers from Benny so that he sleeps on with his knees spread to the sun and the front gate; his cock an acorn between rugby thighs. My throat is tight with suppressed laughter, but I will be careful to remain awake or Keith may have me similarly exposed. As I gather my strength to rise, I see my left foot has lost its shoe to the robbers passed through during the day. Keith leans forward urgently to command my attention to the tale of his most secret ambition and the scarred green velveteen behind him is for a moment magnificently restored by an angle of the sun. Yet another lovely colour, and I am brought before the one stained window of the small Te Tarehi church where my grandparents so loved to sing to the tune of Saffron Walden and the sun through tones both musical and visual made patterns on their faces.

Oh, how young I am. See me disreputable with Keith and sleeping Benny on the verandah. I have a whole life in store — it seems to me.

A Message For Life

Yesterday I heard a cuckoo's chime from the Montford spinney. It rang across the crocus strewn lea on the still air and took my attention from the study desk, and my article on the significance of the horse chestnut in British arboreal history. I couldn't begrudge the interruption, for isn't there a message for life here, perhaps? In our busy round amidst the jostling ambitions and responsibilities of modern living aren't we all inclined to neglect the everyday sights and sounds which succour us; which are the constant reward, even reason, for our passing life. I put aside my work for a time with good grace and opened my casement the better to hear the cuckoo's sound. Sing out, cuckoo, I thought and I will relay your message to my friends and fellows throughout the land.

I paid heed to *Cuculus canorus,* crossed the meadow and climbed through Montford spinney, its three great oaks with lichen on their northern backs supreme amongst their smaller neighbours. In the local dialect these last are still known by old identities as stavers, because of their value to coopers through the centuries. They form no barrels now, yet isn't there a message for life here? The usefulness we find in things varies according to time and need. Our relationships with one another are not dissimilar. Parents who supported and served us in early years deserve in due course, like the Montford stavers a time of repose and quiet, when nothing more is asked of them and due respect is given.

From the high point of the ridge above the spinney, a treasured spot for me, I could see the downs undulate towards the far Cotswolds. In late summer when the land shows through its cover most, one can still see in places the cart ruts made during Roman times on the way to Cirencester. On this same promontory almost two thousand years ago a centurion of Claudius's legions may have looked out to choose camp for the night. Two years back, beneath the old stables of the Dubois manor, the owners found the tiles of a villa floor, with fish and serpents still marvellously bright. There is a message for life in that, if we care to ponder it. Too many of us are obsessed with thoughts of ownership and absolute rights. The view from the ridge is a sermon on the stewardship of the land; the responsibility we all have to take our possession of the glebe as a trust to be lovingly maintained and passed on to our children's children. All this I seemed to hear the centurian beside me murmur with Roman *gravitas*. Would that the great ones of the chambered cities would hear as readily.

I came back by way of Beck Lane, past the hawthorne hedge with delicate damsel lace amongst it in blue bloom, and a badger trail clear enough for those who know country ways. I loitered there, hoping to see foxes, for several times I have glimpsed a young vixen at the place; tail held higher as a token of her sex. The scene, dappled with low sun through the hawthorne and stavers, remained empty. I was about to move on, disappointed, when my gaze fell on a doric jasper moth, so rare and lovely, which was perched on the fustian of my sleeve. I wondered how long I had been staring past it, ignorant. There is a message for life here, don't you agree? Often we feel let down when existence doesn't provide the object we have demanded of it, yet all along other things of equal worth are there if we but adjust our mental focus. Some humility is needed to be at one with nature. The poet Herrick despised the rustic simplicity of his parishioners at Dean Prior so much that he trained a pig to be his boon drinking companion. Amusing perhaps, but comparisons could be made both ways.

At the pool below Rupert's Crossing, so called because the Cavaliers allowed their horses to drink there in 1645, the sound of frogs resonated from the rushes and rampling weeds. The clear centre flowed placidly, as did the Cam I remember from Peterhouse days. Dooley Meek was fishing there, and touched his cap as his family has to mine through generations. Dooley's grandfather had been village mole catcher, and on his tombstone was his chosen epitaph, 'I be mole here now'. Surely there is a message for life in that. Old Meek never set himself above nature as so many of us are wont to do, but saw his life as part of that round of perpetual decay and regeneration which is the divine theatre. If more of us were brought to that sobering realisation then the greater would be our sympathy and contentment.

These are simple reflections from a rural day my friends, yet when I partake of a glass of my own cider and sprawl within my study with a brochure of the new Daimler; when I consider this column syndicated in forty-seven newspapers and magazines, when I relax while you tramp to work for Leviathan — isn't there a message for life here, perhaps?

PLUTO

I saw him first in the pool — a blue, free standing motel pool set in high duck-boards and with a fence of the same boards for privacy, and to stop toddlers from straying in to drown. Wesley Smith was very thin. He gripped the pool ladder and floated like a spider monkey, with his arms and legs spread yet bent. His feet were lunar pale beneath the clear water, and his shins sunburnt. I don't suppose there is a great opportunity to build up a tan in prison administration.

My wife and Jean had taken a liking to each other as soon as they met in the motel laundry. They had been to the gallery together; to the shops. 'Her husband runs a prison,' my wife had told me. It was an indirect introduction to Wesley Smith, and I briefly indulged the fancy that he was the Mr Big who manipulated the occupants and staff of all the cell blocks, although I knew that even such a power would hardly be on holiday in a Tahuna motel. 'Don't be absurd,' Liz said. 'He's the governor or whatever there.' And so he was; the head of the largest prison in the nation, and getting away from it all by having a fortnight in Nelson.

'Ah yes, of course,' he said as Jean and Liz introduced us, and from a sense of courtesy he came out of the pool to talk to me. The dense hair of his arms and legs lay in scrolls from the play if the water, the shaving line on his chin was blue-purple, and within his rather taut face the eyes were oddly lustrous, expansive. 'Our wives have decided that we shall be friends,' he said, 'and so we must comply.'

I brought out to the poolside a carafe of the local apple wine, and the four of us got on with friendship. Wesley told a story against himself as a city man getting lost in a shopping mall at Richmond, and in the relaxed mood of holiday we were all able to stretch to an anecdote or two, so putting our best feet forward in acquaintanceship. We were couples of a similar background, outgrown by our children and without any clash of temperament. It is no disrespect to marriage to say that there are times on holiday when another couple are welcome. My wife was glad of a more knowledgeable shopping companion, and I found that Wesley was a golfer, and not intimidated by silence. It was in fact that casual friendship hoped for while on holiday, and uninhibited by any likelihood that I would fall within Wesley's workday jurisdiction, or he within mine. He already had a competent dentist; I could tell by the quality of his capped upper incisors.

I wouldn't class myself as a particularly curious man, not prying into other people's lives I mean, but it was difficult to be with Wesley Smith without wondering at times about the nature of his job: the responsibilities of it and the special pressures of the whole criminal and penal aspect of our society. With just a few people it's like that; a poet maybe, or a professional soccer player, and you wonder how their special frame of mind must affect their view of the day's ordinary experience that you share.

Occasionally when we were walking up to the tee, or tending the motel barbecue, just saying commonplace things, or nothing at all, I would look at thin Wesley and imagine his gaol with its tiers of mezzanine cells and similarly hierarchical prisoners, exercise areas, security devices, staff with needs for promotion or counselling, and all that bitterness, deceit, despair, malice, pressing outwards. Dentistry certainly isn't an ideal lifestyle: working in people's mouths all day is a good living financially, but not an easy one, and the figures show the profession has one of the highest suicide rates of any career, but I imagined that Wesley Smith would smile at any stresses I could mention.

Jack Spratt could eat no fat and his wife could eat no lean the old rhyme says, and I normally expect the close proximity of personality in marriage to highlight differences, but Jean and Wesley Smith seemed similar in essential temperament; both intelligent, self-possessed, slightly rueful. Jean had her weaving which success had made more an art form than a hobby, and Wesley was a wood carver with his work in several important collections.

It was wet on the second Monday of our vacation, and cool as well. The city was swollen with campers with nowhere else to go, and the concrete block cathedral tower at the head of the main street was a fulcrum for an uneasy swirl of cloud. After leaving Jean and Liz at an exhibition of pottery, I drove back towards the beach, and later went over to Wesley's unit to find him carving; his tools on the window sill and the chair as close as possible to seek the light. Wesley's carvings were smaller and more elaborate than I had expected. Two of them stood on a tray by the motel window. One was a wood pigeon in kauri, the painstaking and precise detail of the feathers only partly complete. The other was carved in a macrocarpa canker, Wesley said, and the grain had a wonder of its own. It too was incomplete, but enough had been done to show that one pygmy had snared another with ropes about a tree trunk, and with exultation yet caution leant forward to torment his enemy with a spear. The whole thing no more than 10 centimetres high, and yet scores of hours needed to show the two creases on the crouching pygmy's belly, or the pattern on the woven twine that held his enemy whose individual fingers had been carved around the coil he tried in vain to keep from pressing on his throat.

I won't presume to make comment about artistic merit, or the talent of the carver, but fine work is an element of my profession also; almost a worker in ivory I could say, and I could appreciate the patience and precision that amount almost to a trance to work such detail on such a scale. Wesley had a wooden vice with padded jaws and a suction base, and over this in the window light he bent to carry on his almost oriental art. We talked for some time of the levels of dexterity needed, and he was very interested in the added constraints imposed by working inside somebody's mouth. He had in fact been considering buying one of the old dental service treadle drills he told me, and he asked me questions concerning them, and also the advanced, high speed modern drills. Wesley said he often did a model in soap first to check on balance and technical problems before committing himself to wood. He'd done some scrimshaw work he said, and some in meerschaum, sandstone and jade, but hard wood he loved best of all. Wesley said carving was popular with the long-term prisoners, and that he took a class himself of the three or four who grew to love it: their obsession perhaps to blot out the reasonable, unreasonable world. When Wesley told me of the most skilled prisoner I had a sense of undeclared envy in his heart that the man had more time than the governor himself to perfect his craft. From the motel window I watched the rain bounce on the road in a sudden fury and the water flow off its curve and fill the hollows of the lawn alongside as Wesley quietly talked.

The leisure of a wet day can be a time for confidences, and the carvings, the discussion of common practices to an extent, had moved us on from our usual trivial subjects. I had a measure of natural curiosity about the prison and his work there. His eminence in an unfashionable career: what it was like to be in charge of the underworld that society wished to see only through safe and entertaining fictions. 'What do you imagine it to be?' Wesley said. He loosened the carving of the pygmies from the suction vice and put it gently aside. He leant back and drew his finger along the blue-purple rasp of his chin. I was close enough to see the grey, downy light reflected in the noticeable curve of his soft eyes.

'I visualise a job demanding a good deal of administrative skill, and judgement as well, and elements of sympathy, even compassion.'

'The system squeezes out compassion,' said Wesley. 'Perhaps you will understand that everything there has to do with responsibility and power. We have all the responsibility and barely enough power, strange as it may seem. They have no responsibility and considerable power. Think of me as a general manager of a firm whose clients are willing it to fail. There's no goodwill, and the best of policies, the most secure of theories, can be destroyed by apathy, by spite and viciousness.' Wesley and I watched the rain, and he twirled the most slender of chisels in his fingers.

'It can't be easy,' I said.

'Not a week passes without a stir of some sort: an effort to screw the system. Not a week without accusations from inmates or their outside supporters, and whatever deceit or animosity is discovered they suffer little and just lapse back sullenly to await another opportunity. But oh, let there be a hint of negligence or oversight on our part, something not done quite by the book, and it's a different story. I can be front page news then.' Wesley's eyes lit, and his voice, still quiet, had nevertheless a tone of savage fun. 'We're never bored,' he said. He smiled at me, as the veteran smiles at the new chum who cannot know the significance of what he hears.

'I can imagine that,' I said.

'It's a difficult game when only one side is bound by any rules, and when it's only us who have anything much to lose, any character to be discredited. Do you see what I mean? One of my best department heads is fond of saying that we manage the anal end of society. No one else much wants to know how things are in our prisons, our psychiatric wards, our front-line welfare services.'

'You seem able to cope with the pressures well enough.'

'When has the pitcher gone too often to the well though,' said Wesley. 'That's a question isn't it.'

I thought about that when we drove back through the cool rain to collect our wives. It was the only talk of that sort we had, for the weather cleared for the remaining days, and Wesley put away his carving and his frankness, for golf-clubs, tourism and studied cheerfulness again.

We worked something out for the last day of the Smiths' holiday. They were to drive their rental car through the Lewis Pass and fly out from Christchurch in the evening. Liz and I took our car with them as far as Shenandoah, and we found a picnic spot there with meadow grass on one side of the river and native bush to the water's edge on the other. Wesley loved the bush, Jean said. She and Liz had made a special picnic lunch with fruit and fresh rolls, and I brought a bottle of Barossa red to mark the parting of the ways. It was a hot, blue day and the sunburn was intensified on Wesley's thin legs and the shoulders of our wives.

We got on well till the very last, and were I think sorry to part for more cause than just the recognition of another holiday's conclusion. Jean said it was time Liz and I moved to the main city, and Wesley said that instead of being content with just one captive at a time in my chair, I could become the official prison dentist with as many patients as I could manage, and paid with no bad debts by the state as well. We talked in an inconclusive way of meeting again during next year's vacation; the Coromandel perhaps, or even Singapore said Jean hopefully. It could all be worked out in letters we agreed. Growing sleepy in the sun between the cars, and with the red wine drunk to mark our parting, we allowed our personalities a certain abandon before return to workaday selves.

The Smiths left before two. We waved them out of the meadow grass and bush at Shenandoah. Wesley held up one slender hand and wrist in salute, and Jean smiled back until the corner. There was anti-climax of course with their departure, and Liz and I had only two more days ourselves before returning to the world which had caries at the bottom of its garden.

I was asleep on the tartan rug in the shade of the car, and Liz was reading, when Jean came back to Shenandoah alone in the rented car. Liz woke me even before Jean had stopped, and in the stupor of that sudden awakening in the heat I was at a loss for a moment to realise that Wesley should be with her, and both of them over the Lewis and on their way to Christchurch. 'I didn't know what else to do,' said Jean, embarrassed by her return. 'Wesley didn't come back and I waited and waited, and then I went into the bush a little way, but you can't see anything; there's no tracks.' Liz put an arm around her shoulders.

'It's all right. You'll see,' she said

Jean explained that just past Springs Junction the trees crowded the road, reached over it almost for one lovely section of the growing slope before the top of the pass, and Wesley had pulled over to stop and enjoy the bush: a last opportunity before the barren heat of Canterbury on the other side. A last walk in the calm trees, hundreds of years old, before he was back to work. He just walked in, she said, and he never came out.

Oh, we said that he'd be waiting on the roadside now, sure enough; that he'd be wondering where she'd got to, but I had a feeling of desolation about it right from the start. When has the pitcher gone too often to the well, Wesley had said. I packed up in a hurry, even in those circumstances struck by my own selfish concern at not being able to find the red thermos top.

Jean came with Liz in our car, while I drove the rental after them back towards the pass. Just a few kilometres past the buildings of Springs Junction was the place where Wesley had gone missing, and it was beautiful right enough. The bush was drawn up to the sides of the road and formed a canopy so that the road was part shadow, part dappled sun in degrees of direct and indirect light. The air was tunnel cool and fragrant; the banks plump with moisture which kept a rich green in the tumbling ferns. Liz pulled over where there was a slightly wider road edge, and Jean was standing amongst the first trees when I joined her. There was no sign of Wesley. The road ahead wound out of sight towards the summit; the bush was high on our right and undulated away down the valley on the other side.

'He must have lost his way, or twisted his ankle,' I said. 'He's sensible enough to work his way down the watershed if he's got lost, and so come out further down no worse off and just feeling a bit foolish.' I wasn't convinced: why should Jean be? She must have understood her own husband; had some knowledge of the things which would make Wesley walk into the bush and not return. I walked in myself so that it might seem I was taking positive action. I followed the direction Wesley had taken, and within a few metres the road was lost above me and the bush closed up in intense scrutiny. The punga ferns were clumped at head height and great sooty trunks slid up into the shifting forest canopy like the poles of a Big Top. I called Wesley's name, and heard no reply. There was just the noise of my own feet in the sloping leaf mould, and a chorus of cicadas far louder than I had ever heard before.

Maybe Wesley Smith was watching me; sitting amidst the fern and lancewood with his thin, hairy arms around his knees, and his lustrous eyes wide in the shadows. Maybe he was watching me go through the routine. It wasn't that I didn't care, but that I didn't believe he was lost in the way it would be assumed he was lost; in the way that would be reported in the papers. Prominent penal administrator missing: Dr Wesley Smith lost in Lewis Pass wilderness.

I made my way back up the slope towards the road, and came out fifty metres or so from the parked cars. I stood to catch my breath before walking down to Liz and Jean; before travelling back to the Junction to make the necessary report. Perhaps I rested also so that Wesley would have just that much more time to do what he wished. Within me was a conviction that Wesley would never be found, though god knows what it is makes a person step away from wife or husband like that, from life, and walk into the bush. Afterwards when there was all the speculation about whether he was still alive, still out there, my own interest and sympathy, my own guilt even, was not at all for the consequences of his action, just the motivation.

The Staff Clerk
Department of Standard Punitive Levies and Assessable Arrears
Private Bag
Wellington 1.

Dear Staff Clerk,

Supplication For Position 735/A86 As Advertised
In Metropolitan Newspapers

I have decided, Staff Clerk, to take a fresh approach in regard to this position and in respect of our relationship. For this reason I have ignored form PS17a, which has failed me in the past, and which is difficult to obtain here in any case. I have discarded also the professional detachment and predictability of those former applications to the tribe of Staff Clerk who are Janus at the portal of the Civil Service. I'm weary of shaping myself for the minds of others; attempting to be tailor-made for a position as I must imagine it; to be tested by you, Staff Clerk, as a child's block is tested in the shaped vacancies, to see if I pass through to the inside. Fain would I be seen as individual, capable of growth. There is an element of ploy in this novelty, I must confess, but message there as well.

From my hut, Staff Clerk, overlooking the Te Tarehi lagoon, I can hear the ocean in lazy play behind the bar, and on the other hand see thick bush of wonderfully contrasted greens along the estuary, and crowded back inland. What do you see I wonder, on your left hand and your right; within your typical New Zealand. There is a sort of Spanish moss hangs from the trees here, Staff Clerk, along the river banks. I've not seen it elsewhere. And sometimes at first light the condensation drips from filigrees and branches through the river mist which smokes from the smooth water, and beards up to match the drooping moss.

You see that I have a sincere intention to present myself to you candidly. Let us be truthful, you and I. I am a conventional age for an applicant, 35, and received an education in Auckland, city of my birth. I was in the academic stream in Sledgeham High. In my U.E.year I was not accredited because of a personality clash with the Headmaster (since retired), but in the external exams I achieved marks of 63 in Chemistry and 74 in history. I failed U.E. that year however, because I thought the English exam was in the afternoon, but it was in the morning. Even now, Staff Clerk, the thought of it brings the copper taste of terror to my throat. My conversion to Islam has given me a bulwark against such dependence on worldly things ever again. I completed my U.E. in a second sixth form year at Sledgeham, during which I was canteen monitor and considered unlucky not to be a prefect (the Headmaster had not then yet retired).

As I write this, rain has begun here at Te Tarehi, Staff Clerk. The sky and estuary are fused by the flux of it; the noise drowns the play of the sea. The rain cloud is moving round me from the hills. I am a sort of Crowhurst, drifting here, able to create my own record of the world, for there's no other human observer. The leak by the fireplace has begun again, into the pan I've positioned there. This is a prodigal part of the world, Staff Clerk.

I attended the University of Auckland for two years, and passed Maths and Classics. In addition I took an active part in student affairs, being nominated for the position of student sexual harrassment officer, and narrowly missing out at the vote because of feminist lobbying. Allah meant men to excel: good women are obedient said the Prophet. In 1977 I decided to interrupt university studies on the understanding that I had the inside running for the post of assistant meteorological officer on the New Zealand Antarctic Wintering Over Party of 1978. Unfortunately my landlord's efforts on my behalf were undermined by political favouritism, and despite passing a three week voluntary snow survival course at Mount Cook, I wasn't offered the post. I had also strengthened my professional background by correspondence courses in meteorological methodology. But what do such disappointments matter in the end, Staff Clerk. Our poet Ma'arri said this world resembles a corpse, and we around it dogs that bark.

Today, Staff Clerk, I shall have whitebait for both meals: whitebait fried in egg and dashed with vinegar. Whitebait heaped up on my enamel plate in defiance of conventional poverty. And for one of these meals I'll have a second course as well: my steam pudding recipe with golden syrup sauce. The Prophet taught that occasional physical indulgence is the means to rid ourselves of bitterness.

After meteorology was closed to me, I spent several years in pest eradication. Do you know the Basin at all, Staff Clerk? It is country difficult to forget. It was my living to kill a great many creatures of the Basin. Rabbits, hares, wallabies and the rest of them, but do you know of the vast flocks of Canada Goose in such places, Staff Clerk? And how they're thinned as flappers, or when moulting. Though it should not, the scale of death has always increased its impact. A magnificent and wily bird, the Canada Goose, who has succeeded as a pioneer here. I began reading poetry in the Basin; Irish mainly, and Australian. Down from the tussock ridge-line, out of the direct wind, I would have my lunch beside the issue Yamaha, and feed on words.

I left the Basin to become co-founder of Aorangi Fitch Breeders Ltd. My partner in this venture was Wally Volper, with whom I had much metaphysical discussion. Wally was temperamentally drawn to existentialist thinking. Our philosophical stock increased; but unfortunately the fitch breeding business received a fatal check when lightning struck our shed in October '83 and destroyed nearly 100 on heat fitch females. Yet all is as Allah wills it, and I had become gradually aware of a fundamental incongruity between my killing occupations and my beliefs. Killing needs to be better paid than I found it; and in more than cash.

Here at Te Tarehi, Staff Clerk, the air is always cooler after rain, and you can hear the water long afterwards still dripping, trickling, running in the bush; evened out so that the last of one day's rain is joined by the first of the next. There are peat and moss bogs here, Staff Clerk, as you would read of in Old Ireland; but no stone fences and no bombs. The fern fronds are brown arms as if from chimpanzees, and there are fantails who pine to be admired like chorus girls stumbled on in exile. Also a plague of evening sandflies to prevent a paradise. At night the moon is a bright bone on the water of the lagoon, and the sea shovels the stones endlessly on the other side of the bar: perpetual navy navvy. In those nights are ancient, indistinct New Zealand shapes and sounds along the estuary.

I joined the Islamic commune at Colenso in 1984, after a spell on the oyster boats from Bluff. Comparative religion fascinates us, Staff Clerk, don't you think, once we begin the reflective phase of our lives. We define ourselves by our beliefs; and only the most wise and most stupid never change. I was in charge of hydroponic vegetable growing at the commune, and had a regular correspondence with the DSIR on the subject. I had success with succulents, but was never able to reach the target of self-sufficiency. That wasn't the reason that I left however: ideological considerations have always been my priority. I was opposed to the move away from collectivism towards an insidious form of charismatic leadership which was undermining the commune. No one would listen to me. I have remained a Moslem, but grown suspicious of institutional links. More and more, Staff Clerk, it is the mystical tradition of Sufism which appeals to me. Of the five pillars of Islam only the pilgrimage has not been followed by me, but I have time to achieve it.

So I am here at Te Tarehi beside the lagoon: antipodean Walden's Pond for scrutiny both outward and internal. A white heron was in the estuary last week, Staff Clerk, it stood in Japanese simplicity against the dark background of the trees. There are still wild cattle from generations back, small and shaggy. I've seen them burst from the flats into the bush when they're disturbed.

You won't dismiss the general nature of this supplication I hope, Staff Clerk. I want to present a *curriculum vitae* of attitude as well as mere event you see. In my new approach perhaps the hem of bureaucracy can be lifted to let in the Indian summer of Te Tarehi: wasps curled in ecstasy upon the fallen fruits, and recollection of sky broken into blue and golden darts by the partial masking of the leaves above. Don't assume either, that it requires no courage to live calmly and alone and listen to your life passing.

Call for me, Staff Clerk, and I will shave my face and hood my eyes; will place a tie around my neck, will break the days and nights to hours again, will learn whatever sub-paras and subsections apply in each case, will be punctilious as well as punctual in all the Department may require. I will combine with you to serve the questor of Standard Punitive Levies and Arrears; keeping all criticism to professional confines.

The estuary is mottled, Staff Clerk, with the shadows of the trees, but my fresh whitebait on the bench are still transparent as if of ice. I feel a sense of incipient competence in the tasks you may assign.

Staff Clerk, I wait for your reply.

Bruce Vancelea
(now Harun)
The Wold Jar Hut
Te Tarehi Lagoon
Summer of '86

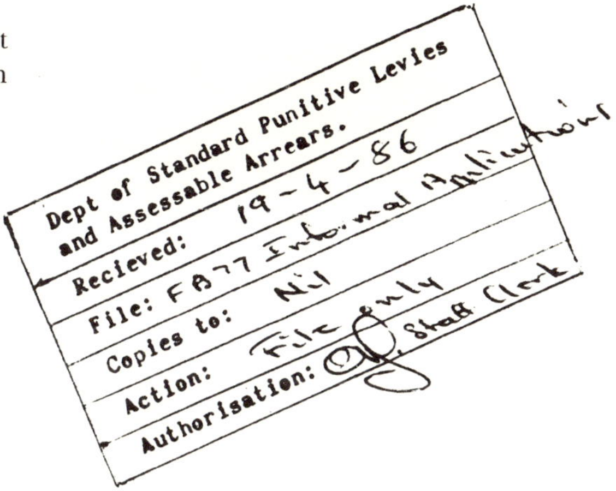
Dept of Standard Punitive Levies
and Assessable Arrears.
Recieved: 19-4-86
File: FA77 Informal Applications
Copies to: Nil
Action: File only
Authorisation: Staff Clerk

The Man Who Discovered The Body

Prior ended up at the Smiths' house above the lagoon by a process of algebra: or rather what she recalled of algebra from distant, failed experience. How A and B start out as utterly distinct in an equation, yet are shuffled in a hugger-mugger way and prove to be on the same side after all. In the living algebra Prior had never met the Smiths before, had no knowledge of their existence in the house above the lagoon; yet there she was, abruptly cognizant of Smith's thatched moustache, and a tinted photograph of his farm upon the wall.

'So you are in Gill Crosbie's four,' said Smith.

'No,' said Prior. Mrs Smith laughed.

'Don't be dense,' she said. 'Didn't you hear her say she played for the other four. You never listen do you. I don't know. You never listen.'

'All right,' said Smith.

It was bowls that brought it about. Two teams selected from the clubs to travel to the tournament, and the usual confusion with the rides, you know the sort of thing, so Prior was left waiting with the Smiths to be collected. Life is spent in such ways.

'I'd say the competition will be pretty fierce,' said Prior.

'What's that?'

'The tournament standard; pretty tough.'

'I'd say it would be,' said Smith. His moustache continued up his nostrils, and each breath was like the sound of the wind in a birch thicket.

'You've never been before, so how would you know?' said Mrs Smith to her husband.

'I can read can't I. I can talk. I know what teams will be there don't I?'

'We won't make the post-section play,' said Mrs Smith. 'You need an experienced skip at that level.'

'Who is your skip?' asked Prior.

'Him,' said Mrs Smith.

'Well, I'm sure he —'

'Just remember a skip's only as good as his team,' said Smith.

'Yes, well I'm sure you —' began Prior.

'You can't tell me you don't need a good skip in fours. You can't tell me that,' said Mrs Smith.

'I'm not telling you that. If you'd listen to what I am telling you, you'd learn something, but you never do listen to the point of anything.'

'No, you can't tell me that you don't need a good skip,' said his wife.

The lounge had no fireplace: instead a heater with a moulded top of plastic logs which would flicker red in winter. Yet alongside it was a set of brass shovel, poker and brush on a stand. Who knows what ashes they were intended to dispose of. 'It's certainly a nice day for it,' said Prior. Mrs Smith had pale skin despite the farm. Her eyes, ears and lips had slightly red rims, as though the blood had retreated there. Her eyes were the milky green of thaw water.

The Smiths and Prior looked from the lounge window over the slope of the farm to the lagoon, with its dark, flat water, and the shingle ridge that blocked it from the sea. The wind of Smith's life reverberated within his hairy face.

'Something's been scaring the hens,' said Mrs Smith.

'Well all the dogs are tied.' Smith's breathing was so insistent that Prior found herself breathing in time with him. Mrs Smith seemed not to breathe at all. Her eyes cast back the light, and her level lips, pink rimmed, had a stark bitterness that was almost beauty.

'Something's scaring them,' she said.

'Knock it off,' said Smith. He looked over a mile of land and the lagoon as a city man might regard a window box, or a single crab apple tree. 'Yes, it was down there,' he said.

'Oh, Christ,' said Mrs Smith.

'Pardon?' said Prior.

'Down there; the body,' said Smith. He leaned back with a smile that could be perceived as a ripple in his moustache.

'Pardon?'

'Oh, Christ.'

'The Anna Milligan murder,' said Smith. 'I found the body in the lagoon; March thirteenth, '85.' Smith had established his true credentials. 'You remember of course?'

'It's coming back to me. The Milligan murder, of course.'

'I found the body,' said Smith.

'That must have been a shock.'

'Don't ask,' said Mrs Smith.

'I could see it on the high tide mark, showing up from a long way. Odd, but the dogs showed no interest at all. All that time in the water had taken the scent I suppose. No clothes on at all, you'll remember.'

'Hurry down, you may find another,' said Mrs Smith. Prior glanced to the lagoon again; to see perhaps a pale, star-shaped figure in the mud.

'Nothing but a steering wheel cover tied round her waist. That's what convicted the bloke in the end. That's how they got him.'

'Was it,' said Prior. She meant to indicate agreement rather than interest or doubt, but Smith blossomed from his chair, and strode into the next room.

'We haven't time now, for God's sake,' cried Mrs Smith, but in reply was just the sound of a lemming host through leaves, Smith's breathing, from the other room. 'You shouldn't have asked,' said Mrs Smith before her husband came back with the newspaper pages.

It was all there: a picture with Smith in the foreground pointing down to the lagoon margin where he found the body of Anna Milligan. Because of the poor quality of the photo Smith's moustache was indeterminate, spreading across the picture and into the shadowed side of his face.

'It's all there,' said Smith. All about what happened in the sand dunes, the clue of the steering wheel cover, the demand for more severe sentences. Each time Smith's name appeared it was underlined in red biro. He leant over Prior's shoulder, his breath causing her dress collar to hover. 'Here I get commended for not interfering with the body in any way, you see,' he said. Mr Smith was to be commended it said for having the acumen not to disturb the body in any way before contacting the Police. 'I had a fair idea,' said Smith. He went back to his chair by the window. 'I had a fair idea of procedure in murder cases, and besides when I seen it I pretty much twigged that it must be the Milligan girl. Read on a bit,' he said, as Prior was allowing the paper to settle in her lap. Prior read on, positioning the paper between them.

Mrs Smith left the room abruptly. 'She suffers from one of these women's things,' said Smith in a confidential bellow. 'But she'll be all right at the bowls. She's good at bowls. I'll say that.'

'Uh-huh.'

'Actually I don't get the hang of this business of women's ailments, you know. It's a mystery over nothing much it seems to me, for one sex is no more complicated than the other is it? I've had to watch my own workings from time to time, but you never hear me complaining.'

'So the body was just lying there on the edge of the lagoon,' said Prior. 'Goodness.'

'It's an odd thing about a drowned woman's body,' said Smith, 'how short the arms and legs seem.'

Prior looked to the sea beyond the bar: so different to the flat, trapped pool of the lagoon. The sea was free in its own immensity: the rhythms and colours of it altered according to depth and clouds and currents, and more intrinsic, secret qualities. It was self-sufficient and bided its time.

'There's an odd softening of outline after so long in the water,' said Smith.

'Gilly Crosbie said that she thought the greens there would be faster than any of the ones we play on,' said Prior. She tried to remember how far it was from Smith's house to the road gate, and wondered if she had the nerve to say she preferred to go and wait there. 'She played there last year and found them hard to handle,' she said.

'Is that right,' said Smith. 'You'll see there in the write-up it says that there was no sign of a struggle on the body. No contusions it says; that's bruises. They were wrong there though. There were bruises on the shoulders and thighs. I can vouch for it and I was the first on the scene after all. I rang the paper about it afterwards, but they never printed any correction.'

'Gilly went through to the quarter-finals of the nationals one year, but the arthritis affects her play now I think. She doesn't say, but her delivery's not as smooth any more.'

'At that time of the morning,' said Smith, 'when the air's cool, you can see from one side of the lagoon to the other. I could see the colour of the body. I had a feeling it was going to be something like that.'

Mrs Smith had her bowling hat in her hand when she returned, and her face was even more pink and white. 'Has he finished yet?' she said.

'I suppose you've heard it all before,' said Prior. Mrs Smith looked at her husband and gave a smile quite beyond Prior's comprehension.

'All of it and more,' she said.

'She never went down to see it,' said Smith. Each breath was audible disparagement. 'There was time before the police came, but no, she wouldn't go down.' He drew his hand over his moustache so that it lay over his mouth like the tassel of a mussel.

'He keeps waiting for his M.B.E.,' said Mrs Smith. He laughed, but with a sense of grievance. His sideshow teeth were a picture of uniform strength. Prior wondered what life must be like in that house when they were alone. A what-not in the farthest corner had a ginger jar on each shelf; two green, one blue, with arched oriental bridges above the pools of golden carp and trees of conscious artistry.

'I think that's Gilly now,' said Prior, at the sound of a car in the drive. She took her bag and went out with the Smiths. When the introductions were over, Smith stood with Gilly Crosbie by the car, and the lagoon was visible between the sheds. Smith's breath rustled in his moustache.

'You see that lagoon down there,' he said. 'The south end; that's where the body was found of course. March thirteenth, '85. The Anna Milligan murder.' Smith laid an arm on the car roof for comfort.

'Is that right,' said Gilly.

A View Of Our Country

Simon Palliser had spoken to the Blenheim Rotary Club on his experiences as a noted traveller, and I agreed to drive him down to Christchurch so he could see something of the country on the way before flying out to Paris via Singapore. I was going on business anyway, and the President thought that I could do our scenery justice, so Palliser would have an impression of the place to take with him.

As we crossed the high bridge close to Seddon, Simon Palliser looked down to the blue, wild flowers and the pooled water. He asked me if I'd ever been to the Ivory Coast. 'I flew in to Abidjan,' he said. 'Some fifteen years or so I suppose after they got their independence from the French. The heat was killing, and after a few days I decided to move into the hinterland. I hired a car and drove to Yamoussoukro where the President had his palace. I'm telling you this because crossing that river reminded me of the crocodiles of Yamoussoukro. I drove 240 kilometres to get there, through Ouossou and Tomumodi, along a road more and more enclosed by jungle and the red soil the jungle fed on. But at Yamoussoukro itself the jungle had been cleared and a modern city built alongside the President's family village. Great plantations had been laid out too, of mangoes, pineapples and avocados. Down one side of the President's palace an artificial lake had been created and stocked with turtles, catfish and crocodiles. There had been no crocodiles in that district before, I was told.

'The crocodiles were fed late in the afternoon, and the hotel hired a driver from the Baoule tribe to take me to view them. The driver met me on the broad boulevard in front of the foyer entrance. He was a cheerful and talkative man with fair English. He began to tell me about his country as we walked to the carpark.

It was a little cooler than the coast, and a mist gathered in the city of Yamoussoukro; at once such a modern place, yet the site of chiefly power for hundreds of years.

'There was a causeway across the lake to the palace gates lined with coconut palms and iron railings, and at the gate the Presidential Guard stood sentry. The crocodiles waited with their mouths agape, on a shelf of sand between the embankment and the lake, and the feeder came in a pick-up truck and took buckets of meat to feed them. He called lovingly in French as he threw pieces down to the crocodiles who seemed short-sighted and inefficient eaters. It began to rain heavily, and colours came up on the backs of the crocodiles, and more crocodiles and a few turtles came out of the lake. The mist crept closer and the rain dimpled the surface of the lake. The feeder then took a chicken from his truck, and swung it back and forth in the rain above the railings; all the time appealing in French to the crocodiles. Then he tossed the chicken into the air.

'The chicken gained courage from being free in the air and rain. It flapped stoutly and landed over the heads of the crocodiles and in the lake. As it landed a turtle surfaced, as if it had duplicated the flight beneath the water, and the chicken was seized. It was an auspicious thing to happen. The feeder was alarmed and angry; my Baoule driver was glum. The feeder climbed the fence and ran towards the water across the sand to frighten the turtle. Instead one of the largest crocodiles jumped forward like an ungainly rabbit and had the keeper's leg in its mouth. There were perhaps twenty or thirty people watching, and the feeling of all seemed not one of horror, or even active concern, but a deep hopelessness. The crocodile backed into the lake, giving several gulping changes of grip which drew the feeder more firmly to him. The feeder called out once in French, then was silent, and his long robe trailed behind him. One of the guards fired into the air, and the keeper's wide eyes were fixed on us, his audience, even as he disappeared.

'The rain dimpled the lake surface just the same; turtle and chicken, crocodile and man were gone, leaving us powerless in the wet. "Quickly come away with me now," my driver said. I was thinking that there had been no crocodiles at all at Yamoussoukro until the lake had been dug for the President's palace.'

It was a dry year in Marlborough. When we stopped a little past Ward for a thermos of tea, the hills were very brown and the heat confused their outlines. Palliser said it reminded him of Spain. 'Emotionally, Spain was a turning point for me,' he said. 'A woman I was very much in love with, left me to take up a United Nations job in the Mato Grosso, and I drifted south into Andalusia and was very drunk for several weeks. You know Andalusia I suppose? Of the several weeks I can remember nothing; a blank in my life, then I sobered up in the little town of Baeza in the hills above the Guadalquivir. I can feel the very evening; the air heavy with jasmine and orange blossom, the soil red as a heart. There were prickly pears at the roadside and within some of them the torreo bird had picked out small nests, and their heads watched at the entrances as I passed. My friend took me to the café to hear the gypsies sing the cante jondo, and all through it the more stolid locals sat at the back tables and continued with their dominoes. I didn't drink, and watched the gypsies under the influence of wine move from the plaintive cante jondo to a wild flamenco; all castanets and exclamation. In the midst of it a farmer brought in a lynx he had killed in his fields, and hung it from a beam by the door for his friends to admire, or to attract a buyer for the skin perhaps.

'As the gypsies danced and sang, as the domino players became steadily more absorbed in their own purpose, I sat with the scent of jasmine and orange blossom through the cafe door, and the Persian gleam of fur upon the lynx. It turned slowly on the cord, first one way then the other, as if its tufted ears still sought some magnetic north of freedom.'

The seaward Kaikouras crowd the main road to the ocean's edge south of the Clarence river and rise abruptly to over 3,000 metres. Simon Palliser had a love of mountains. 'Of course Switzerland has been something of a second home to me,' he said. 'Several times between expeditions I rested at Brunnen on the shores of Lake Luzern. Do you know it? A town of solid, unpretentious houses on a flat strip of land, while beyond it the steep, glaciated slopes descend into the lake like the sides of a fiord. I made a base at the guest-house of the Gotthardt's usually, and from my upstairs room I had a view of the small steamer berths, and the many trees of that part of the town. I remember on one of their election days taking the rack and pinion railway from Brunnen to Axenstein, a high resort with magnificent views across the lake. Because of the elections and the season there were few people travelling, and in my compartment only one other person; a Swedish woman, beautifully dressed, who spoke excellent German. She told me in a gentle, quite unselfconscious way that she had been travelling to overcome her grief at the recent death of her husband, and that her main difficulty was coping with the loss of sexual satisfaction brought about by the abrupt end of her marriage. She had found no opportunity for solace not repugnant to her she said, until seeing me who bore a singular resemblance to her husband.

'It was all so natural, so kind, so tinged with inevitability. We stood close in the corner of the rack and pinion carriage, with her lovely skirt folded up. Her tears were wet on my cheeks; perhaps I cried myself. She clasped her hands at the small of my back and pulled strongly. Past the blond hair fastened back from her smooth face, the lake seemed quite calm from such a height and pine forests rose up to the snow line on the mountains above the water. She murmured her husband's name through her tears, I recall. Have you travelled to Sweden? Sven is a common Christian name there.'

As we drove down the coast close to Kaikoura, Palliser thought he saw a seal on the rocky shore. He was interested because of the heavy swell also, and the scene reminded him of British Columbia. 'I had a temporary job in conservation there,' he said. 'I was camped in the magnificently unspoiled Pacific Rim National Park on Vancouver Island. My main task was checking on the sea lions which lived in groups on rocky islets off the coast. On the one day in three or four the swell allowed, I would circle the outcrops in the small boat provided, count the sea lions and record the colour of any tags recognised through the binoculars. Most days I couldn't go out, and I would walk through the stands of Sitka spruce which fringed the beaches, or I would push into the rain forest further inland. The garter snakes would sidle under salmonberry bushes as I approached, and in the cathedral quiet of the rain forest could be heard just the organ music echo of the great Pacific rollers breaking on the first American coast to obstruct them.

'It was cool rain forest, without many birds, and often difficult to walk through because of the swampy places and fallen trees. Ferns and mosses thrived on the decay, as did puff balls, stallion heads and frilled fungi which added the only vivid colours: visceral gleams of red, yellow and spotted black orange, powdered horns like those of a myriad snails sprouting electric blue from the cancerous side of a log.

'After storms I would walk the grey sand of the Pacific beach, see the heaped driftwood, whole trees sometimes, and piles of rotting seaweed which were alive with jumpers. Some of the driftwood still had soil and stones in its roots and gum on its branches, other pieces had been fully digested by the sea and were worn and pale like old soap. On one morning I was amazed to see the vast horns of a caribou caught in the cleft of a tree close to the water line. The tips of the tines were four metres apart, and the antlers would make an arch that two men could march through without stooping. I couldn't dislodge it from the driftwood, and overnight everything was carried away again by the tide and the storm. So are opportunities lost and nothing can be done. I've often thought that the only explanation of such size is that the horns and skull that held them must have been a prehistoric find, carried down to the sea at last from Alaska or the Yukon where some great bull died ten thousand years ago.'

Simon Palliser slept for a while then, his head jogging on his shoulder, and woke when we were coming through Parnassus. I was going to explain the origin of the name for him when we saw a small girl and her doll waiting patiently for the rural delivery man on the grassy roadside by her farm mail box. 'She reminds me of a child I met once in Mexico,' said Palliser. 'On my way to Tierra del Fuego I stopped in Mexico and took the opportunity to visit the Mayan ruins at Chichen Itza. I drove out from Mérida after a meal of tamale with black beans. Rather than the pyramids and temples it was the sacred well of sacrifice that interested me. A huge, circular limestone opening, and twenty metres down sheer rock walls to water which is twenty metres deep again. Young men and virgins were sacrificed in full finery there; the remnant of the jutting altar can still be seen. Government divers have recently managed to recover gold masks and skulls from the mud.

'I had my lunch of chocolate and melon by the stones and shadow of the well's lip, and some Indian children squatted around me to beg a share. I could hear the murmur of the visitors and the more assured, single voices of the guides. I could see people clambering up the stepped side of the pyramid. I thought how this setting of absolute tyranny and religious death had become with time a picnic spot and oddity; the stones and pits denied the sacrifice which had given them their significance. When they had eaten my food the children left me, except for one small girl who calculated that I must have something hidden, or that I would tip her for the privilege of being rid of her. She sat by the rim of the well of sacrifice, and childlike twisted her fingers into the cracks of the wall while watching me intently. All in an instant her fingers drew out a ring of gold with blue amethyst centre, which had lain so long so close to all the people passing. While my mouth was still opening, she rolled the ring once in her fingers as a pebble, and still with her eyes fixed on mine, reached her thin hand over the rim of the well and dropped the jewel to the water and mud far below.

'She must have seen something in my face then that dismayed her, for she bounced up and skimmed away through the heat of Chichen Itza to join the other urchins. There was nothing I could do, you see; nothing that would bring back such a chance missed.'

I thought the Canterbury plains a good contrast to the landscape earlier in the day, and I told Palliser that the Waimakariri which was coming up, was one of our major rivers. 'For me,' he said, 'the river which has my soul is the Okavango, and I've seen both Niles, the Mekong, Mississippi, Rhine, Ganges, Amazon, Yangtze, Congo, Euphrates, the Don and the Orinoco. The Okavango flows away from the sea into the Kalahari; wonderful incongruity. In ancient times there was a huge lake over most of Botswana, but earthquakes altered the courses of the other rivers which fed it, and now only the Okavango continues spreading over 18,000 kilometres into a million channels and lagoons: the inland estuary of a once inland sea. The great Okavango flows into the sand, holds back the shimmering menace of the desert each year. It's one of the most beautiful and luxuriant places in the world, and protected from the worst of modern encroachment by the tsetse fly and sleeping sickness. I've been drawn back again and again, as perhaps you have yourself. On an early visit I was charged by a tusker while hunting zebra, and had to shoot. The authorities made me pay an excessive elephant license fee despite my protests that I had acted only in self-defence. The ivory was confiscated, although I kept the tail and later had an ebony stock fitted to it, making a fly swat.

'On that visit to the Okavango old Johannes de Wette was still alive, and living on one of the estuary islands in the south. He was 87 years old and his brother in law had captured Winston Churchill during the Boer War. De Wette was one of the true white hunters and we sat overlooking the papyrus beds, listening to the slap of catfish and myungobis, the ugly cries of the malibu stork, while he told me of the old days on the Okavango. They used to make hippo rafts to navigate the swamps by shooting four hippo in the head and sewing their mouths closed. After twelve hours the heat so blew their bellies up that they had the buoyancy of gigantic corks, and were used one at each corner of a log raft. De Wette and his comrades would drift through the channels raised up on hippo carcases as if on a dais. Among the Botswana in those days they were treated like royalty, and de Wette said that a bed of Botswana maidens was provided for the hunters — 18 or 20 girls, their bodies gleaming with fig oil, would lie with arms and legs intertwined to make a couch for the night. De Wette's seamed, Afrikaner face was impassive as he told me, but his deep eyes were wistful as we watched a magnificent white-necked fish eagle plummet from the sky into the deep channels of the Okavango.'

As we came into the quiet, spread suburbs of Christchurch, Palliser contrasted them with the intensity of Calcutta. He had come down from Tibet to convalesce he said, after suffering from frost-bite, and to avoid the tourist traps had found a room in the Ashin district of Calcutta. 'It's always been my object to take part in the real life of any place I find myself in,' he said. 'You will remember no doubt the typical stench that part of Calcutta has; the cooking fires, exhaust fumes, oil and dung, the smell of the river and of the cremation grounds further out. Part of that smell too is poverty and loss of dignity. All within sight of the domed Victorian Railway Terminus, memorial to the Raj, and not far from the *maidan* — the lungs of Calcutta.

'My room was made of tar paper and the sides of packing cases from the Bala engineering works. As I lay on my sleeping bag at night I could see stamped on the boards above the curtained doorway the words, Store Away From Boilers.

'My small-time landlord liked to entertain me by taking me to the bazaars in the evening, spurning the untouchables from our path with the hauteur of a man of property. Street after street where life went on; everything is done in the streets because there is no option. Past the pumps in the street for household water, past the stall holders and beggars, the people crouched in doorways, the goat boy selling milk as required from his animal's udder, the banana sellers, hooded rickshaws with their drivers squatted between the poles and resting. One night we saw a goldfish and ball-bearing eater outside a flower shop and a potter's. There are no ends to the way a man can be demeaned in search of a living. Up to ten goldfish and ball-bearings I saw him swallow, then sing for a while, then regurgitate them into a plastic bag of water, so that they swam again apparently unharmed. In the narrow alley at the side of the potter's shop were piles of clay and wood, shards of pottery, trays of small images of Kali set out to dry. The sideshow swallower may have noticed me watching with more interest than most of the passing crowd, or perhaps it was just as a European who gave him an American dollar that I received attention. He stood before me with a smooth, handsome face, and swallowed five ball-bearings the size of golf balls and in good English told me that he was a B.A. "You are seeing what a person will be doing for sake of family," he said. "What we are brought to is a terrible thing." Behind his personal misery was all the beauty of the flower shop; garlands of jasmine and marigolds from the red soil, roses even, and a few sacred lotus blooms set further back. The swallower became vehement at his plight; shouting to be heard above the transistors and bazaar noise. In his misery he forgot to maintain muscular control of the ball-bearings in his gut, and they must have moved down for suddenly he screamed with pain and fell back amongst the marigolds and jasmine. It drew more people and more interest than his former act, and all the watchers loudly gave advice as to the best way to cure him. The flower seller called loudest of all about the dying man. I asked my landlord what he was saying and was told the vendor demanded to know who would pay for the crushed jasmine and roses.'

I left Simon Palliser at his hotel by the Square. He was grateful he said to have had the opportunity to see something of the nature of the country here, and to spend time getting to know me. We could see the Cathedral quite clearly, and Palliser said as I left that it reminded him of a peculiar thing that happened while he was staying in Strasbourg some years before.

GLASNOST

What might seem the most difficult thing is often the easiest to account for. Peter Belikov, beloved in his own Ukraine and of some repute elsewhere, attended the International Festival of Landscape Poetry in the Barossa Valley, and so did Nigel O'Kane. Thus they met. Belikov was almost a name of course, while O'Kane was no name at all. New Zealand PEN initially nominated Tucker, but at the last moment he suffered a sports injury, and the secretary remembered O'Kane's 'Kurow Triptych' in 'Agapemone' magazine. The secretary was not well up on South Island landscape poets, but was determined to find one. She assumed that as there was more natural landscape per capita in the South Island, the standard of its poetry must be correspondingly higher. O'Kane had a part-time job under one of the government employment schemes checking for carp infestation in the hydro channels of the southern lakes, but the threat posed was not thought such that he couldn't be spared for a few days.

No, the difficult thing might be thought an explanation of why amid one hundred and seventeen male and eleven female nature poets concentrated in the Barossa, the Ukrainian Belikov, almost a name, and obscure O'Kane of the Waitaki, should form any sort of friendship at all.

The answer lies in O'Kane's state of mind at the first plenary session. He had once been overseas before, but only to the North Island, and the flight to Australia made him agitated. On landing he had to stifle his anguished cries as what appeared to be a portion of the wing disintegrating proved to be merely airbrakes. As the sole New Zealand poetic representative he knew no one on the mini-bus to the Barossa: no one in the multi-coloured marquee which stood in the scented gardens for the first evening plenary session. The name tag he was issued, registered him as O'Kay, which he was philosopher enough to accept as a favourable omen. Alone at such a function he did what all alone at such functions do, he drank more heavily because of it. The Barossa reds were particularly robust that year, and the nibbles well hidden.

O'Kane found Dutch courage enough to cheer the Colombian representative who spoke out bitterly against the cancer of industrial society, and to smile into his neighbour's Hamitic face when the chairman, a Tamil professor of Asian Literature, told a joke which proved he was a personal friend of Seamus Heaney, or Nissim Ezekiel.

O'Kane was most conscious of his obscurity when the formal part of the evening was over, and the poets began to mingle. Many appeared to be acquainted from the trail of festivals, launchings, readings, conferences, exchanges and academic fellowships which criss-crossed the world. The talk and laughter rose so that the marquee began to swell like a bull frog, the candy stripes tightening in the light temporarily strung. Midges and moths were drawn in enquiringly from the twilight Barossa, and hovered as parentheses about damp, open mouths.

The Chairman made himself heard with an Asian gong, and suggested an impromptu reading. An accomplished chairman, he had cunningly forewarned some poets and had them planted in the throng. Before any of these could rise to their cue however, O'Kane, driven by alcohol and the heady presence of so much poetry, stood on a tubular steel chair and recited Baxter's 'Rocket Show' from memory.

It was then that Belikov first saw him. As he watched, as the talk in the marquee died until the only sounds were the breaking of wind and plastic wine glasses underfoot, Belikov felt his heart tighten at the true demonstration of a poet's love for his profession. The front legs of O'Kane's chair sank gradually into the wine-soaked soil, and he steadied himself with one hand on the back. His running shoes had from long usage come to follow the shape of his feet perfectly, his grey trousers were worn at the knees from obeisance beside the water channels, and his natural wool jersey was unravelling at the band. His name tag hung out the more he had to crouch, and those nearest could clearly read that he was O'Kay.

There is a fitness in a poet's poverty, Belikov considered. A rich poet is like a fat ballet dancer, both gross failures in the essentials of their art. Even those listeners who had difficulty with English, or O'Kane's accent in its use, could respect a consciousness of a love for the words greater than his unpractised delivery was able to express. He received a good-humoured reception as he toppled forward at the poem's conclusion, and the chairman quickly moved on to another poet whose spontaneity was more expected, and more in keeping with the hierarchy of those present.

Overawed by his own presumption, O'Kane burrowed his way to another part of the tent where he could be insignificant once more, and Belikov left his small retinue and tried to follow. O'Kane was fortunate enough to find a plate full of asparagus shoots wrapped in ham and held with toothpicks, that had been put down and forgotten behind a rubber plant. He ate eleven of them, which served to regain his composure, and Belikov found him there in time to eat two of the last remaining with him.

Belikov and O'Kane talked not of poetry, but of their lives, which is the way of true artists. It is the difference between the spring and the trough. The Ukrainian spoke of his home town of Osipenko on the shores of the Azov Sea, and O'Kane asked excitedly of Chekhov's Taganrog and Babel's Odessa in the region. O'Kane described the treeless slopes of the inland basins of his South Island, with the tussock undulating in the unchecked wind and the scree slopes glistening in the iced water of the thaw.

Belikov was on the rise. He gave a speech at the Festival's second day on the lyric pessimism of Ukrainian poetry. It was rumoured that he would appear on Australian television, but for some reason it didn't happen. However, he gave several radio interviews and readings. Despite his position and responsibilities, despite his established acquaintances at the Festival, Belikov made a point of talking to young O'Kane at least once each day. Belikov was not so far from his days of full blown poetic idealism that he was unmindful of its wonder and passion, its obsessive innocence, and before the two poets parted at the conclusion of the Festival in the Barossa, Belikov gave O'Kane his home address and a copy of his ninth volume of poems — *Dusk Upon The Asov Sea.* In return O'Kane wrote out for his new friend the 'Kurow Triptych'.

O'Kane returned to his brown valley and his search for fish no longer content with Mandarins' gardens. It suited his whimsical humour when he was asked his occupation to say, carping. He supplied PEN with a report of the Barossa Festival as required; some 5,000 words which the secretary reduced to 200 in the newsletter, for since her invitation to him it had been pointed out to her that O'Kane was utterly insignificant as a poet, and lacked any acknowledged publishing or critical history. Yet O'Kane could not be deprived of his experience, or his friendship with Belikov, and he wrote every month; long letters of the milky flow of the Waitaki, of the dust billowing from the Hakataramea in wind storms, of the delicate pulse in a gecko's throat and the flight of a hundred Canada geese in a necklace against the setting sun. He shared the inspiration for his in progress, 'Sonnets of Otematata'.

And Belikov replied, despite his many correspondents, describing the majestic steppes, sturgeon fishing in the sea mist, the reed beds of the Yevpotkin, and his growing reputation which necessitated ever more frequent visits to Kiev, Moscow, and outside Russia to represent his country in America, Britain and so on. Belikov became a name; a small major poet rather than a large minor one. He was included in a 'Time Magazine' article on the leading contemporary Soviet poets, and he was awarded the Nekrasov Medal for his lyrical 'Return to Osipenko'.

Art is however a jealous god, and Belikov suffered a severe stroke thirteen months after the Barossa Festival while reading a letter from O'Kane. His memory and movement were desperately impaired, and only his last thoughts about O'Kane were clear in his mind. His wish to see him finally became evident to doctors and family. The brother, Andrey Belikov, told of 'O'Kay' O'Kane's letter found clutched in Peter's hand, and the earlier letters were recovered from the poet's files.

In the spirit of glasnost the tender story was told not just in Russia, but the world. A small enough piece of news perhaps, for the literary community is always despised by media power, nevertheless it was human interest, and there was an element of hands across the political waters as well which was an angle worth working.

The Ukrainian Academy, benevolently regarded by Moscow, was permitted to approach the New Zealand Minister for the Arts through the Soviet Ambassador to invite the poet O'Kane to visit

Belikov in the Dostoevsky Clinic at Rostov. The Minister called upon the Arts Council to identify O'Kane, the Council called upon the Literary Fund, the Literary Fund called upon PEN, and PEN heaped praises on their secretary who had shown the perspicacity to recognise O'Kane's talents and send him to the Barossa Festival in the first place. There was even a brief discussion in the Prime Minister's office as to the implications of accepting the Soviet offer to meet the expenses of O'Kane's trip, and it was decided New Zealand should provide the funds and so present the visit to the ailing Belikov as a gesture of goodwill from New Zealand to Russia.

Oh yes, it was quite a thing for a time. There were photos of both Belikov and O'Kane in the papers, excerpts from the letters, and mention of the 'Time' article to establish Belikov's significance. The nickname O'Kay O'Kane provided a pleasing tag which no journalist strove to overlook, although certain senior common room staff with a sense of irony spoke instead of Arcane O'Kane. The MAF when approached described the poet's responsibilities with them as conducting a survey of the comparative distribution of freshwater Cuprinidae. PEN dug out O'Kane's original 5,000 word report on the Festival and published it in full. 'Landfall' claimed an interesting editorial correspondence with the southern bard, saying that it had rejected his work it was true, but had never rejected it out of hand. Several anthologists contacted O'Kane in order to obtain permission to include his work in forthcoming definitive collections of New Zealand poetry, and the Ngaitahu recognised O'Kane's spiritual affinity with the land and presented him with a twenty-seven inch bone fish-hook pendant to carry to the indigenous people of the Ukraine.

Traditional poets and critics came forth from the woods and gullies all over the country to beat post-modernism over its fictive heads with O'Kane's success. It was rumoured that the as yet unfinished 'Otematata Sonnets' displayed a textural richness and sacro-guilt symbolism which rivalled Baxter himself, but 'Kurow Triptych' was the only published work available and so it received considerable attention. The coda was much quoted.

Christ is advent anew in the black stilt
On a braided crucifix of silt.

Nigel O'Kane coped with it all. Innocence can be its own protection in such things. In the same, soft running shoes he made his pilgrimage to the Black Sea to meet his friend Peter Belikov, who was by then unable to give a greater recognition than the clasping of his hand. Before returning to New Zealand O'Kane visited Taganrog and Osipenko; stood himself on the loved shores of the Asov Sea. He was amazed that what seemed so insignificant and hemmed in upon his home atlas, should be in truth so vast, so calm, and so uncaring.

Other news supplanted O'Kane soon after his return, but his story was too much the stuff of literary anecdote to be entirely forgotten. He went back to the solitary pursuit of art and carp convinced he was a man of letters, and he was still young enough to think it was his poetry which had done the trick.

The Dungarvie Festival

Ivan and Len worked together for two years, and then by chance got to know each other on the summer day they didn't make it to the Combined Local Bodies Civil Defence Seminar in Dunedin. Each council had to send two representatives, and there was a good deal of duck-shoving to sort out who had to go. Ivan was landed with it because he was a comparative newcomer, and wouldn't be missed anyway. To show that the council was taking Civil Defence seriously there had to be a chief as well as an Indian, so Len, who was Administration Officer, had to go.

He came around early to pick Ivan up, so that they could be away in good time, and Ivan saw that they had been given the oldest vehicle in the fleet. They would be the Kettles come to town in Dunedin. The ute's left front guard had been in pink undercoat for years, and in the back was an assortment of road signs and three boxes of poisoned carrots that someone kept forgetting to set out around the treatment ponds. Low on both doors were paint bubbles, showing where the rust was eating through from the inside.

Len knew he looked incongruous. His good suit was already picking up a variety of rubbish from the wool sack which covered the front seat. Neither of them said anything about the ute though, and Len drove as befitted a chief, and Ivan sat on the pink wing side as the Indian. Len's manila envelope with the programme for the seminar lay on top of the dash, so Ivan put his there as well. They didn't discuss the programme: it had headings such as statutory responsibilities of local authorities, and counter-disaster logistics for rural communities.

Reticent, I suppose, is a word that you could use for Len, and professional would be another. He did his job from day to day without malice or favour, and without any inclination to pry into the thoughts or lives of colleagues. A working relationship over two years had for Ivan merely confirmed those aspects of Len's nature that he had recognised within the first week.

'We've drawn the short straws,' said Len with a smile.

'It looks that way.'

That's all they said for a while, but to be fair to both of them the ute didn't encourage conversation. The motor laboured and the road signs and poisoned carrots in the back had a disappointing fellowship. Also there was the threat of the Central summer, even at that time of the day. The ground had little cover, and the schist outcrops were bright, scaly, with no sweat to give.

'I don't much like the sound of the old girl,' said Len when they were close to Dungarvie, and as if by speaking of it he gave recognition, even acquiescence, the motor sickened in that instant and then died. They drifted, with just the road noise and the diminishing quarrel of the road signs and carrots, almost to the restricted speed zone of the village, and where they should have reduced speed the ute stopped completely.

'Ah well, Jesus,' said Len.

'At least we're not far from a garage. That's a welcome fluke.'

'That's true.'

There was a garage at Dungarvie. They could see it clearly. In fact all of Dungarvie could be clearly seen ahead: on the left the garage then a community hall, on the right three stock crates jacked up on a section until needed, then the gap of a lucerne paddock before the store. Past the store was the only separate house they could see for all Dungarvieites. Len tried the starter several times without success, then went to the front of the ute and looked at the engine, more from a sense of responsibility than any hope of finding what was wrong. Ivan stood by him, but looked along the flat road to Dungarvie. He saw no one; nothing moved, and in the time between the ute stopping and their walk to the garage beginning, only a blue Triumph passed them, paying no heed to them or the restricted speed zone, disappearing down the road before they had taken many steps.

Len and Ivan took off their ties, and folded them and put them in the pockets of the coats they carried as they walked into Dungarvie. 'I suppose I should have rung up the yard yesterday and insisted on a better vehicle,' said Len. 'I just never thought we'd end up with that ute. I mean they knew we were going through to a meeting in Dunedin. It's poor.'

'I suppose it's mostly bad luck really.' Ivan was more accustomed to being given the ute as council transport.

'Yes, but after all we are going to the city as representatives of the council, aren't we.'

Ivan could feel his lips drying as he walked. He licked them, and moved his coat from his shoulder where it was making him sweat, and let it hang over his wrist. Through the thin soles of his best shoes he could feel the unevenness of the seal. It seemed to take a long time to walk the two hundred metres or so before the garage. Some barley grass heads had attached themselves to his trouser legs. He felt his face screwing up against the glare of the sun.

The garage was wooden; so old and so high that it may once have been a smithy. There was no one amid its work-day untidiness, although a transistor radio, hidden like a cicada in the jumble of the side bench, sang on. Ivan and Len were not surprised. They knew that in a country district one mechanic is thinly spread. They kept walking and even before they reached the hall, the sound of laughter claimed them: laughter despite the few, quiet buildings and the sky burnt to a powder blue. The laughter billowed from the community hall, but then lost its force in all the calm, surrounding space. Laughter at once natural and engaging, asking to be found out, yet also with defiance perhaps at all that emptiness; all that press of the given moment which there was no movement to disguise.

The hall was representative of a persistent species: outside all cream weatherboards and bleached red tin roof, inside a wooden floor with chairs stacked to one side, and on the walls the district rolls of honour for the Great War 1914-18 and the Second World War 1939-45. At the far end was one door to the committee room, and another, plus a slide to the 'facilities'. A rolled bowling mat leaned like a furled flag in a corner and on top of chair stacks were three jars of dried flowers and an unclaimed cardigan.

The laughter came from the far end of the hall, in the open door of the facilities, but Len and Ivan found it difficult to see the people there at first because of the alternate shadow then the fierce shafts of light from the windows as they walked the length of the floor. Two women and a man sat on chairs and peeled potatoes. One woman had yellow shorts, matching sneakers and the ease of attractiveness; the other had a floral dress and a laugh like a string of firecrackers. Their helper was a Maori, very thin, wearing a green army singlet, shorts and heavy boots. Even carrying their coats and ties Ivan and Len felt over-dressed. The three had a sack of potatoes and two enamel basins at their feet. They washed and peeled the potatoes in one basin and laid them in the water of the other so they wouldn't brown.

Ivan and Len had found their mechanic it turned out — Charles. Evonne had the Hollywood legs, and Judith the laugh which made every speaker feel a wit. The two of them were mother helpers for a guide camp being held in the domain next to the hall. It is the way sometimes that the more random the meeting, the more relaxed the mood. They all fitted in; there was not a nark amongst them. By rights they should never have met up at all. Ivan and Len should have been on their way to the seminar in Dunedin; should have been through Dungarvie too quickly to have heard the laughter from the hall, or to have seen the red crosses by the names of soldiers who had fallen. Yet Ivan could smell the bowling mats, and old paper lining cupboards; see the withered flowers in their jars, and the table tennis challenge ladder which displayed its champion so aptly as C. Meek.

Ivan sat with Evonne and Judith, offered himself as a replacement potato peeler, while Charles and Len went back to examine the ute. 'Does it matter much if you're late getting to Dunedin?' asked Evonne.

'We're supposed to be going to a civil defence meeting.'

'I don't know much about civil defence,' said Evonne, 'but then I don't know much about Girl Guide camps either, yet I'm here.'

'All camps have certain fundamentals, like peeling potatoes.' Ivan was flattered by Judith's laugh into imagining he had made a joke. She threw a potato into the basin with such force that the droplets as they scattered were caught in the sun from the window and for an instant held all the colours of the rainbow within themselves. Judith and Evonne began their story of all the indiscretions and mistakes they had committed as mother helpers, and of the Guide Officers who never failed to discover them. As Charles, Len and Ivan held no rank within Guides they were seen as reassuring envoys from a more tolerant world.

Carrots had replaced potatoes by the time Len and Charles returned, and Ivan had joined in so completely that the other men returning had to break the circle. 'Charles says it will take a while: probably something electrical,' Len said.

'Could be the distributor,' said Charles. Judith laughed and Evonne joined in. 'Heh,' said Charles, 'I've told you before there's nothing the matter with my name. I bet plenty of mechanics are called Charles.'

'How many Maori ones?' said Evonne. Judith's laugh, so sudden and so complete, drew them all in. Afterwards Charles looked at Len and Ivan. He tried to make his thin face deadpan.

'These women are trying to offend me,' he said.

'I rang the office,' said Len.

'What do they think?' asked Ivan.

'Well, they want us to go on if we can be on the road again before midday, otherwise we might as well wait here and bring the ute back when it's fixed. Someone would only have to be driven over to get it anyway.'

'Right.'

'I'll tow her in and have a look at things now,' said Charles. 'If you come up in an hour or so I should know what the story is.' He took a carrot from Evonne's hand, as if she should know better than to grip such a thing, and walked back through the hall. His shoulder blades showed clearly under the singlet and his boots seemed clumsy on the ends of such thin legs.

'Goodbye Charles,' said Judith sweetly. He didn't turn at their laughter, but waggled his fingers with his hand behind his back.

As a break from the vegetables, Len and Ivan were taken through the back door of the hall to be shown the camp. There were no goal-posts on the domain because of summer, but at the far end some pony-jumps were still set up, and on the hall side two lines of bell tents with a flag-pole in between. Ivan thought the scene like a limited budget set for a Boer War movie, with a minimum authenticity of the grass worn between the two rows of off-white tents, the flag-pole, the heat shimmer beginning over the brown landscape, and the blue, hollow infinity of the sky. He thought things might look like that at the end of the world: all people spirited away and just the props, the objects, left to get on with it.

'Where are they all?' said Len.

'They're on a badge trek in the hills. A six-hour round hike from the dropping off point and they have to carry their lunch and emergency clothing in case the weather turns. All the qualified people have gone with them, and we're left here to prepare tea,' said Judith, 'and look after Suzie Allenton who was sick last night and is sleeping now in her tent.'

'We're supposed to make an inspection of the tents sometime during the day,' said Evonne, 'and give points to the tidy ones which go towards the top tent competition.'

Ivan was about to ask what happened if the Boer commandos attacked while the camp was undefended, but he remembered he had said nothing to the others about the impression the tents had created. Yet he imagined Botha's or de Wet's horsemen cantering in to surprise the mother helpers and sick, sleeping Suzie Allenton. 'Were you ever in the Scouts, Ivan?' said Len from the back steps of the hall.

'No.'

'It wasn't my thing either. I never had anything to do with Scouts or Boys' Brigade, and although I was roped into National Service the only tents I remember were bivouac things which we had to carry ourselves.They were so small you had to crawl into them.'

'Time for your confessions now,' said Ivan to Judith and Evonne.

'I was brought up on a farm,' said Judith. 'I could never be in group things.'

'I was in the city, but don't remember going to Brownies, Guides or anything like that. I don't think anybody ever invited me.' Evonne looked carefully at the tents and flag-pole, as if for the first time. 'Have I missed out on something important do you think?'

'You can do your penance as mother helper,' said Len. 'Girl Guides, like any other army, march on their stomachs.'

'I'd like to march on the stomachs of a few of them,' said Judith.

The direct sunlight was intense. Len's head lolled back to rest against the door jam, and his eyes closed. The others rested their heads in their hands, and supported both by propping their elbows on their knees. Ivan wished he had a hat, and found himself breathing through his mouth. 'Should we make a round of the tents now?' said Evonne after a time. The two women lifted their heads enough to see across the grass to the tents, and assessed the effort it would take to visit them all, and compared that with whatever energy and duty they felt.

'Maybe later,' said Judith.

'I'll just check on Suzie then,' said Evonne. She stood up, pulled her shorts down at the back of her thighs, and walked across grass so dry that it crunched beneath her sneakers.

'I could sleep the day away in a tent myself,' said Len. 'The less you do the less you want to do.'

'She's a good sort,' said Judith, watching Evonne as she neared the tents. 'Her husband's wealthy, but she's still come to take her turn. She pitches in just like everybody else. She even cleaned up on the bus when one of the girls was sick after fish and chips. It's not very pleasant then in the confined space of a bus when you're travelling so far.' Ivan and Len watched Evonne at the tents; her banana shorts and sneakers, her graceful, brown legs. The men kept their faces non-committal in Judith's presence, and they made no comment. 'Yes,' said Judith. 'Beaut legs. She's lucky there, don't you think? Mine keep getting thicker year by year.' She pulled her dress up to show her strong legs and big knees with a smiling crease on each. 'What about your legs?' she said to Ivan.

'Skinny and hairy. Not a pretty sight.'

'It's just as well we're both wearing longs,' said Len. 'I've nothing much to offer in the way of legs either.'

'Charles's have a good natural tan, but they're skinny too,' said Judith.

'Evonne will have to win first prize for legs then,' said Ivan. Evonne looked back towards the hall and laid her head to one side on her hands to show that Suzie Allenton was still sleeping.

Len and Ivan didn't wait for Evonne to reach them across the domain, but gave a wave and told Judith that they might be back if Charles wasn't able to fix the truck in time.

'Oh, god,' she said. 'Do come back and rescue us.'

'We haven't lost a mother helper yet,' Len said.

Once the habitual responsibility for events had been shifted from him by forces beyond his control, Len became increasingly relaxed. He was in no hurry on their walk back to the garage, and he talked with Ivan of seeing the original sub-division plan of Dungarvie in the council files: two hundred private sections had been surveyed in the flush of colonial enthusiasm, and sites for shops and churches, but even the gold rushes didn't create that Dungarvie, didn't build its churches or fill its cemeteries. Dungarvie had never been much more than they could see. Ivan noted that there was not even a pub in the place, and his interest was not historical. At least the high, red barn of the garage offered some shade.

'She's never been any Rolls-Royce,' said Charles when they joined him. 'However you shouldn't have any trouble getting to Dunedin and back.' Len and Ivan looked without enthusiasm at the ute; its patch of pink undercoat, soft tyres, and stains weeping from the various rust spots on the body. The carrots in the back were bleached and wrinkled: a sign face-up announced road works ahead. Len thought of the drive to Dunedin in the heat, and the attention that would be drawn to them by their late arrival at the seminar. 'On the other hand,' said Charles as one of life's entrepreneurs, 'we could declare a Dungarvie Festival if you wanted to stay for a while, and give Evonne and Judith some company. I've even got a carton of beer that we could all chip in on.'

Len opened his mouth as if to say no in his role as Administration Officer, but then was seized by the wonderful implausibility of it all as he stood in the garage doorway. The few ill-hung bell tents he could see not blocked by the hall, the dozing store, the barley grass in the free sections, the sheep crates with dung burnt to an inoffensive crust, the old smithy garage he stood in, Charles smiling from the shadows which matched his skin. 'Well why not,' Len said, and having said it and not been struck down by conscience or by lightning, he repeated it boldly. 'Well why not. We're too late to bother going on anyway, don't you think?'

'Yes,' said Ivan and Charles with certainty. Charles hoisted the carton of beer into the back of the truck, and they drove back slowly towards the hall through the welling shimmer of the road and grass.

The mother helpers had gone inside again, and were preparing a vat of mince and onion to go with the potatoes. The sight of the beer on Charles's shoulder was enough to start them laughing. The sooner the meal was prepared, the sooner they could relax, Judith said, so Ivan and Len chopped carrots directly into the mince while Charles sliced onions. Tears ran down his face, and his brows lifted oddly as he tried to keep his eyes from closing.

'Come on, come on,' said Charles. The women took some apples and apricots, everyone took a mug, and Charles led the way across the domain to the culvert where the road crossed the stream. There was a small, scoured pool where the concrete ended. Charles took the bottles of beer from the carton, and dropped them onto the shingle bottom, reaching down till his shoulder was in the water so that the bottles would land gently. Part of his singlet became bright again with the water, and the drops skated across the oil of his hands. There were small grasshoppers at the pool's edge, and a silver skink for a moment on the concrete of the culvert bridge. Len tasted his share of the first bottle, which was given no time to cool.

'I love the salty taste good beer has,' he said. 'Ah, it's needed in this weather.'

They surrounded the small pool. Len and Judith stepped over the trickle of its outlet and sat on the other side, but that put them hardly any further apart than the others. All of them were soon barefoot. Charles's feet were dainty alongside his workboots. Judith tucked her floral dress up like pantaloons, and hung her legs in the water so that the effect of refraction had them broken at the calf. Ivan leaned forward to eat a ripe apricot so that the juice would fall onto the grass and not his best shirt or suit trousers. He had knotted the corners of his handkerchief, soaked it, and it lay on his dark head as a first defence from the sun. Occasionally a truck or car went by in the midday heat. The growing whine of any approach gave all five a chance to compose their faces. Sometimes drivers or passengers happened to look down and saw with envy, surprise or condescension the group around the culvert pool celebrating the festival of Dungarvie. But as time went on, the road, its travellers, its starting points and destinations, ceased to be a relevant awareness, and no disguise or provision for them was made at all.

'Let's hope no one breaks down,' said Evonne to Charles, 'other wise you'd have to leave our picnic and fix the car.'

'Actually I never meant to be a mechanic,' he said. 'I wanted to be a physicist.'

Judith's laugh exploded pod-like in the dry air. She had difficulty in holding her mug of beer. Len's laugh was almost as loud, almost as distinctive; high-pitched and abrupt it was not the social laugh that Ivan had heard from him in the past, but a new laugh. It was a laugh of instinctive delight and lack of inhibition. 'No, I did, fair go,' said Charles. Laughter feeds on itself, so that they were all drawn in. Charles himself found his voice so collapsed with laughter that it was husky when he managed to carry on. 'Look, look, I was a marvel at physics at school and could have easily gone on, but at Vic I got side-tracked into a heavy metal band, and lost my bursary because I failed everything except physics.'

What a depth of humour and irony there is in actuality. Evonne lay back because her stomach was sore from laughing. There must be a hundred reasonable ways to explain the move from physics and a Wellington rock band to sole charge of the Dungarvie garage in the old smithy. It had the freakish likelihood of truth. 'I wanted to be a wildlife officer,' said Len, sudden in his decision to be confidential as well. He had dipped his hands into the pool, and cooled his face with the water. The hair of his forehead was stuck together. 'I wanted to save the black robin, the takahe, the kakapo and so on.' At his ears amid the short sideburns were the first grey hairs, and on the sides of his nose the sheen where his glasses normally rested. 'More than anything else that's what I was set on doing, and somehow I've ended up as an accountant; a Council Administration Officer.' He was still sufficiently self-conscious to add that of course he had remained a financial member of the Forest and Bird Society. It set the others off again, particularly Judith. She considered it a great one-liner. Her feet jerked beneath the water and her laughter cracked like a stock-whip across the domain. Did any accountant ever dream of becoming an accountant, any more than the day-shift foreman of the chicken nugget factory dreamt of his success, or a man sold his soul to the devil for the right to be caretaker at the Shangri-La Lodge and Cabin Park? How many shopping reporters, high school language teachers, rural delivery drivers, one term politicians, or Pleasant Valley inmates, could point to a constant ambition?

The bottles of beer lay on the gravel bottom of the pool, and quivered like trout in the ripple of Judith's feet. The stones had a fuzz of slime because the water was barely flowing; the label from one bottle had come adrift and undulated like a fin. The pool had a thin lip of green cress and clover before the brown grass began. 'How can you work day after day in this heat?' said Evonne to Charles, who was reaching down into the pool to bring up another prize.

'You tell me,' he said. 'This part of the country is stranger to me than to most of you, I'd say. I'm Tuhoe you see, children of the mist, and so on. This isn't my place.' It was a final incongruity. Len was delighted with it.

'I don't suppose there are many Tuhoe physicists in Dungarvie when you come to think of it,' he said.

Everything seemed amusing to them in that afternoon. Sometimes there is an intoxication of the heart which has little to do with drink: some combination of circumstances and personalities which slips past defences and brings a mood of goodwill and acceptance. All of which may be just another way of saying how hot it was in Central that day, how influential the beer and fruit on empty stomachs; how each person felt release in a new role and company knowing it was just for one day. Ivan noticed that Len rolled his trousers higher as time went on, and that his face at times was almost impetuous. They had left the office, yet not arrived at the seminar. They had shrugged off routine, yet not assumed interim responsibility. They were in a pleasant limbo, and yet with some excuse.

'Me?' Evonne was saying. 'I wanted to be a school dental nurse and make snowmen with red ink faces from cotton wool wads. The uniform quite suited me I thought, and as well you had your own special room. Instead I'm just a rich bitch I suppose.'

'A toast to the mother helpers,' said Charles amid the talk of Bertie Germ and money, and the mother helpers drank deeply to themselves as a sign that they recognised their worth.

Ivan wondered about himself; what he had intended as distinct from what he had become. The physicist, the wildlife ranger, the dental nurse, and Judith still with her mystery, all wanted to hear of his lost life. Judith shaded her eyes the better to watch him, and her mouth was open for her explosive, benevolent laugh. 'An actor,' he said. There was joy that he had not disappointed them. Charles threw his head back as if to dislodge something in his throat. 'I did a fair bit at school and then a Polytech course. We had a group that toured schools and hospitals, but when the funding was withdrawn I switched to office management.' As he said it, he was amazed how the exigencies of the moment become in retrospect a seamless process of inevitable selection.

'Oh, but you would have been good on the stage,' said Evonne loyally. 'You could be a gentleman caller for Laura, or a rebel in a kitchen-sink play.'

'Or the fool in Lear,' said Len, 'who knows more than the king.'

'Give us something now,' said Judith.

'I've forgotten it all.'

'Yes, come on Ivan,' said Len. He was delighted that his colleague had revealed such an exotic past. A chant began.

'We want Ivan. We want Ivan.'

In any other setting, any other time or people, Ivan would have suspected an edge of vindictiveness, an underlying hope of some humiliation, but the Dungarvie Festival was all goodwill None of them knew each other well enough to wish for any harm. Ivan stood up to free his breathing, and gave them one of Biff's speeches from *Death of a Salesman* about the dangerous gap between self-image and reality.

As part of his concentration on it, Ivan had an exact awareness of the others listening; their combined physical existence on the grass there, around the culvert pool. A grass stem turned in Len's fingers, and on one pale ankle bone a green vein was looped. Judith's sunburnt face was full on to him to give support, and Charles nodded as he listened and dabbed an insect from his beer. The Boer War tents were in their two rows at a distance; the hall and store and garage becalmed in heat and time. Then Ivan quoted Willie to his friends in the Dungarvie domain; isolated from the rest of the world with a bird singing up high somewhere, one great, strutted pylon glinting on the hill, two lines of sagging tents, and in one of them somewhere, sick, sleeping Suzie Allenton whom he never saw.

Ivan had his immediate appreciation however, and a stock truck happened to pass at just that time and made a roar of approval upon the little bridge above them. Judith had seen the film version, and talked of it with Len and Evonne, while Charles gave Ivan his ideas on the importance of sustaining enthusiasms. Ivan was breathing heavily because of the heat and his nervousness at reciting. He was content to listen for a while. 'You must keep the idea of your life being special,' Charles said. 'Of it having nothing to do with any historical generalisations or social trends, but instead is a free-wheeling thing with all the possibilities still there if you want to explore them.'

'There's an underlying feeling of time past,' Ivan heard Judith saying, 'and it's pressing forward into the present and the future more and more.' For a moment Ivan thought that Charles would accept that as an answer in their own conversation, but Charles still waited.

'Sometimes I doubt the depth of what we see,' said Ivan. 'Sometimes despite the exact, connecting detail before us, I feel it bulging, and just a shimmer at the seams to hint at things quite different beneath.'

'That's it,' said Charles, and he topped another bottle.

'Didn't he marry Marilyn Monroe or something?' asked Len. 'I thought I read that he married Marilyn Monroe.' He picked blemishes from his apple with his fingernail.

'At our last staff meeting,' said Ivan, 'we were discussing the computer training programme, and for an uneasy moment the words spoken didn't fit the movements of the people's mouths, and there was the scent of the open sea that I haven't thought of for years.'

'That's it,' said Charles. 'Last week I took an irrigation pump I'd mended back to a cockie up the valley, and at the gate a dog challenged me. Not a sheepdog either, but a Labrador. The sun was going down and this old dog stood right before me, barking hoarsely but it had so little belief in its own threat, or mine, that its eyes turned away as it barked. I had a feeling that it marked something in my life, but I had no way of guessing the significance.'

'Kerouac called Monroe a trash blonde. He met her once and she snubbed him,' said Evonne.

'I've never read any Kerouac,' said Len. 'I come across the name from time to time, but I've never read anything.'

'We'll do our Kerouac dance for you,' Judith said. She and Evonne stood up and swung their hips slowly, and undulated their arms. Judith's dress was still tucked in, and her legs were pink with sunburn; only behind the knees still white. Evonne could have been a Marilyn Monroe herself, with smooth muscles on her thighs, and heavy breast. Len gave his new, high-pitched laugh, but much softer than before.

'That's just a hula,' he said.

'Now reincarnation is another thing,' said Charles. The beer had reached his eyes and they had a moist gleam. He lifted the strap of his green singlet, and scratched his shoulder. His thin body was crumpling in the heat and the relaxation of unforced conversation. 'I find myself considering it quite often.'

'You believe in reincarnation?' said Ivan. Evonne and Judith still did their Kerouac dance, and Len clapped in time. It was a leisurely dance because of the heat, and Judith could drink from her mug without interrupting her movement.

'Let me give you an example,' said Charles. 'I had this dream of hunting polar bears from a kayak, and one reared up on an icefloe and I felt all the authenticity of detail in an instant: how the water drummed the kayak's skin against my hips, and the bear's fur yellowed and disordered in the arm-pits as it raised great paws.'

'An Eskimo dream. You didn't,' said Ivan.

'What's this?' said Evonne.

'Charles dreamt he was an Eskimo.' The dancing was over and Evonne and Judith sat down to laugh again.

'You didn't!' said Len.

'Only a few nights ago,' said Charles. 'It was so true that it woke me up. It took a while for the Arctic chill to pass. I got out of bed and went to the window. I could see some of the hill facings full to the moonlight, and a fence-line across them. But there wasn't a polar bear in sight.'

'Perhaps an Eskimo has had a vision of Dungarvie as recompense,' said Ivan. 'The view from your window with the dark gullies and moonlit tussock slopes of the Old Man Range, and a single fence-line to divide one side of emptiness from the other.'

'Or the festival now,' said Judith. 'Us at our picnic here when we're all supposed to be somewhere else. But it's so hot. You'd hardly dream such heat.'

Even reincarnation and the Kerouac dance couldn't protect them all forever. The afternoon was well on, and consciences were stirring. No one voiced it, but they had a small fear that the Guides and qualified instructors might return from training and they would have to see themselves reflected in scornful eyes — five feckless people, moist faced and idle in the sun from an excess of goodwill and beer.

'I suppose we'll have to go,' said Len, but he continued to lie back, his suit trousers rolled below the knees. 'I haven't enjoyed myself so much in ages.'

'We've still got our inspection to do; and poor Suzie Allenton,' said Evonne.

'And the meal,' said Judith.

'You didn't give the mother helpers any of the carrots from the truck did you, Charles?'

'Why not?'

'They're poisoned.' Len knew this would set Judith off again.

'That's the sort of lunch issue our council runs to,' said Ivan. Amid the laughter, Len clumsily stood up, but was unable to find his balance. Too many factors were combined against him: dizziness from standing up suddenly in the heat, pins and needles in his left leg from the hard ground, the flattery of beer and laughter, the loss of steadying inhibitions. He began to fall sideways despite whirling his arms, and the laughter increased. He tried to turn his fall into a leap across the pool, easy enough, but hit the far edge with an outstretched leg and half fell in. Had it meant his death, the others could not have stopped their laughter, which went on as Len hobbled in a circle on the grass to get his jarred leg moving properly again.

The incident allowed Ivan and Len to make easy goodbyes, with no scrutiny of the day attempted. Laughter and spontaneous acceptance had been the start of their trivial festival; with laughter and openness they kissed and parted.

Ivan and Len carried their shoes across the domain, and when they reached the truck they opened both doors, but stood outside for a while until the cab was a little less stifling. 'You'd better drive,' said Len. 'I think you drank less than me.' They could see Charles fitting his heavy boots as they pulled away, and when Ivan gave a farewell on the horn, Charles, Evonne and Judith raised their hands, and even at that distance and above the noise of the ute, there seemed an echo of machine-gun fire which might have been Judith's laugh.

Dungarvie fell over the edge of the world behind them; soon they could see just the top of the high smithy garage. The morning's trip seemed a life away. 'We're not much further ahead on civil defence,' said Ivan.

'The farmers round here say that disaster struck some time ago anyway, and today's seminar was too late for that.' Len was dusting his feet with his socks while Ivan drove, then he rolled down the legs of his suit trousers and began picking out spears of barley grass. 'I never knew you'd been an actor,' he said. 'We should see more of each other and talk about those things.'

'We will.'

'Judith was the only one that didn't tell us what she wanted to be. Did you hear her say that she was going through a break-up with her husband?'

'No.'

'She told me while you were talking to Charles about reincarnation, or his time at Vic, or maybe his Eskimo dreams. Being a mother helper was a chance to step back from normal things and sort herself out.'

'She could laugh anyway.'

'That's true. You meet interesting people by accident at times, don't you. Scores of times I must have been through Dungarvie and I don't think I've ever stopped. Yet today was some sort of fun wouldn't you say?'

They talked easily in the afternoon sun. The Dungarvie Festival had been one of those oddities — a oncer — like a freak giant hail storm, or the escape of zoo leopards into the suburbs. Those things which happen once in a blue moon, and which bind those caught up in them with a sharp sense of comradeship, and of life's possibilities after all.

Tomorrow We Save The Orphans

My final voyage, a winter's night, and Dubois accompanies me as a courtesy of farewell. After more than a year at Acme Textiles I have been appointed a researcher with Statsfact Polling Agency. Dubois is piping me ashore. 'I might do the same at your age,' he says, 'but later you'll see the advantages of night work. Fewer people and more interesting ones.' He's right; they drop through the sieve of daylight employment to a nether world. The most fallible of fools and perverse of the profound.

The breath that forms Dubois' words is a plume in the freezing air as we stand beneath the water tower and check the sacking on the pipes. Appearance is most marked and memorable on the day that we meet a person, and the day we part. Dubois' continental good looks are in some way debased, the casual, toss away features of a circus rouseabout, but his eyes and hands have individual authenticity. Dog killing hands, strong and supple, with muscle raised between thumb and forefinger, and eyes that will not tolerate deceit.

'I've been reading more about castle development and the influence of the Crusades. Brattices and the advantages of circular masonry,' he says.

I returned from Europe with an innocent bladder infection and a debt of over three thousand dollars to my parents. Acme Textiles was unimpressed with my education, but when I crooked my arm to make a muscle and talked of labouring in Wolverhampton, the personnel manager said okay, I'd got it; night work, but only if the caretaker liked the look of me. I never saw the personnel manager again. He was the Charon who delivered me to the underworld. His name was O'Laughlan. The managing director, whom I never met at all, was called Jim Simm, and the caretaker was N.F. Vincenze Dubois. Life is full of such splendid ironies.

On this last night, a winter round, Dubois seems willing to put aside all except that final cover which is the necessary reserve to keep the glare of other people from our soul. At farewell to comradeship and proximity it matters little if some confidences are shared which might be awkward if you had to meet again. We all learn to jog along in our relationships, not expecting too much, not admitting ambitions we can afterwards be beaten with. 'Have you really been here fourteen months,' says Dubois. He has a muslin cleaning rag knotted around his neck for warmth and the collar of his tartan jacket turned up against the chill. 'Fourteen months. Fourteen months,' he says, 'and I don't remember more than two or three things in that time, apart from the Middle Ages, that I care a damn about. I hope it's different for you.'

Night has a stark effect. A liposuction that removes the inessential until the bones, the sinew, the organs only of an impartial world remain. The dump skips cast perfect shadows from the moon across the frosted shingle and dirt of the yard. Larger stones are rising up like mushrooms, and cats troop Indian file silhouettes upon the wall at Pine Light Engineering with shoulder bones that undulate against the sky. Grass which grows three stories up in the gutterings gives a faint, prairie whisper in the barely moving air, and hedgehogs fossick out from weed and fennel corners to feed.

Frontages of industry present the latest faces, but the backsides retain the scars and emblems of old allegiances. Pine Engineering was once the warehouse of Pacific Skins Ltd, and Acme Textiles itself incorporates amongst others the bulk of Aldous D. McManus and Sons, Pastoral Agents and Scourers, estb 1862. The brave, old lettering can be seen behind the fire escapes. Dotty Standish has come to one of the small side-doors to cry, as she does most nights. Her husband died three months ago from cancer of the bowel. Dubois will not fire her yet, as she has been a good cleaner for several years.

'I could have made you assistant caretaker, or night-watchman, if you wanted to stay on, even though you're no good with your hands,' says Dubois as we check the loading bay doors. Our steps echo on the hollow, wooden ramps and between the echoes is the sound of Dotty snivelling not far away. 'I heard a new dog barking last night,' says Dubois. 'A Labrador, or Labrador-Cross I reckon, at the refrigeration depot, or perhaps further over at the seed driers.'

Dubois is chunky and middle aged, but nimble still. In the main machine room he vaults to the top of the spinners to check them. He leaps from one to the next. There are fourteen French Bavantés and six Wisconsin Hammonds; the names in proud red and green bas-relief on the sides of the casings over which Dubois strides. He has come to check on the Hinkles' electrician. As caretaker Dubois has patronage to dispense; not just cleaning for the women of his choice, but suppliers and tradespeople. The Hinkles' man has finished with the freight lifts, and tells us they should get their certificates of worthiness now.

'I meant to say,' says Dubois, 'that my tele is playing up. The sound cuts out every now and then.'

'I'll call in on my way out,' says the Hinkles' man eagerly.

'Would you.'

'No sweat, Jesus no. If it's anything serious we could let you have a nearly new set we've repossessed.'

'Tell Keith I'll probably need someone out to fit new flourescent lighting in accounts. I'll know for sure in a week or two.'

'Right. No sweat. See you then,' says the Hinkles' man. Dubios conducts the conversation from the height of the spinners, which accentuates his mastery. He now climbs higher as the electrician leaves. Into the steel rafters he moves to check his rat baits, disturbing delicate colonies of wool fibres built up over the years. Some lightly fall in clumps like vari-coloured lichens, others disintegrate and drift for a time before the lights as a haze of green, or gold, or blue.

'The bastards have been at it.' His voice is tight with satisfaction. 'Oh rat, rat you'll feel thirsty now.' Dubois half swings through the bolted rafters above the machines, leg and arm, leg and arm, careful to protect his head. 'Rat, rat,' he says, 'you feel the thirst of death.'

The factory at night is a titanic; dimly lit and throbbing. A place of many levels and decks, with lives a world apart separated by just a bulkhead, or a narrow stairway which says factory staff only. The boiler pipes are never silent in this season, the air conditioning fans resonate with individual melodies from deck to deck. A persistent vibration gives a sense of movement, of voyaging, so that Acme Textiles is pressing on over the sea of the night.

Vincenze Dubois is more absolute captain of the firm by night than Jim Simm ever is by day. In trading hours the place is subject to the compromise and transactions of the world, taking cognizance of powers of equal, or greater, strength. But Dubois has a concentric empire: a ship of the night that rumbles self-suffiency and to which only minions from the outside come. This caretaker knows the place as an extension of himself. The cleaners and the routine of their tasks, the machines in all their variety, rat paths in the ceilings and cellars, the seventh skylight in the warehouse which leaks after hail. He knows the stalagmites of borer dust glinting on the lower beams of the acid store, the folded blankets behind the dye crates where the works supervisor takes Sarah from reception during breaks, the blue pigeons which have pushed past the netting on the east gable, the forgotton box of Chinese silk cocoons above the cupboard in the old boardroom presented by a trade delegation in 1949. Dubois knows Stevens of personnel picks his nose, that the three original doors nailed shut behind boxes in the old storeroom are solid kauri, that the morning sun strikes Acme first on the rusted iron above the blue pigeoned east gable. There is a piebald rat in the boiler house, Dubois tells me, which eschews all poison, and antique green jars in wicker work ignored beneath the dust and spiders' lace of the upper gantry. Cannington writes old-fashioned poetry on the firm's paper, and Tess Eggleslee hides stolen lipsticks in the ledge above the toilet cubicles. There is a faint stain on the smooth wooden floor of the press room. Dubois points it out as the blood of Kenny Donald crushed there seven years before by a fork lift carrying the umber bolts of commercial grade which were so popular at the time.

'Remember we talked of mead,' says Dubois. 'I've had some working; several batches in fact with different herbs, but it's difficult to control the fermentation. I'm not very hopeful and honey's bloody expensive.' We are in the first storey offices which have imitation wood grain formica desks and vinyl swivel chairs with corrective backs. There is not a cobweb, or a textile thread, in sight. From these windows the freight yard is a bleak field. In the summer the security beams suffuse the penetrable and billowing air, but now their light is fractured, crystalline in the frozen night. The Tuki sisters watch Dubois check behind the wall heater and beneath the photo-copiers.

'You won't find anything there, aye,' they say.

'I'll catch you one night,' says Dubois.

'Promises, promises,' they say.

Dubois will miss the Medieval Age I suppose. As well as women and machines, he likes discussion of the origin of heraldic devices, and how donjon, Norman-French for tower became corrupted by time and usage into dungeon. Dubois likes me because I am an intellectual and simpleton. I am without authority or skills in the nether world, yet have information he finds interesting. 'There was a Dubois with William at Hastings,' I say, 'and Cardinal Dubois was Premier Minister in 1772 and in effect the ruler of France.'

'I was told that Dubois meant by the wood. My grandmother always said we had property in New Orleans.'

'Edmond Dubois-Crance served in the Royal French guard, but became a leading Jacobin in the revolution and organised its armies.'

'There's a negro branch of the Dubois in the States,' Dubois says.

'What did you do before?' I ask him.

'Before?'

'Before becoming a caretaker,' I say. Dubois leans away from me to peer behind the drink dispenser.

'Charlotte, Charlotte,' he calls, and Charlotte comes from one of the corridors. 'There's cardboard cups squashed down the back here. Get one of the girls to poke them out with a broom handle please. Michelle, perhaps; she looks as if she'd be better with that end than the brush.' Charlotte laughs, nods, walks away; says nothing. 'Charlotte,' calls Dubois again a little while after. He has found something else to rectify, but Charlotte is out of earshot. 'Charlotte? Ah, never mind. Do you ask a lawyer or an architect what they did before? Do you ask a headmistress or a mercantile banker what they did before?'

'It's just that...'

'It's just that you can't imagine an eighteen year old deciding to make a life career as a custodian, right.'

'No, it's not that,' I say, but it is exactly that. Caretaking is something that you end up doing, surely, as a result of compromises and expedients. A wintering over until you line up something more in keeping with your view of yourself. There is something in the concept of caretaker that suggests the pathological poles of murderer or poet.

'It's my life's job,' says Dubois. 'I started out as a primary school caretaker and I've done pretty much all sorts. The more night work the better though, because I'm interested in freedom, see, which is a form of power.' Dubois hears a hoon car in the alley, and leaps up onto one of the canteen tables so that he can watch the lights pass his domain. We can hear the car back-firing as it slows to turn into Astle Street.

Charlotte comes in to release the *Phantom of the Opera* in volume from the cleaners' transistor. The Tuki sisters three doors down, start to sing along and before Charlotte can go back to work, Dubois begins to dance with her. How well they dance on the white and yellow of the cafeteria floor, amid the chair legs upturned on the tables, and spun by the swelling music of the night. Dubois is handsome and the muslin cloth a cravat at his throat. There is no parody in the care and skill he shows, and Charlotte's calves are well muscled above her working shoes. Faces and voices at the doorways as the other women watch them dance, and when it is over they go back to work the better for it. Dubois is unselfconscious regarding the life he leads.

On our way to the boardroom, Dubois and I are talking of tallage and the earliest practice of paying in kind. And the tax which was a further burden on the serf. The boardroom has Boardroom in gold pretension on the door, in case there may be confusion with other rooms with a fourteen berth, pale pine table and better than average, blue vinyl chairs. Dubois smokes a black cheroot, but we don't sprawl, for it is too cold in this part of the building. Our hands are in our pockets and we shrug our shoulders for warmth. On the wall there hang the managing directors: Jim Simm will be added in good time, but their *doppelgängers* of the night perservere only in the minds and hotel stories of casual workers. Even Dubois can remember only the caretaker immediately before him. A twenty-first battalion man whose stashes of gin still turn up from time to time. However complete and despotic their reign, caretakers go largely unrecorded. So Earls and Barons pass into history by virtue of their rank, while butlers who bestrode a world below the stairs are forgotten when their subjects die.

'So heriot was the death tax,' says Dubois. 'Nothing much alters in the state's greed does it.' I am so close I hear the outside leaf of his cheroot crackle as he draws in and the red rim moves. 'Let's talk of Sir William of Cabagnes who captured King Stephen in battle,' says Dubois, his finger checking a window catch. I am sentient of the subterfuge and interlock of time and place in that instant. The moonlight winking on Dubois' thumbnail at the window, my rather nasal voice pronouncing the vowel in mace, my torso shrunk within the heavy clothes of winter, the words Alistair P. Brigeman beneath his proud black and white face on the wall. A tremor through the carpet from the Phantom's songs beneath. Then time moves with a whisper and again we bowl on towards our end.

The cleaners are nearly finished for the night. The long watch is an exclusively male affair. They walk past us in the shadowed corridor. Dubois asks me to check the fire-doors on level three. He'll catch me up shortly, he says, and as I go on he steps out to separate Carol from her friends; guiding her towards the switch room with the pressure of his hip. 'Wait your patience,' Carol says, so as not to seem too amenable while still in view.

The fire doors are as safe as most excuses. I decide to walk back outside the loading bays. Dubois has told me it is important not to become too rigid in one's routine, for that could be exploited by a thief. I doubt for the moment that he is following his own advice. An angel swish; high on the factory side above me a muffled thump, and a mallard drake falls to the frozen dirt and stones of the moonlit yard. I turn a full circle with a sheepish smile to see who has played this joke, but there is no-other-body. The drake's sleek head follows me. I don't want the responsibility it brings and try to shoo it away. In response the duck rolls on its side, almost like a cat to have its stomach scratched, but one wing extends in a tremor of departing life and in the soft, body feathers where two legs should be, is only one and a little blood. Something terrible has been happening further in the night.

A car without lights is driving slowly down the yard. The gravel crunches sharply in the cold air. It is only Ransumeen who works for Sleaptite Security. Ransumeen is an idle, moaning sod who has been an insulation salesman, grader driver, post tanaliser, and now despite his complaints will see time out in the security business. 'It's an agony my back,' he says. He gets out and falls into step beside me, pulling on a balaclava to wear beneath his uniform cap. Ransumeen has no regard for me, but seeks anyone to talk to on a lonely shift. 'It's an agony. Too small for my build. I've a good mind to tell them that I'll have to toss it in unless I get a better car.'

'Right,' I say. Ransumeen has a habit of arriving at the Lintell Street entrance after ten o'clock when the women are leaving. He hopes to entice the younger ones with an offer of a ride home in the security car.

'I could do with a workout for the old mutton gun,' he boasts. But Dubois has warned the women against him, because he considers Ransumeen workshy and unreliable. 'I suppose the cleaners have almost finished now?' says Ransumeen. The balaclava does nothing for his looks. 'That Eileen's got a nice pair on her: a very nice pair.' He sees the women coming from the lighted doorway in twos and threes, and hurries from me to offer them double service.

The full moon this mid-winter night has a round, idiot face. My nose is putty, and all of us are made slump shouldered by the cold. This stark, dead duck yard of Acme Textiles has no links with the expansive world in which the same night-staff played volleyball last Christmas. On that night the air had rolled languidly amidst us, heavy with fragrance of the chocolate factory, the wheat silos, metallic cinders from the foundry, the sharp tar and salt from the harbour, and the plebeian scents of weeds along the fences of stained factory yards. I was in charge of the beer and fruit juice from the munificent management, and took it from the cafeteria into the summer night where Charlotte, Carol, Rua, Eileen with such a good pair, the Tuki sisters and the other chased a yellow balloon as their volleyball. It was a mutant version of the office party, or the true one perhaps, with Dubois as seigneur, myself as squire in the medieval sense. The cleaners were boisterous and obscene, because they were all female together, away from their families and knowing they deserved better than the treatment they received.

The world is a thousand worlds and our experience of it is determined by the point of vantage. The history of one moment in one place is a thousand histories which are horror and joy apart, men and women apart, old and young apart, worlds of temperament and esteem apart, of education and expectation apart. Our own vision is a lie to the rest of the world who jog beside us. Eileen and the Tukis had leapt for the balloon into the tar and wheat scented summer night, and Dubois gave gifts of pantyhose purchased from his own wages.

I say nothing to Ransumeen of these recollections. Disappointed in his advances he heaves phlegm in the moonlight, tells Dotty he's not going her way, and complains of the rigours of the job as we head for Dubois' winter headquarters in the boiler room. 'Where is that mad bastard,' says Ransumeen. 'A good Kiwi name I must say; Dubois. Jesus.' The furnace is now kept going all night. Dubois is there before us, his face cherry red in the glow of the drip-feed and his hands clasped around his enamel mug as if in prayer. There is a low, wooden form that we sit on, and the great pipes lead off above our heads, each one lagged with sacking held with hoops of tin. This is the vibrating engine-room of our night ship and almost I can hear the ocean of the outer world surge past. Dubois has made a line of blue plastic binding tape which stretches between the pipes and dries his jockies, woollen work socks and heavy shirt.

'I've been thinking about the three field system,' he says, with only a nod to Ransumeen, 'as the means of maintaining some level of fertility in village soil. It's the tie to the seasons surely, one spring sowing, one autumn, one fallow, that explains its importance more in the north.'

'I suppose so.' Dubois is at his most scholarly in the post-coital glow. The fly of his work trousers is still partly undone and the corner of a green shirt can be seen, yet the collar of the one he wears is grey. Ransumeen is a reluctant audience on the occasions when Dubois and I discuss feudalism. He is not aware of any connection between the past and the present; those not alive have never lived. His perception of life is reptilian: conscious only of the sun which warms his blood during the day, and the frost which slows him in his night work. He can barely maintain a latitudinal interest in things around him unrelated to his appetites, let alone a longitudinal one in the past and the hereafter. Only the concept of *droit de seigneur* appeals to Ransumeen from talks between Dubois and myself in the boiler house, on our rounds, or in the gully of the roof where we have sat on pigeon blue summer nights.

'So the big cheese of the district could have every sheila on her wedding night?'

'It was a prerogative not often enforced in practice,' I say. Ransumeen doesn't want to know that.

'They knew how to live in those days,' he says. Ransumeen's response assumes I suppose that he himself would have been the big cheese.

The warmth of the boiler room is having an effect. Ransumeen lifts his cap to remove his balaclava. 'There's a bloody vicious Dobermann at Fraser's yard,' he says. 'A real goolie cruncher. The police and our guys won't check anything on those premises.'

'Fraser's. Fraser's,' ruminates Dubois.

'Grocery warehousers, down from the coolstores.'

'Of course,' says Dubois. 'A big Dobermann, aye? They have tender feet.'

'A real bastard. He tore the cheek off a boy whose bike threw a chain there. He had to have his arm grafted onto his face for ages.' Ransumeen gives me the thumbs up so that Dubois cannot see. He knows the caretaker's interest has been aroused: an odd passion whetted.

'If you're passing again in a couple of hours with a mate who'll take over here, then we could pay this Dobermann of yours a visit.' Dubois takes up a stick, and thumps along the overhang of the boiler house roof until a deadened sound tells him that Pongo is lying in his coats there for the warmth. 'I know you're there, Pongo. You remember that anything goes missing round here and you're for it.' I have never climbed up to the roof to see Pongo, but passed him once in the yard. He is quiet, gingery, and on winter nights creeps up to the boiler house overhang in Dubois' fiefdom.

As we begin another round, Ransumeen takes his cue to leave. He complains about his car again. The yard lights and the moon make geometric patterns of the skips and pallets, the high building walls and roofs. All that the day will prove worn and soiled has a bridal veil in the winter frost. How cold it is. Can this be the same ground over which Dubois saunters in summer nights, coming from the staff showers back to his humble rooms by the incinerator. I have seen him with a towel as a skirt, and carrying just his trousers and soap. Parrots and roses climbed on his back: tattoos of green, vermilion and purple. Parrots and red roses while I explained to him that steward was originally sty-ward to emphasize the importance of swine in medieval times.

With Ransumeen gone we check the west doors and go in again. Dubois continues to give me company on this my last night. He is thinking of agriculture again. 'Why didn't they use horses to plough with more?'

'Horses were few in number and expensive,' I say. 'The ox was the draught animal for ordinary people; healthier over its life span, giving more work from poor fodder and the people didn't mind eating it at the end. The Church then forbade the eating of horse meat.' We talk of medieval stock practices as we patrol the factory. Dubois stops abruptly to feel the air. Niceties of movement and temperature, which I cannot register, tell that a window has been left ajar. Complacent people think that occupations of little status can have no special skills: that any fool can be a lobster catcher, gardener, or poet. The main cleaners' storeroom is ajar, and Dubois' quick instincts lead him to investigate. There lies Dotty with her head on the orbital polisher and her feet amongst the mop handles. Her thin legs are hairy, and her breath comes as quickly as if she were climbing the Matterhorn.

'She's taken all her pills at once again,' says Dubois, and lifts her easily in the fireman's hold to carry her into the cafeteria. 'No. No, Dotty, there's no easy death for you here,' he says, and gives me the daughter's number to ring. It's not the first time, but the last cannot be far off. While we wait and talk of Agincourt, Dotty moans beneath the drug. Dubois has placed a bag of cleaning rags beneath her head, and she smiles fatuously despite the noises she makes. Dotty's daughter and her husband are ashamed of her. They come quickly. Without thanks to us, or more than angry solicitation for Dotty, they bear her away. 'Poor Dotty,' says Dubois. 'She's about come to the end of her tether.'

Ransumeen blows his horn after midnight, and it is sharp in the cutting air. He is back with a friend who will patrol while we go to punish the Dobermann who bit off the boy's cheek.

Dubois armours himself in his dog fighting kit, which I have seen only once before; in October when he killed a roving Alsatian which kept shitting by the boiler house door. More than anything else he looks like a samurai; black breast-plate, wickerwork and elbow guards. The orient had a modern feudal age, I remind Dubois. 'Know your enemy,' says Dubois. 'It's the head and hands you have to be most careful of.' He has tubular steel finger stalls within his fireman's gloves, and tells us that a fully grown Great Dane has a bite that will shear three millimetre aluminium, while a bull mastiff damages mainly by shaking. 'I come crawling for a big dog,' says Dubois, 'but it's me that walks away. Get past the shock impact and the bite, and dogs rupture internally quite easily really. Sudden, full-body weight even from a kneeling position is too much for them. Rottweilers are sensitive to that despite their reputation. You see dogs are not meant by nature to be individual fighters.'

Fraser's is well away, among the newer factories on low lying ground. Ransumeen switches off, and the car glides down the empty street and up to the gates so as not to antagonise the dog until Dubois is ready. There is a straggling, knee-high mist from the sea, and beyond the street light is a main pylon with its own barbed wire enclosure. The thick cables droop and glisten between that pylon and the next. From its skeleton knuckles of insulators hang to grasp each wire, and the electricity crackles and snaps so loudly in the winter air that it is difficult to hear what Ransumeen says in his voice at once ingratiating and confident. 'The mad, mad bastard,' he says. 'No one would believe it, would they.'

Dubois is fighting the Dobermann on all fours. Neither of them makes any deliberate noise. The dog has Dubois' left arm in its teeth and shakes its head; wrenches suddenly with an instinct unpleasant to see. All the while it keeps its body away from the caretaker, who shuffles in a circle, attempting to come to it. The sparking of the pylon lines is amazingly loud; the breath rising from man and dog mingle in the broken mist. The fight is difficult to watch because of the many shadows despite the moonlight.

In the entire time the Dobermann does not release its first hold. 'Get the bastard. Stick the bastard,' hisses Ransumeen. His greater animosity is expressed towards the dog, I think. He glances behind to check that the street is empty. Dubois and the dog drag and circle their way to the heavy netting of the inner fence. There Dubois is able to get the Dobermann side on at last and bring his elbow down with the weight of his body behind it. Abruptly a sound like the first harsh burst from bagpipes. A second time the sound, and the Dobermann scrambles lop-sided away with its head low. 'The bastard's done for. It'll die soon,' says Ransumeen. I see in my mind's eye the duck again; its irridescent head, and the wing fretting on the yard. I hear Dotty snivelling. I tell myself I should have no sympathy for a dog that bites a boy's face.

Dubois gives no commentary on his actions as we drive back to Acme Textiles, and does not immediately take off his helmet. It is metallic blue, with half-visor that modern helmets have. Perhaps he wants time for his civilised face to reassemble behind the mask. The leather padding of his left arm is bright with the Dobermann's saliva. Ransumeen catches my eye and smirks.

We have coffee and brandy in the boiler room on our return. What envy might Pongo feel, only a thickness of tin, and a world, away. Ransumeen tells his colleague how Dubois got rid of the Dobermann, but is cut short by the caretaker. Ransumeen's work-mate, who is a keen Salvation Army man, takes the opportunity to produce three glossy, foolscap posters promoting an orphans' fund, and he asks Dubois if they can go up in the staff canteens. It is little enough return for his surveillance, and Dubois puts them aside with a nod, close enough to the furnace to have the flames flicker on the beseeching faces of the orphans as Ransumeen tells the story about the staff nurse and the elephant. It's not well received: Dubois and I have heard better punchlines, the Salvation Army man doesn't like the genre.

'They can't be regular partners,' says Dubois as we watch the Sleaptite couple from the boiler room door. The moonlight and the frost grip ever tighter, and the world outside is motionless except for Ransumeen and the Salvation man squeezing into the small security car. 'There were some 25,000 slaves entered in the Domesday Book,' says Dubois, 'but the numbers gradually diminished.'

'They joined the rank of the half-slaves; the villeins.'

'The luck of birth meant more then.' He seems to have forgotten the posters, but when I remind him that we will be passing the cafeteria he waves a hand. 'This is your last night as castellan,' he says. 'Tomorrow we save the orphans.' So the orphans remain in the glare of the drip-feed together with the jumble of samurai armour.

We decide to begin through the piece room whose arched windows cast the dense, quiet light of the moon like cheeses on the concrete floor. 'Did I tell you of Hugh the Brown, Lord of Lusignan? A wonderful crusader who was victimised by King John,' I begin. Dubois does not answer me. He is lost for a moment behind the curtain of epilepsy. These *petit mal* attacks come only occasionally, then he picks up again without realising that he is ten seconds behind the rest of the world. Here is matter for metaphysical speculation; the brief loss of synchronisation might in the puzzle of time and events either kill or save him. I saw him have a more serious attack only once, after he came from fighting a schnauzer in the docks, and a fierce, spring hailstorm then blocked the gutterings so that the water banked up, flowed down the walls of the computer room and into the switchboard beneath. We were coming back through the nanny presses, having done what we could, when Dubois began soft noises which were no words, took with the urgency of a lover one of the press covers to lie on as he felt the aura. He sat down and held up the palm of one hand as a sign to me that what was to happen would be over without harm, or revelation, without need of any intervention. Convulsive trembling, harsh breath, the glimpse of a parrot's head upon his shoulder, then calm in which his face was innocent. Soon he had been up again and taken up his command.

'I find the guilds interesting,' says Dubois. He is bending at the grating of the ducts to check the air flow. 'Furriers and glaziers, silversmiths and ironmongers, doublet and hose makers, glovers, cobblers. They were unions in their way.'

'But including employers as well as workers. Setting up standards of the craft as well as conditions. I suppose more like the Japanese *zaibatsu* than unions on a British model.'

'A personal approach.'

'Things suited the scale of commerce; the scale of population then. The people of London would come out to see their king, or a hanging, quite literally. In William the Conqueror's time London was the size of Oamaru.'

'No,' says Dubois. He slows to consider it.

'It's true. Much of England was forest, and wolves ran in packs through Shropshire.'

'Ah, I can see it,' says Dubois. Our checks have led us outside again and our faces shrink in the cold. It seems that he is going to see the whole shift out with me. He flashes his torch behind the loading bay door handles. He has put some blacking there as a test of Ransumeen's efficiency. 'That whining bastard's not done a check. I'll have him out.'

Dubois turns to look across the yard. He shows his teeth, and draws his breath deeply in defiance of the temperature. 'This is my weather as a northerner,' he says. 'A people get acclimatised over thousands of years, and function best that way. I can't stand too much heat. A cold day and a stiff wind makes something in me stir. I'm at my most alert and ready. I have this awareness of my origins.'

'It's sound enough reasoning,' I say. 'Clear genetic links with environment are proved. Look at those Andean Indians with special respiratory adaptations for altitude, and Kalahari Bushmen who hardly sweat.'

'In this weather my tribe stirs inside me.'

'You might find that you suddenly come out with the words of a Frankish warcry,' I say. I wonder however how the boiler room fits Dubois' hypothesis.

'I'm rusty on the Franks,' says Dubois, 'except for Charlemagne. I remember that he could hardly write.'

'Yet he spoke popular Latin as his mother tongue and was also fluent in German and classical Latin.'

'Tell me something else.'

'The Basques had a rare victory over him at the Roncevalles Pass. About 780 — no, I can't remember. Anyway that's where the epic hero Roland died.'

This is the trivial way I can be of help to Dubois; some recompense for lacking the skills of a handyman. I owe my job at Statsfact Polling Agency to the Acme Textiles testimonial Dubois provided. The managing director's stationery was from Jim Simm's office, and Dubois asked Noreen to do the typing. Noreen was a cleaner, but had been a secretary before she started having children. Dubois suggested the sentiments and in-house detail; Noreen the authenticity of phrase — such as, throughout his successful time with us, and, it is with pleasure and no hesitation that I recommend. I like best of all the part referring to my grasp of corporate sales strategy and my progress in the fast track executive promotion scheme.

'When he was old and sick, he had to campaign against King Godfrid of the Danes, and as the Franks marched north through Saxony the Emperor's pet elephant, Abbul Abbas, died. It was seen as a terrible omen,' I tell Dubois.

'Abbul Abbas,' says Dubois meditatively.

On our way back to the boiler room Dubois detours through his maintenance workshop, where his tools line the walls. All have blue paint on their handles and are stamped with the letters V.D. to lessen the likelihood of theft. I have accustomed myself not to smile, or pass any comment. Through the cavernous main factory we walk and Dubois is contentedly imagining his poison at work above us. 'Rat, rat,' he says, 'you begin to feel the thirst of death.' So might we all in time of course.

Furnace light flickers on Dubois' clothes strung to dry and the orphans who still await a home. The great pipes rumble in this engine room which powers Acme Textiles through the night. It is like this with heaven and hell perhaps: no spatial difference, just that Lucifer leads the night shift and employs the same means to different ends. Dubois untucks the muslin from his neck, allowing it to hang as a scarf. 'We'll have a last cuppa, then you might as well go. No sense in two of us hanging on till the last.' Not once during this last night has Dubois said that we might meet again; that any possibility for the continuation of our acquaintanceship exists. He is too honest and too wordly, understanding the contacts of labour. We have spoken more of manors and garderobes than our own lives, but then who wishes to be told the details of other people's problems; it is sufficient comfort merely to know that they have them.

Dubois comes out to see me leave. He challenges the winter air with Merovingian equanimity, and shows the white of his eyes at the offensive sound of a dog somewhere beyond the engineering works. His hair is greying, but only at the edges so that it appears frosted like all else around us. Even the flat surfaces of tin or wood have fine hachures of frost; not shiny at all, but feathered almost, grey-white in the moon and security light like a blossoming mildew. The puddles by the freight entrance though do have a crystal surface, and creak beneath our feet. From illogical habit we stand out from the shadow of the factory, although the lighted yard will be no warmer. 'Things will go all right for you,' and Dubois takes a hand from his pocket to shake with. There is music for this white winter night. Pongo is playing his mouth organ. No doubt he has been kept awake by the comings and goings of this last voyage.

For every place there is the official and accredited view; and for every place there is a reverse of which only intimacy allows knowledge. From our lives we can all demonstrate the truth of that. So at Acme Textiles I leave a population known only by those who must board each night. And Vincenze Dubois is its strange captain.